DON PENDLETON'S

STONY

AMERICA'S ULTRA-COVERT INTELLIGENCE AGENCY

MAN®

SKY SENTINELS

D1496550

A GOLD EAGLE BOOK FROM

WORLDWIDE®

TORONTO • NEW YORK • LONDON
AMSTERDAM • PARIS • SYDNEY • HAMBURG
STOCKHOLM • ATHENS • TOKYO • MILAN
MADRID • WARSAW • BUDAPEST • AUCKLAND

First edition October 2009

ISBN-13: 978-0-373-61987-0

SKY SENTINELS

Special thanks and acknowledgment to
Jerry VanCook for his contribution to this work.

Printed in U.S.A.

SKY SENTINELS

PROLOGUE

Wilson "Pat" Patrick took a seat on the rocky ledge and pulled the strap of his canvas briefcase over his head. As he set the bag down at his side, he turned to Buford Davis and said, "Make sure you get those colors flying high, Buff. We can't be more than a quarter mile from the border."

Davis had already found a crack between the craggy rocks and jammed the steel pole down as far as it would go. A light wind caught the flag and flattened it out so it could easily be read.

Noncombatants! the slick flag proclaimed both in Farsi and Arabic. And below that was written *Newsweek magazine,* followed by the periodical's logo.

Patrick opened his briefcase and pulled out a small tin lunch box. Davis had found another relatively flat surface a few feet away from Patrick and dropped to a sitting position, temporarily setting his camera bag behind him. From somewhere inside the light bush vest in which he carried everything from camera lenses to a

Swiss Army knife, he produced a paper sack. He pulled an egg-salad sandwich out of the bag.

The two men heard the tromping of feet behind them and turned slightly to see six members of the FOX News team approaching. Jason Kapka, who was toting a heavy video camera, was the only one Patrick knew. Kapka made the introductions.

Patrick opened his lunch box and pulled out a peanut-butter-and-jelly sandwich as the FOX crew found rocks or ledges where they could stow their gear and sit for lunch. Patrick finished his sandwich and opened a small bag of Cheetos at the bottom of his lunch box. He looked down into the valley that separated them from Iran. A trickling stream of water passed over the rocks at the very bottom of the valley, and although it was actually a few feet inside the Iraqi border, it was generally regarded as the separation line between the two countries.

As he watched broken twigs, flowers and strands of grass float by, he suddenly caught movement in the corner of his eye.

Patrick spotted the heads of two men appear as they marched purposefully over a hill and into view. Both wore red scarves around their necks, earmarking them as members of the Iranian Revolutionary Guards. Officially known as the Pasdarans, these special forces Iranians were fully decked out in khaki uniforms, web gear and carried either American M-16s or Soviet AK-47s.

The M-16s, Patrick knew, were left over from the days when the Shah had ruled Iran. The AK-47s had been acquired from the old Soviet Union, which had been more than happy to arm the Iranians while they held the American hostages shortly after the revolution.

"What do you suppose those two are up to?" asked Court Hough, one of the FOX crew anxiously. Before anyone could answer, another pair of heads appeared. Then another. And it continued until roughly two dozen of the Pasdarans had marched over the hill into view.

"Just out on patrol," Davis said around a mouthful of egg salad. "Flexing their muscles for us."

The Americans continued eating their lunches. "They'll stop down by the stream," Jason Kapka said. He reached to his side, unzipped his bag and pulled out his camera. "Might as well get some footage of them, though," he added as he turned back around and rested the camera on his shoulder. "It's been a boring day. But the suits back home'll still want tape of some kind."

The routine-patrol explanation seemed to have calmed the FOX men. When Roger Stehr spoke up, his voice was steady. "Well, I'm sure you *Newsweek* liberals can find a way to make it look like it was all the U.S.'s fault," he said.

"And I don't doubt that by the time we finish lunch, you FOX guys will have written that they killed two dozen babies in some sort of Satanic Muslim ritual," Davis retorted.

All of the journalists laughed.

But their laughter had an edge to it.

The Americans continued eating as the men with the red scarves around their necks made their way down the embankment to the water. But they all stopped in mid-bite when the Pasdarans sloshed straight across the water and began climbing the bank on the Iraqi side.

Patrick looked quickly to the side and saw that the breeze still held the noncombatant flag straight out. There was no way the Iranians could miss it. And there was no doubting that they knew they were invading another country.

"What the hell are they up to?" Court Hough said in a shaky voice. "Don't they know where the border is?"

"They know," Davis said as he continued clicking away with his camera. "They just don't care." His eyebrows furrowed. "I don't like this. No, I don't like this at all."

As the squad of Iranians continued to make its way up the hill, one of the newsmen stood. "Look," he called out in a loud voice as he turned slightly and lifted his arm, tapping the media patch on his shoulder with the fingers of his other hand. "We're newsmen."

As he turned and pointed toward the flag Davis had jammed into the ground, one of the lead Pasdarans raised his AK-47 and shot him through the heart. The newsman fell down the bank, past the oncoming Iranians and finally came to rest in the stream, turning the water a dull red as the blood drained from his body.

All the rest of the Americans froze in place. A few seconds later they were completely surrounded.

"Stand up!" an Iranian with sergeant's stripes ordered as he jammed the muzzle of his M-16 into Patrick's chest. The Americans complied. Turning to his side, the sergeant rattled off orders in Farsi and a second later four men hurried forward, searching the Americans head to foot and confiscating their equipment and bags.

One of the Pasdarans suddenly turned toward the

sergeant and spoke rapidly, holding up a North American Arms .22 Magnum Black Widow he had found. The sergeant stepped away from Patrick and walked toward the two men. Holding out his hand, he took the tiny hideout gun and lifted it to his eyes. "What is this?" he demanded in perfect English. "A toy?"

The American newsman saw a possible opening and took it. "Yes," he said emphatically. "Just a toy gun. I found it and planned to take it home to my kids to play with." As soon as the sentence was finished he held his breath.

"I see," said the sergeant. "So, if it is a toy, this should not hurt." Pressing the barrel of the little pistol between his captive's eyes, he cocked the hammer and pulled the trigger.

The .22 Magnum round exploded in the newsman's brain, sending blood, flesh and chips of skull out both the front and back of his head.

The sergeant turned toward the rest of them. "It seems it is a dangerous toy," he said, smiling. "It should come with a warning on the box."

The air filled with laughter.

But it was all Iranian.

The sergeant barked out more orders, and the soldiers who had searched the American newsmen gathered up both the still and video cameras. But instead of taking them as Patrick expected them to, they piled the cameras into the arms of one of the FOX correspondents.

The sergeant looked the man in the eyes. "Take your tape, and your pictures, back to your President," he said. "Tell him that if he can invade other countries, so can

Iran." Then he aimed the .22 Magnum at the FOX man's foot, cocked the hammer and pulled the trigger again.

The American's howl of pain was almost as loud as the explosion.

"That will slow you down a little," the sergeant said. "But you can still make it back."

The FOX man had dropped the camera bags and now more Pasdarans lifted the bags and slung them over his shoulders again.

"I think I will keep this toy for myself," the sergeant said, grinning. More orders in Farsi followed, and suddenly Patrick and Davis found their hands cuffed behind their backs.

"Congratulations," the sergeant said. "You have the honor of becoming our guests." He turned one last time to the FOX man who was sweating and trying to stand on one leg, his face contorted in agony. "Go now," he said. "And tell your president that this is only the beginning."

A moment later Wilson Patrick, Buford Davis and the remaining three men from FOX were trying not to fall as they were escorted down the embankment toward the stream.

Patrick glanced over his shoulder to see the FOX man begin limping back toward the American base camp.

He wished he had paid more attention to the man's name.

CHAPTER ONE

The three members of Able Team wore skintight black combat suits as they fell through the sky over Oklahoma City's south side. Below, Carl Lyons watched the traffic on Interstate 44 as he prepared to pull the ripcord on his parachute.

Local law enforcement had already set up roadblocks surrounding the strike zone. There were already hundreds of law-enforcement officials on the scene. But they had been ordered by the President himself to wait for Carl "Ironman" Lyons, Rosario "Politician" Blancanales and Herman "Gadgets" Schwarz, the three men who made up Stony Man Farm's crack Stateside counterterrorist squad known as Able Team.

At the last possible second, Lyons jerked his cord and looked up to watch the parachute canopy open above his head. A few feet to the side and a mere foot or two above the canopy, he watched Blancanales and Schwarz do the same.

The three men's black combat boots all hit the

asphalt parking lot of a deserted Pizza Hut in front of the large church at almost the same time. Wasting no time, they cut the lines to their chutes and let them blow away in the strong Oklahoma wind.

Somebody else could pick them up. Right now, Lyons, Blancanales and Schwarz all had more important duties to perform than to worry about littering.

Lyons glanced at a cardboard sign in the otherwise empty window of the Pizza Hut building. It read Future Home Of The Southern Hills Baptist Church Youth Group. He wondered just how many of those young Christian boys and girls would still be alive once the building had been remodeled. Unless he and his team were successful, the purchase of the former Pizza Hut might turn out to have been a bad investment for the church.

Terrorists dressed in khaki uniforms had taken over the sanctuary at approximately ten-fifteen that morning, just as the musical portion of the service was ending and the sermon was about to begin. Some had moved in through the sixteen entrances to the sanctuary with submachine guns and smoke and stun grenades, while others had taken over the balcony and rounded up miscellaneous personnel from the offices and other rooms inside the church. At least one man—an off-duty police officer—had been killed during the siege. The small .38 Smith & Wesson Chief's Special in the pocket of his sport coat had proved to be no match for the superior fire- and manpower of the invaders.

As Lyons straightened, a burly man with sandy-brown hair, a well-trimmed mustache and wearing a brown suit walked up to him. "I'm Langford," he said simply. "You must be the guy they called me about?— Agent Lyons."

Lyons let the M-16 fall to the end of the sling over his shoulder and shook the man's hand. From the briefing Able Team had held via cell phone as they flew to Oklahoma City he knew that Langford was the director of the Oklahoma State Bureau of Investigation.

"Give me a quick rundown on the situation, will you?" Lyons asked.

"Not a lot to tell you that you didn't hear during the flight," Langford said. "We've had some sparse communication with the men inside. We're estimating that there's about three dozen, total."

"Any other Feds shown up yet?" Lyons watched the OSBI man's eyes carefully as he spoke. As a former LAPD police officer himself before joining the Stony Man crew, he was more than familiar with the turf wars between law-enforcement agencies. No one liked having what they thought was his responsibility taken away from him. But he saw no jealousy on Langford's face as he questioned him.

"Just the OKC office of the FBI," Langford said. He looked toward a group of men in carefully tailored suits who stood huddled around a minivan. "They got their little feelings hurt when I wouldn't let them take over the show." He paused to draw in a breath. "I think they're arguing about what dry cleaner is the best at stuffing their shirts right now."

Lyons wasn't known for joviality, but that one made him smile. "They're good at that," he said. Then, changing the subject, he said, "Have the men inside ID'd themselves or given out any demands?"

"No demands yet," Langford said. "It's almost like they're waiting for us to get set up on purpose in order to make the biggest splash possible."

"That's a legitimate possibility," Lyons said, nodding. "Any idea who they are? The briefing we got on the plane said they were all dark-skinned, wearing khakis and shouting what sounded like Arabic to a kid who got away."

Langford nodded. "We had a brief conversation with the boy. They didn't claim to be a terrorist group at all. They said they were Iranian Revolutionary Guards. Sounds like a load of crap to me."

"Me, too," Lyons said. "The Iranian government *openly* sponsoring a terrorist attack on a Christian church inside the U.S.? That's like declaring war."

"My thoughts exactly," Langford said. "But they could be Iranian rather than Arabic. Most people around here wouldn't know the difference between Arabic and Farsi if they heard it side-by-side."

Schwarz and Blancanales had so far remained silent. Schwarz looked at Langford, "You have any idea where they are inside the church?"

"That kid that sneaked out right at the beginning," Langford said. "He'd been in the bathroom when the shooting started and the grenades went off, and he ran for the closest exit. He said it looked like they were taking everyone into the sanctuary."

Lyons felt his jaw tighten as he nodded his understanding. That meant explosives. If the terrorists were armed only with firearms, they'd have spread the hostages out throughout the building. The Able Team leader was about to speak again when a dark red Toyota Tundra pickup pulled up, followed by two black-and-white OCPD cars, sirens blaring and lights flashing. It had obviously run one of the roadblocks.

A man wearing a large turquoise bolo tie, a gray suit, black cowboy boots and a white straw fedora stepped out of the truck while a woman Lyons assumed was his wife stayed inside.

Officers from the two squad cars leaped out after him, guns drawn. Ignoring them and the other officers stationed around the church, the man in the bolo walked toward Langford and Lyons.

Langford held up his hand and shook his head to the uniformed men. They lowered their weapons.

"Somebody you know?" Lyons said.

"Oh, yeah." The OSBI director grinned. "Retired agent. And I'd forgotten he went to this church." He paused a moment, then said, "Carl Lyons, meet Gary Hooks. Former agent and close-quarters-combat expert with and without weapons."

The two men shook hands.

"You're a little late for the service, Gary," Langford said.

"We always are," Hooks said. "My wife can't stand that canned music they play on Sunday mornings. So we get here just in time for the sermon and sneak into a back pew." He looked around for a moment, taking in all of the other officers, weapons and equipment. "Then again, maybe God made me late on purpose," he said.

"My guess is none of you know jack about the layout inside of the church."

"No details or schematics," Langford said.

"It's fairly simple," Hooks said, tightening the turquoise bolo around his neck. "Right behind those front doors is a foyer that is about ten feet wide and circles the sanctuary. But it's a killing ground. They—whoever *they* are—could stand just inside the sanctuary itself, with the doors propped back, and kill every one of us who opened one of the outside doors before we even got inside."

"Any other ways in?" Blancanales asked Hooks. "Ways these guys wouldn't know?"

"Well," Hooks said, squinting slightly, "this isn't ancient Rome and we don't have any catacombs to hide in. But there's a way in they may not have thought about, particularly since they're Muslims and particularly since this is a Baptist church." He looked up at the roof of the large building. "There's one way in I think enough of us could use to get the drop on them. That'd give the rest of these guys time to come through the doors," he said, then cleared his throat. "Your team, Lyons, plus Langford and me. Our job will be to take out the sentries at the sanctuary doors from behind so the SWAT teams and other officers can come in and join us."

"And just how do you plan to get behind them, Gary?" Langford asked,

Hooks grinned. "Since you're a Methodist, I wouldn't expect you to know," he said.

Langford laughed, and it was obvious to Lyons that this was an old joke between the two old friends. "Don't worry," Hooks said. "I'll show you all the way. But we've got to spot and disarm whatever explosives they've set up, too. And that could get tricky." He paused a second and cleared his throat. "You know what this is, Dwayne," he said, using Langford's first name. "One giant suicide bombing. Those men inside plan to blow themselves up along with everyone else, and you know it. I know that because they haven't paid a bit of attention to what we're doing outside here. Has anyone so much as seen a face in any of those windows?"

Langford shook his head. "But you're retired, Gary," he said. "You don't have to—"

"I'm not retired when somebody tries to blow up my church," Hooks said. He glanced around. "You've got some good men out here," he added finally. "I know, because I trained most of them in close-quarters combat. But none of them know the inside of that church like I do."

Langford laughed softly again, then looked at Lyons. "He never was worth a damn at taking orders," he said.

"I think what he's saying makes sense," Lyons said. "We need Hooks to come with us."

"Then let's get on with it," Gary Hooks said.

"I know this is a foolish question, Gary," Langford said. "But do you have a gun on you?"

"One or two," said Hooks. "But I need one more." He turned swiftly and returned to his pickup, kissed his wife, and came back carrying a worn canvas briefcase. A moment later he produced a 5.56 mm Kel-Tec PLR-16 pistol and began stuffing extra loaded magazines into the pockets of his gray suit.

As soon as he returned, Langford turned to a man at his side. "Give me your AR, Don," he said.

As he grabbed the AR-15 from his subordinate's hands he said, "Everybody ready?"

Lyons nodded. "Then let's go. You know the layout," he said, looking to Hooks, "so you lead the way."

A second later they were following the man in the gray suit and turquoise bolo tie around the building to the side of the church.

THE RECENTLY PURCHASED Pizza Hut building was not the only addition the Southern Hills Baptist church had planned. A vacant lot where an old crumbling wood-frame house had been torn down stood adjacent to the church's gymnasium, and the workmen who were building new Sunday-school classrooms had left several ladders at the site.

While Blancanales stood watch through the windows into the gym to make sure no curious eyes were on them, Lyons, Schwarz, Hooks and Langford hefted the tallest of the ladders and hauled it to the side of the church.

"See anything?" Lyons asked when they had the ladder resting against the brick.

"Nothing but basketball goals and foul lines," Blancanales said.

Lyons led the way as the other men steadied the ladder, then turned and assisted each of the other men up onto the asphalt roof of the church.

The men made their way as quietly as possible across the top of the building. When they reached an airshaft roughly halfway toward the front of the church, Hooks stopped. "This leads down into the dressing rooms behind the baptistry," he said. "From there we can step down into the water itself. There's a curtain that'll cover us from sight."

Lyons nodded. It was at this point, he knew, that the leadership of the quickly formed five-man team should return to him. Hooks looked him squarely in the eyes and nodded his acknowledgment.

"Okay, guys," the former LAPD detective said. "I'll go first. None of us hit the water until we're all down. Got it?"

Four heads nodded back at him.

With Hooks's and Langford's help, Lyons pried the metal shaft off the hole leading down into the building. His Randall Model 1 fighting knife took care of the screen, and then he lowered himself through the passageway to the tile floor. His boots tapped as they hit the floor and he heard the curtain in front of the water start to move.

Someone had heard him.

And there was absolutely no place to hide.

Ignoring his own order of a moment earlier, Lyons lowered himself into the water of the baptistry and ducked his head beneath the surface, pressing himself as tightly as he could against the wall directly beneath the curtain. Through the water, he could see the curtain move. A bearded man wearing a red scarf with his khaki fatigues and BDU cap peered through the open window.

But he didn't look down. And a moment later, the curtain closed again.

Lyons rose slowly through the water, acutely aware of the unavoidable sound he was making. But it was evidently not as loud as his drop had been because the curtain remained closed. Climbing up the two steps and back onto the tile floor, he looked upward and motioned for the next man to come down. Lyons caught Schwarz's legs before they hit the floor, then lowered him silently.

Together the two Able Team operatives did the same for the remaining three men.

Holding a finger to his lips, Lyons then gave hand signals to direct the other men down into the water. He remembered the red scarf the terrorist had worn as he looked through the curtain a minute earlier, and frowned.

These terrorists had claimed to be legitimate Iranian troops. And the red scarf was official issue to the Revolutionary Guard—like the green beret to U.S. Special Forces.

The president of Iran was crazy—few people would argue that point. But was he crazy enough to actually send official troops inside America's borders and attack a house of worship? Of course anyone could buy a red scarf and tie it around his neck and call himself anything from Revolutionary Guard to Gene Autry if he wanted to. The terrorists could easily be al-Qaeda or Hezbollah or Hamas or some other group simply masquerading as Pasdaran troops.

At this point it didn't matter. He and the rest of his men could sort that all out after the thousand or so hostages on the other side of the curtain were safe.

Lyons's M-16 was already soaked with water from

his earlier dip beneath the curtain. But that mattered little with modern firearms. It would still fire. So holding it in front of him, he moved slowly to the corner of the curtain and used the barrel to push it slightly to the side.

Directly through the window was a large choir loft, with terrified men and women dressed in robes still sitting in their chairs. Mixed in with them were more men in khaki uniforms and red scarves.

One of them had to be the man who had almost spotted him earlier.

Behind the pulpit, and making full use of the microphone in front of him, another terrorist dressed in identical fatigues and a red scarf stood spouting Islamic terrorist propaganda in broken English. Lyons could hear him demanding that the congregation all convert to Islam immediately or be killed and go directly to Hell.

Other men with AK-47s, Uzis and a variety of other weaponry stood next to the speaker. Still more patrolled the aisles, and in the balcony Lyons could see that the same thing was going on. These men in red scarves—perhaps Iranian Pasdarans, perhaps simple terrorists in disguise—were covering their hostages from every angle.

What interested Carl Lyons most, however, was a red-scarfed man on the stage sitting next to a Caucasian in a blue suit. Lyons suspected the man in the suit was the minister. In his midforties, he had slightly graying hair. He sat quietly. But his face showed no fear. If anything, what emanated from the pastor was confidence and determination.

Next to the minister, on the floor, was a sinister-looking device that appeared to be comprised of Semtex plastic explosives and a glass container that held a dull, cloudy liquid that was turning yellow.

Nitroglycerin. Most people thought it was clear, and it was when it was new. But as the explosive aged, it took on more color.

And more instability. It might even be set off by the vibrations of a gunshot. It was a true IED—Improvised Explosive Device. Unprofessional and unpredictable.

In addition to a pistol in one hand, the man next to the minister held an electronic device that resembled a television remote control in the other. But Lyons knew this device had only one channel.

Explode.

Lyons stepped back through the water. He could never crawl through the window and get to the bomb or the man with the detonator before the bomb was detonated. And if he shot the terrorist, the gunshot itself might cause the explosion of the shaky nitro. Lyons stood there while the rest of his team took turns looking through the curtain to access the situation for themselves. All of them looked at him when they'd seen the explosive.

The Able Team leader moved back to the corner of the curtain and brushed it slightly to the side again. He looked out to lock eyes with the minister he had seen only moments earlier.

Somehow, for whatever reason, the preacher had turned in his seat enough to stare at the baptistry. And somehow Lyons had known he was going to do just that even before he moved the curtain.

The minister slowly nodded at Lyons.

Lyons nodded back. Although he wasn't sure why or what the nod meant. He only knew that to do nothing meant the sure deaths of two thousand innocent people seated in the congregation.

Turning toward the rest of the men next to him in the water, the Able Team leader whispered individual assignments. Langford and Hooks would take out the guards at the main doors while Schwarz and Blancanales dived through the opening to handle the terrorists on the stage and in the aisles.

Just before he was about to seize the curtain and jerk it back, Schwarz grabbed his sleeve. "What about the bomb?" he said.

"I'm taking care of it," Lyons said.

Schwarz frowned, then slowly nodded.

Carl Lyons reached up and grabbed the curtain with one hand, holding his M-16 with the other. He took a final look at each of his men, then suddenly ripped the curtain off the front of the baptistry so hard it came completely off the rings that had held it in place along the top of the window.

HAL BROGNOLA was a well-known face to the Secret Service agents stationed at the White House. So when he walked purposefully through the final metal detector and sent a loud buzzing down the hall, all he got from the men in the dark suits were nods of acknowledgment.

Brognola nodded back as he strode toward the open door to the Oval Office. Stepping inside, he saw that the chair behind the huge desk was empty. But that wasn't unusual.

So he turned to his left.

Few Americans knew it, but the Oval Office was used primarily for news briefings and meetings with foreign dignitaries. It was a show office. Most of the papers the President reviewed and signed, as well as the rest of the actual work he did, was conducted in a much smaller, more businesslike room next door. And it was from this door that Brognola heard the familiar voice say, "In here, Hal."

Brognola crossed the freshly vacuumed carpet and entered the work office. The Man was seated at one end of a long leather couch with stacks of paper arranged next to him.

When the President pointed toward the other end of the couch, Brognola dropped down beside the stacked papers. He wore two hats in the U.S. government. To the public, he was a high-ranking official within the U.S. Department of Justice. But behind the scenes, he was also the Director of Sensitive Operations for Stony Man Farm.

Today, however, he had no doubt which role the President would be expecting him to assume. Had the Man simply had Justice Department business on his mind, he'd have conducted it over the phone.

"I guess I don't have to tell you about the situation at the Iraq-Iran border," the President began.

Brognola shook his head. "I haven't seen a news tape replayed so many times since Rodney King," he said.

"You realize what the Iranian president is trying to do, I'm sure," the Man said.

"Sure," Brognola said. "They're trying to suck us into another Iraq. Crossing the border and killing and kidnapping American noncombatants was an act of war. Clean and simple. They're daring us to invade Iran."

The President nodded. "Exactly," he affirmed. "Right now, the sympathy of the rest of the world is with us."

Brognola grunted sarcastically. "That won't last. Particularly if we start bombing Tehran."

"You know, I know and Iran knows that we can kick their butts nine ways to Sunday if we want to," the President said. "But unless we nuke them out of existence, we'll have to send in more troops to keep order, and it won't work any better there than it has in Iraq."

"Or Vietnam or Korea," Brognola agreed.

"Right," the Man said. "It's pretty much all or nothing. We'd have to just forget about civilian casualties altogether and wipe them out. Or sit back and do nothing for years like we did when the Shah went down." He paused a moment, then said, "But there is a third possibility. A surgical strike that frees the hostages but doesn't do much, if any, collateral damage. It's slim, but at least it has a chance."

Brognola knew what was coming and remained silent.

"Where's Bolan at the moment?" the Man asked.

"Haven't heard from him in several days," Brognola said. "He's tied up with some things in Bosnia right now."

"Able Team and Phoenix Force?" the President asked.

"Able Team's in Oklahoma," Brognola said.

"Ah, yes." The President nodded. "The church situation. I understand it's Iranian-backed terrorists there, too?"

"Maybe yes, maybe no," Brognola said seriously.

"There's a rumor going around the intel agencies that the men who took over the church are Iranian Revolutionary Guardsmen. Pasdarans, complete with their red neckerchiefs."

"And Phoenix Force?" the President asked.

"McCarter and his boys are catching a few hours of well-deserved sleep after that affair in South Africa. But I can have them up and ready within the hour."

The phone on the desk suddenly rang.

"Get that, will you, Hal?" the President said. "Put it on speakerphone."

"Certainly, sir." Brognola rose to his feet, took two steps to the desk and pressed the intercom button on the phone.

"Nan, I told you to hold all of my calls while Mr. Brognola was here," the President said somewhat testily.

His tone didn't seem to have any effect on his receptionist. "I know," the voice on the other end of the line said confidently. "But you'll want this one."

"Who is it?" the Man asked.

"Javid Azria," Nan answered.

The President looked at Brognola.

Brognola looked back.

"Put him on," the Man directed.

A click sounded over the speakerphone and a moment later an Iranian-accented voice said, "Mr. President?"

"Yes, Mr. President?" the Man said back.

Brognola stood where he was, waiting.

"In addition to the church in that cowboy state of yours," the voice said pompously over the speakerphone, "the third suicide bomber I sent to Israel has just eliminated close to four hundred infidels by detonating himself in one of the decadent Western-inspired night clubs in Tel Aviv."

The President remained cool. "I hadn't even heard of the first two yet," he said, glancing at Brognola. "They must not have been very big."

The voice that responded turned angry. "They were big enough," it growled. "Exactly the size I *wanted* them to be."

Brognola sat silently. He was listening to one of the biggest egos he'd ever encountered in his long career.

"And, Allah willing, there are far bigger things to come," said the Iranian president.

"Are you declaring war on the United States, Mr. Azria?" the Man asked, using the Iranian president's name for the first time.

But the leader of the free world got no response.

All he and Hal Brognola heard was a click as the line went dead.

THE BAPTISTRY WINDOW was only wide enough to allow three men at a time to crawl through it. And as Hooks, Langford and Schwarz launched themselves upward out of the water, Lyons and Blancanales helped shove them onto the stage.

Counting both terrorists and worshippers, over a thousand heads jerked their way.

As the water-soaked warriors jumped to their feet, the remaining two members of Able Team followed.

It had all taken just enough time for the men in the red neckerchiefs to overcome their surprise and react.

Luckily, Able Team and the OSBI men assisting them reacted a fraction of a second quicker.

Lyons was the first to fire, triggering a 3-round burst from his M-16 into the head of the man who had been shouting from the pulpit. Lyons turned toward where the minister and the dark-complected man holding the remote detonator sat and saw that the minister had already grabbed the other man's hand. He held it in both of his own, his fingers tight around the device, preventing the terrorist from entering the code that would bring down the entire church.

Hooks and Langford knelt on both sides of the pulpit. The OSBI director was firing his AR-15 steadily in semiauto mode, taking out one door guard per round. Return fire whizzed back toward him, some of it striking the pulpit while other rounds perforated the large cross hanging just above the choir loft. Occasionally a round flew past them into the baptistry and a plopping sound echoed forth as it spent itself in the water.

The members of the choir had all hit the floor. Next to him, Hooks fired his Kel-Tec PLR-16, which had obviously been converted to full-auto. Each tap of his forefinger drove another khaki uniform and red scarf to the ground.

Schwarz and Blancanales were firing their own M-16s into the red-scarfed terrorists in the aisles and balcony. In addition to these warriors, several men and one woman within the congregation itself had risen to their feet and joined the battle, killing the terrorists near to them with hidden pistols. These off-duty cops and citizens with concealed-carry permits had been smart enough to wait for the right time to fight.

Lyons's well-trained brain had taken in all of these facts in a heartbeat, and now he turned his attention back toward the biggest threat in the church—the amateurish improvised bomb that still stood on the floor next to the chairs where the minister and his guard had been moments earlier. The two men were wrestling on the floor, each doing his best to gain control of the remote electronic detonator.

Skipping from the back of one choir chair to another, Lyons made his way down the rows through the choir loft toward the stage. Moan, cries and shrieks could be heard just beneath his boots.

So far, the vibrations from all of the rounds being fired throughout the church had failed to detonate the IED. But that didn't mean the next one wouldn't. Or the one after that. And the minister and terrorist wrestling on the floor were still too close to the device for comfort.

Lyons let his M-16 fall to the end of its sling as he jumped off the last row of choir seats and landed on the stage. A second later he had drawn the Randall Model 1 fighting knife and was diving on top of the grappling men. Lyons knocked the minister to the side, taking his place and grabbing the terrorist's wrist with his free hand. Before the man had a chance to push any of the buttons, the Able Team leader had thrust the point of the Randall's seven-inch blade through his wrist. He twisted the knife back and forth. Ligaments and tendons popped as the Able Team leader literally cut the detonator out of the man's hand with the Randall's razor-sharp edge.

The man with the scarf screamed at the top of his lungs as blood began to shoot from his wrist. Grabbing the detonator from the man's useless fingers, Lyons put all of his weight on the Randall, feeling it cut through to the other side of the wrist, penetrate the carpet below, then lodge itself in the wood beneath.

As he rose off the terrorist's chest, Lyons saw the man try to pull the knife out of his wrist with his other hand. Unsuccessful, he screamed as the pain proved more than he could endure.

The man with the knife through his wrist fell back in agony.

The minister had risen to his feet after being knocked clear by Lyons a moment earlier. The Able Team leader looked at him. His hair and clothing were disheveled and torn from the life-or-death wrestling match in which he'd just been engaged, but his eyes were clear.

Lyons pulled his trademark .357 Magnum Colt Python from his hip holster and twirled it so that the grips faced the minister. "You know how to use this thing?" he asked the preacher.

The man nodded his head. "Cylinder turns opposite from a Smith & Wesson," he said.

Those few words convinced Lyons that the preacher knew his guns. "Keep him here," he said, looking down at the man still pinned to the floor. "Don't shoot him unless you have to. He may have valuable information for us later."

The minister nodded as he took a two-handed grip on the Python and aimed it at the terrorist's head.

Lyons lifted the M-16 and turned toward the congregation. Catching a glimpse of khaki running toward a foyer door at the back of the sanctuary, Lyons directed a 3-round burst into the terrorist's back. The man dropped to the carpet a foot from the door.

Turning slightly, Lyons saw a member of the congregation wearing a plaid sport coat and dark tie aiming a Glock at one of the terrorists. But another terrorist, behind the man in plaid, was aiming an AK-47 at his back.

Lyons swung the M-16 around and sent another 3-round burst over the heads of the people huddling beneath the pews. The bullets all hit the man in the red scarf in the chest, dropping him out of sight a second before the man in plaid triggered his Glock.

The terrorist the churchgoer had aimed at fell to the man's pistol fire. He turned his gun on yet another of the intruders, never knowing that the Able Team leader had just saved his life.

Schwarz and Blancanales had moved down off the stage and were creeping along the sides of the sanctuary, using the pews as cover and targeting any terrorist who presented himself. Hooks and Langford were still battling away from the side of the pulpit.

Raising his eyes to the balcony, the Able Team leader saw that only one of the attackers was still on his feet, firing downward over the safety rail. Raising his assault rifle, the Ironman caught him in the chest with yet another burst of fire. The man screamed. Then his scream was cut off and a gurgling sound replaced it as his chest filled with blood.

Falling forward over the rail, he did a half flip before the back of his head struck the top of a pew. By now, the gunfire had begun to subside, and the cracking sound of the falling man's neck breaking echoed throughout the large sanctuary.

The various law-enforcement officers waiting outside began to enter the sanctuary through the foyer doors, and suddenly the battle was over.

"Check for wounded!" Lyons called to Schwarz and Blancanales. Both men nodded back at him. In the meantime, Langford walked to the pulpit and began talking in a calm voice, doing his best to end the screams of horror and other noise from the people under their seats. In a few seconds, heads began to rise as it became apparent that the nightmare was over.

Lyons returned to where the minister was still covering the man pinned to the floor. "Pastor," he said, "I need a room where I can talk to this guy. Nice and private."

The minister nodded as he handed Lyons's revolver back to him. "I'll take you to one of the Sunday-school rooms," he said. "By the way, thanks." He paused a moment, then said, "You don't look like regular policemen. Not even like special state agents like our own Gary Hooks."

"Nobody looks like Gary Hooks is my guess," Lyons said.

The minister laughed. "He marches to a different drummer, all right. I'm Rick Felton, by the way. Call me Rick." He stuck out his hand. "And you?"

"Just call me Lyons," the Able Team leader said.

"You must be federal agents of some kind," said Felton. "Is that what it is?"

"Sort of," Lyons said as he knelt next to the man on the floor. "It's hard to explain."

Lyons turned his attention to the man on the floor. Reaching down with both hands, he wriggled his fingers beneath the man's wrist, then yanked upward. There was still screaming and loud moans all over the sanctuary, but this terrorist's shriek was loud enough to turn all heads their way.

Lyons left the knife in the man's wrist, using the grip to guide him down off the stage and out through the closest exit. As they descended the steps, he saw both the Oklahoma City Police and Highway Patrol Bomb Squads enter the sanctuary. He pointed toward the bomb behind him, then moved on.

As they neared the door, Schwarz and Blancanales suddenly appeared next to him. "Only two civilian injuries, Ironman," Schwarz said. "Both superficial flesh wounds."

"Lucky," Lyons said as Felton led them down a hallway past the church kitchen.

The minister glanced over his shoulder and shrugged. "I think there might have been a little more than luck involved here, don't you?" he said. When no one answered, he continued to speak as they walked on. "Tell me how I knew you were in the baptistry," he said, smiling. "Better yet, tell me how you knew I'd know, and that I'd be willing to fight for the detonator until you got to me. And tell me why none of the congregation was killed, and why that bomb never went off. By all rights, we should all be dead right now. You think that all just happened by coincidence?"

"I don't know," Lyons said.

Felton glanced up toward the ceiling. "Well, I do," he said, smiling.

Lyons followed the minister to a door with a metal sign that read Adult II Sunday School. Felton pulled out a key ring and opened it, holding the door wide while Lyons led the captured man inside, still holding the knife. As soon as they were all inside the room, Lyons sat the man wearing the red scarf in a metal folding chair. The man was still making low, whimpering noises that the Able Team leader found irritating. Twisting the knife slightly, he made the prisoner scream.

"Okay," said Lyons. "You keep whining like a baby and I'll keep twisting the knife. Or you can act like a man and I'll treat you like one."

Their captive rattled off something in Farsi.

"You speak English?" Lyons demanded.

The man shook his head.

Lyons pulled on the knife again and the man screamed, "Yes! I speak English! I speak very good English for you!"

"Somehow I knew you were gonna say that," Lyons told him. Still holding on to the knife handle, he turned to Felton. It was obvious that the minister was uncomfortable being there while Lyons inflicted even this slight pain on their captive. "Pastor," he said, "you might want to take Hooks and Langford through the church and see if any of these guys escaped the sanctuary and are hiding someplace. On the other hand, there are probably SWAT teams already doing that, so I'd go back to the sanctuary and get behind the pulpit if I were you. I'm sure your presence would be of great comfort to the congregation during this stressful time."

Felton was no fool, and his facial expression told Lyons that he knew the Able Team leader simply wanted him out of there. But he nodded, then looked at the bleeding man in the chair. Even though the terrorist had attempted to murder him, his family and a thousand other people in his congregation, the preacher's eyes held no malice—only a trace of sorrow.

Felton looked up at Lyons, Schwarz and Blancanales. "Do what you have to do to save lives," he said. "And I'll keep working on their souls." He paused for a minute, then started for the door. "Someday the lion will lay down with the lamb," he quoted as he twisted the doorknob.

"Yes," Lyons agreed. "But I'm afraid it's not going to be today."

CHAPTER TWO

"Gadgets," Lyons said to Schwarz, the Able Team's electronics expert, "go double-check what the bomb squads are doing and then hurry back."

Without a word the Able Team warrior zipped out of the Sunday school room door and disappeared down the hall toward the sanctuary.

Lyons pulled the red-scarfed man's arm over the table in front of where he was sitting and braced it with his left hand. "This is going to hurt," he told the terrorist. "Hold your breath."

With a sudden yank on the Randall's grip, he withdrew the blade of the custom-made fighting knife.

The terrorist screamed and jerked the injured limb back against his chest, cradling it like a baby with the other arm.

"Do us both a favor," Blancanales said, irritated. "Act like a man instead of a bitchy little girl. You're a shame to our entire gender."

The prisoner quieted down, but small little moans still came from his mouth.

"Do like he said and shut up," Lyons growled. "Or I'll do the same to your other arm." In truth, the Able Team leader had no intention of torturing the man. Torture was too unpredictable. The subject tended to tell his tormenters whatever he thought would make them stop, and it might or might not be the truth.

The fact of the matter was, Lyons had even found pinning the man's wrist to the stage to get the detonator distasteful. But it had been the only practical way to disarm him. Guiding him into the Sunday-school room with the blade still stuck in his arm had been equally unpleasant. But it, too, had been the fastest and most pragmatic way of getting him out of the sanctuary and to a place where he could be questioned.

Now, as the injured man fell silent and tears streamed down his cheeks, Lyons looked him in the eye. "We've got two different routes we can take here," he said to the man. "You can tell us everything you know about who you are and what your plans were." He paused for a second, then went on. "Or we can play games until you bleed to death." He pointed to the man's wrist where the blood continued to leak in a slow but steady stream. Miraculously, it appeared he hadn't completely severed any of the major arteries in the process of cutting the tendons and ligaments.

But he had to have at least nicked one.

Snatching the red scarf from around the man's neck, the Able Team leader used it to wipe the blood off his knife. Then, dropping the Randall back into its sheath, he said, "Let's start with your name. What is it?"

The man closed his eyes but the tears still flowed from under his eyelids. "Umar," he finally mumbled.

Lyons leaned down, stuck a thumb on top of both of Umar's eyelids and opened them for him. What he saw inside was a man who was as terrified now as the poor, defenseless congregation in the sanctuary had been during the earlier siege. "Okay, Umar," he said. "Tell me who you and who the rest of the men are."

Umar paused a moment, as if trying to think of an answer that would satisfy Lyons but still not betray his countrymen. But when he saw Lyons's hand drop back down to the grip of the Randall knife, he said, "We are the Pasdaran. What you call the Iranian Revolutionary Guard."

Schwarz had reentered the room and now stood on the other side of the man with the punctured wrist. "Right," he said, leaning down on the other side and sticking his nose an inch away from Umar's. "And I'm George Washington, father of this country."

Umar shook his head back and forth violently. "No!" he declared, his eyes still on Lyons's hand gripping the knife. "It is the truth. We have been sent here by President Azria himself."

Lyons straightened but still stared hard at the man across the table. Could that be true? Javid Azria, the president of Iran, was a megalomaniac every bit as crazy as North Korean dictator Kim Jong Il. And regardless of Azria's claim to the contrary, everyone knew Iran had been working on a nuclear program ever since he had taken control of the country. And Azria had either refused or stonewalled all attempts by the UN to inspect that program.

If Azria had already worked out the kinks in his nukes, it might just have resulted in the courage to send official troops onto American soil. That possibility cast a whole new shadow over an already dire scenario.

"What were you supposed to do here?" Lyons demanded.

Umar took a deep breath, then looked down at his wrist, which was still spouting blood.

"I wouldn't waste too much time if I were you," said Rosario Blancanales, who stood directly behind the man. "You've probably lost a pint or two already. Feeling a little light-headed?"

Umar slowly nodded to indicate that Blancanales was right.

"Then I'd talk fast if I was you," Lyons said. "While you still can. Believe me, you tell us the truth—the whole truth—and you'll get immediate medical attention. You've got my promise on that. If you don't, we'll just watch you slowly pass out and then die right here." He leaned closer and added, "It's your decision."

"We are Revolutionary Guard," he said. "And our orders, which came directly from the president's mouth, were to find a large church in the area of the U.S. known as the Bible Belt, take it over during a Sunday-morning service and blow it up."

"And you were planning to blow yourselves up with it?" Lyons asked.

Umar nodded his head, and it was apparent to all

three Able Team warriors that the line separating terrorists from officially sanctioned government soldiers had finally been crossed. It was also obvious that Umar was getting close to the point where he'd pass out.

"So it was a suicide mission?" Schwarz said.

Umar nodded. "Yes," he said, his voice weak.

Lyons knew he'd have to hurry if he planned on getting more intelligence information out of this bleeding Pasdaran. As if to emphasize his thoughts, Umar's chin suddenly fell to his chest and his eyes closed again.

Lyons slapped him across the face. "You're faking it, you little scumbag," he said. "You think we just gave you a way out of all this. You're wrong."

Either the slap or Lyons's words or both brought the Pasdaran's head and eyelids back up immediately.

"So I can assume that you're not the only squad of Pasdarans in the country?" Lyons said.

Umar nodded. "There are dozens," he said.

"Where do we find them?" the Able Team leader demanded.

Umar slowly shook his head, and it was obvious that he really was getting dizzy now. "I do not know." His words slurred like a drunken man's. "Each unit knows only their own orders."

Lyons straightened to his full height and turned away from the bleeding man, his thoughts returning to Iran and Azria and the nuclear program. American intelligence agencies all knew that most terrorist strikes against the U.S. were backed and supported by the various governments of the Middle East. But this was never admitted to by those governments. To openly send official troops—especially troops as identifiable as these men in the red scarves—was unheard of.

Carl Lyons knew that Iran had developed nukes. His gut assured him of that. But did they have missiles, too? Ironically, that was where nuclear programs in rogue countries such as Iran usually got stalled. Building nuclear bombs was relatively easy compared to developing their delivery systems.

Lyons continued to stare down at the bleeding man. Even if the Iranians didn't have missiles to tote the nukes halfway around the world, there were many other ways to sneak them into the U.S. and then detonate them. And even if they didn't attack America, Israel was barely a stone's thrown away from Iran.

One nuclear explosion in Israel and a chain reaction could easily escalate straight into World War III. Such devastation was unthinkable to the average, sane man no matter what his politics or the country he called home. But to a madman like Javid Azria it might seem to be a perfectly logical step.

The Able Team leader turned back to Umar and saw that the man really had fallen asleep this time. "Pol," Lyons said, "go get some cops to wrap this guy up and get him to an ambulance where he can be transfused." He looked at the man in the chair who was still clutching his arm to his chest in his sleep. "And tell them he needs to be arrested and guarded. We may get more out of him later if he lives."

Blancanales hurried out of the room.

Schwarz and Lyons walked out together. They had

taken only a few steps down the hall back toward the sanctuary when Lyons's satellite phone rang. Lyons held the instrument to his ear and said, "Yeah?"

"You learn anything worthwhile?" Hal Brognola's voice asked.

"Just some general stuff. No specifics," Lyons answered. "These guys claim to be official Iranian Pasdaran instead of terrorists, and according to the one who lived, there are several dozen bands of them scattered across the U.S." He paused as Schwarz opened the outer door of the church. "But each squad appears to be autonomous. None of them know what the others' orders are."

"Well," Brognola said, "I can tell you what at least one of them is doing at the moment."

"What's that?" Lyons said.

"I'll brief you once you're in the air," said Brognola. "One of the local PD helicopters will take you to the airport, where Charlie Mott'll be waiting for you."

Blancanales joined them as they walked down the steps of the church. Almost as soon as Lyons had pushed the button to end the call, he heard the chatter of helicopter blades in the air above him. Looking up, he saw a blue-and-white chopper with OCPD markings.

The chopper set down on the grass in front of the church and the men of Able Team quickly boarded. A moment later the helicopter was rising again, headed for Will Rogers World Airport a few miles away.

DAVID MCCARTER came wide awake as soon as the phone rang next to his bed. Before it could chime again, he had snatched it from its cradle. He glanced at the wristwatch on the table next to the phone and saw that he'd had four hours of sleep.

Well, the native Londoner thought, it was at least more than usual. "McCarter here," he said into the mouthpiece.

"Grab your buddies and gear up," Hal Brognola's voice said into the phone. "You're on your way to Iran."

McCarter yawned. "Iran," he said. "Always wanted to go there."

"Well," Brognola said, "you're gonna get the chance. I'm about to land outside and I'll brief you and the other guys once you're on board."

"You're going in with us?" McCarter asked.

"No," Brognola clarified. "I'll just be riding along to run down the situation for you. Jack will fly me back as soon as you're on the ground."

McCarter yawned again. "That's going to cut into your own time," he said, glancing at the wristwatch again.

"Not as much as you think," Brognola said.

"Come again?" McCarter requested.

"You'll see what I mean in a few minutes. Grimaldi's got a brand-new toy."

David McCarter saw no reason to keep questioning Brognola on the subject. So he changed it. "Anything special we need to bring with us?"

"Just your personal weapons and other gear," said Brognola. "Kissinger'll be loading the extras while you round up your men."

"Affirmative," McCarter said. Even as he spoke he was pulling open a drawer filled with BDU clothing. "Just give me five."

"I'll give you four," Brognola said, and then the line went dead.

McCarter donned a clean blacksuit—the skintight, stretchy combat clothing of Stony Man warriors—and zipped up his boots. He reached for the large duffel bag that held the rest of his equipment. He had learned long ago that you packed before you slept in one of the Stony Man Farm bedrooms. Stony Man missions broke quickly, and tasks that required five minutes had to be completed in four.

Or less.

Leaving the room, McCarter walked along the hallway knocking loudly on the four doors he passed. The other members of Phoenix Force knew what the noise meant.

They were heading out again.

Two minutes later, the five-man squad walked out the front door of Stony Man Farm's Main House and headed for the landing strip. Just in time to see a strange plane land on the runway.

"What in bloody hell is that thing?" McCarter said to no one in particular as they walked toward the aircraft.

"It's a Concorde," Gary Manning said. The burly Canadian was Phoenix Force's explosives expert.

"We know it's a Concorde, Gary," said Rafael Encizo. "What our brilliant former British SAS man means is, what's it doing *here?*"

A moment later the five warriors had boarded the bird-looking Concorde, which was being flown by Jack Grimaldi, Stony Man Farm's number-one pilot. Brognola sat in the redecorated passenger's area in a reclining chair that was bolted to the carpeted deck. The other men dropped down into similar seats around the plane.

"Okay," said Thomas Jackson Hawkins in his South Texas drawl. "I give up. Where'd you pick up this monstrosity, Hal?"

Hal Brognola laughed. "Got it practically for a song," he said. "When the Concordes went out of business. As you can see, we've completely redone the inside."

"How come you didn't tell us about it?" Calvin James asked. The former Navy SEAL was from the south side Chicago.

"I wanted to surprise you," Brognola said. "These recliners are great to sleep in. It's going to give you more rest before each mission."

"You'll get no argument from me on that," McCarter said as the Concorde took off down the runway again. "But first tell us why we're heading for Iran."

Brognola nodded, then looked at his watch. "A lot has gone on since you boys shut your eyes in the Main House a few hours ago." He told the men of Phoenix Force about the murders of the newsmen and the hostages in Iran, as well as the attack on the church in Oklahoma City.

"The actual word *war* was never used when the Man was talking to the Iranian president," he said. "But that ratty little bastard might as well have. He took personal credit for his men crossing into Iraq, killing two men from FOX in cold blood and kidnapping the hostages. As well as the takeover of the church." Brognola pulled the remaining half of his cigar out of his front jacket pocket and stuck it in his mouth. "And he promised there was more to come. He even insinuated a nuclear strike on both Israel and the U.S."

"So what is it we're on our way to do?" Manning asked.

"Rescue the remaining five Americans," Brognola said solemnly. "And do your best to stop World War III."

Calvin James reached behind his back and pulled out a twelve-inch Crossada knife. It resembled a mediaeval dagger, and James kept it sharp enough to shave with either edge. "I'd like about thirty seconds with Azria and this," he said, staring at the huge knife in his hand. "Just the three of us."

"Well, you may get your chance," Brognola said. "There's no telling which way this thing's going to go at this point. But I can tell you that the Man in Washington is gearing up for a full-scale attack, both nuclear and conventional. The captive Lyons and his crew took, said there were at least a dozen Pasdaran teams already in the country and getting ready to strike all over the States."

The sentence brought on a profound silence as the Concorde rose higher into the air.

Brognola continued. "We're going to land in occupied Iraq. There, you're meeting a former CIA snitch named Adel Spengha. He's also known as "the Desert Rat.""

"Are you telling us he doesn't mind that name?" McCarter asked.

"Evidently not. He's half Iranian and half Pakistani, and he'll guide you through the mountains into Iran."

"This bloke trustworthy?" McCarter asked.

"Are snitches ever trustworthy?" Brognola retorted. "You'll have to watch him for double crosses just like always. I could count on one hand the number of informants I've had over the years who weren't playing both sides of the fence. And I'd still have enough fingers left over to throw a decent curve ball."

McCarter nodded his head.

"Okay, then," Brognola said. "This Concorde is going to get us where we're going in about half the time we'd make in a regular plane. So if I was you, I'd take advantage of that time to catch up a little more on your sleep." Without another word, the director of Stony Man Farm leaned back in his recliner and closed his eyes.

So did the men of Phoenix Force.

And when they opened them again, the Concorde's wheels were touching down on the runway of a U.S. military base in eastern Iraq.

CHARLIE MOTT was a long time Stony Man pilot. So it was no big trick for Mott to set one of the newly acquired Concordes down on the runway in Oklahoma City. Officials at Will Rogers World Airport had already been contacted by the Justice Department, and the sight of the odd, bird-beak-looking aircraft brought out only a mild curiosity on the parts of the Will Rogers's crewmen who greeted him.

"I wondered what was going to happen to these things after the company went broke," said a white-bearded mechanic in coveralls when Mott walked down the folding staircase. "Who are you with now?"

"The Department of Justice," Mott lied.

"That the truth?" asked the man with the beard.

"Uh-uh." Mott smiled. "But if I told you the truth, I'd have to take you up in it and drop you out at about forty thousand feet." He paused and adjusted his California Angels baseball cap. "Without a parachute."

The man with the white beard laughed. The noise conveyed not only humor but a tiny bit of nervousness, as well.

Silence fell over the tarmac until an Oklahoma City PD sedan, lights flashing and siren blaring, suddenly appeared and began crossing the runways toward the Concorde. "Ah," Mott said. "My passengers have arrived."

The marked unit screeched to a halt and Lyons, Blancanales and Schwarz got out.

"Need a lift?" Mott asked as they hurried his way.

"Yeah," Lyons said. "But where did you get this thing?" He indicated the Concorde with his head.

"Hal bought a couple of them," Mott said. "I think you'll be impressed." Without another word, he turned and hurried up the steps. The men of Able Team followed.

As they taxied down the runway, Lyons said, "Hal's supposed to brief us in the air. Any idea where we're going?"

Mott pulled a headset over his ears and began fiddling with the Concorde's control panel. "As a matter of fact," he said, "I know exactly where you're going. To a suburb of Kansas City called Shawnee Mission."

The Concorde left the ground looking like some kind of a determined predatory bird in flight.

As the trio moved to the reclining chairs bolted to the deck in the back of the plane, Lyons pulled his satellite phone from a pocket. Once seated, Lyons tapped in the number to Stony Man Farm.

A second later Hal Brognola was on the line. And the conversation turned serious.

Deadly serious.

ALL EYES on the ground rose to the air then fell to the runway with the Concorde as it landed at the U.S. military base near Mandali, Iraq.

They stayed glued to the men of Phoenix Force as the five men—all dressed in blacksuits and wearing side arms, as well as carrying assault rifles—walked down the steps to the ground.

McCarter started to lead them toward the buildings in the distance. But before he could even take a step in that direction he saw two jeeps racing toward them. Both sets of tires screeched to a halt in front of the Phoenix Force warriors, and the drivers—both wearing 101st Airborne patches on their sleeves—motioned them to hop aboard.

A few minutes later they were in front of a desk with a nameplate that read Colonel L. D. Brown. They shook hands all the way around, then dropped into five folding chairs that had obviously been brought in just for this meeting.

Colonel Brown might as well have had U.S. Army stamped on his forehead. Although obviously around sixty years old, he still had a full head of hair flattened into a white buzz cut. His face was worn and wrinkled, reminding McCarter of a dry creek bed, and although he was only around five feet six or seven inches tall and maybe 140 pounds, the muscles in his tattooed arms, which extended out of his short-sleeved uniform shirt, would have rivaled those of Popeye the Sailor.

Brown had started to speak when a sergeant suddenly opened the door and ushered a man dressed in robes and a kaffiyeh into the room. He looked up at the colonel to see what his next move should be, and Brown raised a hand and waved him in.

The door to the office closed behind him.

"Gentlemen," Brown said to the men of Phoenix Force. "Say hello to Adel Spengha. He also goes by Desert Rat. And he's worked with the CIA for years."

Another round of handshakes took place and then Brown said, "Rat here, can get you through the mountains and into Iran faster and safer than anybody I know. But that doesn't mean you won't encounter any of the enemy."

The man called Rat had taken a seat in another of the folding chairs, and now he opened his mouth. Speaking in near-unaccented English he said, "The Zagros Mountains, which border Iraq and Iran, are filled with Iran's regular troops, brigands and a tribe of Kurds who got caught in the middle of things when the war first started. All are dangerous." He paused a second, then added, "I must be honest. It would be much wiser not to go."

"That depends on how important a chap's mission is, I suppose," McCarter answered him. "We don't always have the luxury of doing the smart thing. Sometimes we have to do the necessary thing."

The Rat nodded his head. "Yes," he said. "I understand. So, when do you want to get started?"

"There's no time like the present," said McCarter, standing. The rest of the men of Phoenix Force followed.

Brown walked out of the office and down the hall with them. "The jeeps will take you as far as they can," he said. "But then you're on your own."

"That's usually the case," McCarter told Brown. "Thanks for your help."

The two men shook hands once again, then the men of Phoenix Force and Adel Spengha piled into the jeeps.

As they started toward the Iranian border, McCarter saw the Concorde take off again over his shoulder.

CHAPTER THREE

The Zagros Mountains, which separated the northern border of Iraq and Iran, was the largest mountain range of either country. And David McCarter could attest to that as he climbed the final step to the small plateau, then held up his hand for the men behind him to stop. "Fifteen-minute break," the Phoenix Force leader said as he turned around. "Then we move on again."

McCarter took a seat on the plateau, pulled the canteen from his belt and took a swig of water. Swishing it around in his mouth, he swallowed, then took another sip. Farther up the mountain footpath, he could see snow. But even though he and the rest of the men had been ascending steadily for over three hours, they were still low enough that their cold-weather gear was still stowed in their backpacks.

McCarter looked at the snow again, then drank once more. There was no need to save water. There would be plenty of snow and ice that could be melted before this journey was over.

McCarter drank again from his canteen as he watched the rest of Phoenix Force and their guide take seats or lie down to rest upon the plateau. After a short break the Phoenix Force leader glanced at his wrist. It was time to go.

"Everybody up," he announced as he rose. "Time to move on." He smiled slightly as he watched his men almost jump to their feet. There were no moans or any other sounds of distress or unhappiness you always heard when commanding regular troops. The men of Phoenix Force were far above such behavior. They were the best of the best, culled from positions with Delta Force, the Navy SEAL, U.S. Army Rangers and Special Forces, and other special-operations units. McCarter himself, being an Englishman rather than American, had once headed up a team of British Special Air Service commandos.

He was proud of his past. But David McCarter was even more proud of his present. Every single man under his command was a leader, and could take the steering wheel at any time. McCarter considered commanding such men a privilege and an honor.

Adel Spengha was the last to rise to his feet. While he remained as silent as the warriors, it was obvious that he was hardly in the same peak physical condition as the men of Phoenix Force. It was primarily for his sake that McCarter had called for the rest period in the first place.

The Desert Rat wobbled slightly as he walked over to McCarter, and the Phoenix Force leader saw the fatigue in the man's eyes. "I would suggest," Spengha said, "that we soon pick out a place to bivouac for the night." His dark brown eyes rose toward the snowy peaks ahead. "If we keep going, we will have to spend the night near the top and it will be freezing."

McCarter assessed the suggestion. "You're right," he said. He glanced at his watch again. "We'll hit it hard for another hour, then find a place to settle in for the night. Trying to cross the top would be a death sentence. We're going to be walking on ledges covered in ice as it is, and there's no sense in trying it at night."

The Rat's eyes looked relieved.

McCarter was about to announce his decision to the rest of the team when sudden gunfire broke the peacefulness of the mountain. He watched what sounded like a submachine-gun round strike the Rat's bulky robe, then yelled, "Take cover!"

The men of Phoenix Force dropped back down on the plateau, squirming in tightly behind the boulders that surrounded the area.

McCarter had unconsciously reached out and taken the Rat down with him. Now, as they crawled to the cover of the rocks, he said, "Were you hit?"

The Rat shook his head. "I don't think so," he said. "Just my robe."

The gunfire had continued. But it stopped as the targets disappeared. "Anybody hit?" McCarter called.

He got four negative replies from his men.

David McCarter turned his attention back to the steep trail. The gunfire had come from somewhere farther up the mountain. Which meant the enemy had the higher ground.

Never a good thing.

As silence returned to the plateau, the Phoenix Force leader looked back at the Rat again. "Any idea who we're facing?" he asked.

"My guess would be brigands," Spengha said. "Iranian soldiers would have come down the trail en masse. And the Kurds are farther to the south. At least I *think* they are."

"How old is that bit of intel, mate?" McCarter asked.

"Two days," the Rat said.

McCarter's teeth tightened as he blew air out between them. Two days was like an eternity when it came to war. More than enough time for the entire picture to change. The Kurds might have moved north during that time. And he wasn't so sure about the Iranian regulars, either. Iran's red-scarfed Revolutionary Guard—the troops Lyons and his men were now facing back in the States—actually outnumbered the country's regular army both in size and influence.

So he wasn't nearly as sure that they weren't facing legitimate Iranian soldiers as the Rat seemed to be.

McCarter had been wearing a black floppy boonie hat during the climb. But now he yanked it from his head. Draping it over the barrel of his M-16, he slowly poked the hat up over the boulder.

Almost as soon as it became visible from behind cover, a shot rang out. The hat twirled on the rifle barrel before he pulled the rifle back down beside him. "Well," he said more to himself than to the Rat, "whoever they are, they're still there."

The Rat nodded his head vigorously. "We must go back," he said. "We will get killed if we try to continue."

"We're not going back," the Phoenix Force leader said. "We're going into Iran, we're going to find the hostages, we're going to get them out safely and we're going to find out if that little wanker of a president really does have nuclear weapons." He looked the Rat in the eyes. "Now, you stay here."

Without waiting for any sort of reply, David McCarter dived away from the boulder and rolled across the plateau toward where Calvin James had taken cover behind another large boulder. He threw a wild 3-round burst toward the enemy as he rolled, and felt the heat of return rounds sizzle past his body as he moved.

But a moment later he was safely ensconced behind the same rock as James.

The gunfire continued for a moment, then settled down again.

"Cal," McCarter said as he rose to a sitting position next to James, "I believe we have a job for a man of just your talents."

The well-trimmed mustache on the black Phoenix Force commando's face spread wide into a smile.

He already had the twelve-inch blade of his double-edged Crossada out of its Kydex sheath.

CALVIN THOMAS JAMES had grown up on Chicago's South Side where knife fighting was more important than any subject or sport offered by the school system. It was a matter of survival. You either got good or died trying.

And while he had plenty of scars to remind him of past altercations, Calvin James was still alive.

Slowly, the Phoenix Force warrior descended back down the rocks, staying out of sight below the plateau where the other men were still lurking. He knew he had to stay invisible if he was to be successful on this private mission McCarter had just handed him.

James was counting on the enemy staying focused on the plateau. He just needed to move far enough to the side that he could navigate his way up the mountain until he located and identified them.

Finally, when his instincts told him he was low enough to be out of sight, James moved to the left side of the mountain pass, then slowly began to scale the side of the mountain. His eyes stayed one step ahead of his body, always searching for the next hand- and foothold, be it a crevice in the rocky mass or the stub of a tree lacking enough water to grow to its full potential. Every so often, he came to a ledge wide enough to stand on, and he used such places as rest stops, keeping a close look at the chronograph on his wrist and forcing himself to wait a full two minutes before moving on.

It was a true test of strength, skill and patience but soon he had drawn even with the small plateau from which he'd started. Here and there, he could see an arm or leg among the rocks, and knew they belonged to one of his Phoenix Force brothers. But they weren't moving. And there still had been no gunfire since he'd left.

James moved on, the muscles in his shoulders and arms beginning to pump now as blood rushed into them and his legs. When he came to another ledge wide enough for a breather, James looked back down to see that the rest of the men of Phoenix Force and the Rat were completely out of sight. He had begun timing the rest stop when a pebble rolled down the side of the mountain and bounced off his head before falling on.

James looked up to see the boots and pant legs of a man ten feet above him and perhaps a yard to his right. Above the pants, the man wore a brightly striped robe that was cinched at the waist by a gun belt.

James froze in place.

The enemy was using the same strategy that he was. The only difference was that their recon man was coming down the side of the mountain instead of going up.

James watched closely as the man descended toward the same small ledge upon which he was standing. Luckily, the head above the robe was looking over his right shoulder as he made his way down, and appeared totally oblivious to the fact that James was even there.

So the Phoenix Force knife expert slowly withdrew the Crossada from its Kydex sheath, hoping the inevitable swooshing sound it made would not be loud enough to catch the ears of the man above him.

While the swoosh sounded as loud as a tornado in James's mind, it went unnoticed.

The Phoenix Force warrior waited until the man had both feet on the ledge before moving a step to his right and hooking the Crossada around his throat. Pulling him in tightly, he whispered, "I hope you speak English. Because if you make any sound at all, it'll be a race to see if you bleed to death before you get killed by the fall you'll also be taking."

The man remained silent.

"Okay," James said, pressing the razor edge of the

huge fighting knife a little harder into the man's throat. "In the quietest voice you can possibly muster up, tell me if you speak English."

"I speak English," the man whispered in a jittery voice.

"Good," James said. "Then tell me who you are."

"We are what you call Kurds," said the man, his voice still shaking. "And we thought you were either Iraqi or Iranian troops. Which is confusing because we are now speaking English and your voice sounds American."

James hesitated a moment, then slowly withdrew the knife from the man's throat and sheathed it once again. He turned the Kurd around to face him, and shook the man's hand. "We are Americans," he said. "At least, I am. But we've got a Canadian and Englishman along with us, too. We're an international force, and we're not after you."

The man still looked frightened and skeptical. "So, what do we do?" he said.

James frowned for a moment, then said, "How far away are the rest of your men?"

The Kurd's dark brown eyes looked directly into those of Calvin James. "Not far," he said. Then, guessing at what James already had in mind, he said, "They will be able to hear me if I shout."

"Then shout your little heart out," said James. "Tell them we're friendlies, and we want a meeting with your leader." He paused for a moment, drawing in a breath of the thinning mountain air. "But first, what's your name?"

"My name is Mehrzad" the Kurd said.

"I'm James," the Phoenix Force warrior said, then shook the man's hand again to ensure that he knew they were, indeed friendly. "Now, call out to your men."

Mehrzad's voice cracked slightly as he shouted out in a dialect of Arabic. Silence followed his words, then a voice called down the mountain.

After the next exchange, James said, "My turn." Looking down toward the plateau where his fellow warriors waited, he yelled, "These are Kurds, guys. They thought we were Iranian or Iraqi."

"I'm not sure which is the bigger insult," McCarter's voice called up the mountain.

"I say we kill them just for that," Hawkins drawled.

"Some of them speak English, Hawk," James yelled back. "And they may take you literally and not understand that you're making a joke." He raised his voice even louder on the word "joke" in case other English-speaking Kurds above had heard the exchange. T. J. Hawkins was Phoenix Force's newest member, and while he was as good at fighting as any of them, he occasionally let a careless sentence slip out of his mouth.

McCarter's voice came up the mountain again. "Tell them we're laying our rifles down, Cal. And ask them to come on down to meet us on the plateau."

"I heard him," Mehrzad said. Then the Kurd translated the Phoenix Force leader's words in a loud voice.

Above, James heard low mumbling and grumbling as the Kurds tried to decide if he and the rest of these strangers could be trusted. Mehrzad spoke again, then James watched as the members of Phoenix Force rose from behind the boulders and laid their M-16s against the rocks, finally stepping out into full view.

A few moments passed, then the heads of more

Kurds began to appear above them. They all moved toward the pathway that led to the plateau.

James realized he had been less than ten yards below where several men had been hiding behind an outcropping in the rocks. If Mehrzad had not come down the mountain first, James would have been filled with automatic fire as soon as he'd climbed even a few more feet.

Calvin James raised his eyes toward the sky and grinned from ear to ear. "Thanks," he said.

Then he and Mehrzad made their way across the mountain to join the rest of the Kurds going down to meet Phoenix Force on the plateau.

CARL LYONS leaned back in his reclining chair on board the Concorde and pressed a button on the control panel to his side, answering the call from Hal Brognola. "Lyons here, go ahead. We're all listening. Where are you?"

"I'm on my way back from dropping Phoenix Force off in Iraq," Brognola explained. "Here are the facts as they stand right now. Another squadron of Pasdarans have taken over an entire shopping mall on the Kansas side of Kansas City. There's no runway close by that even Grimaldi can set the Concorde down on, so I've arranged for a Kansas City chopper to be ready for you when you set down at Kansas City International."

"Great," Lyons said. "But I want Jack flying it."

"I've pulled some strings and arranged that, too," Brognola said over the speakerphone. "They weren't all that happy about turning their bird over to somebody they didn't know. But I convinced them it was a good idea."

Lyons chuckled under his breath. Hal Brognola had

the ear of the President any time he wanted it, and he suspected the Stony Man director might have had the Man call himself. "How long ago did they take the mall over, Hal?" he asked.

"Shortly after 1300 hours," Brognola said. "It's Sunday, so it hadn't opened until noon. They gave it an hour to fill up with customers—a lot of them church-goers who'd stopped in on their way home from services. The first communication to the KCPD came in at 1312."

"You suppose they did that on purpose?" Lyons asked.

"I'm certain of it," Brognola said. "They told the KC cops that themselves."

As the Concorde flew on, Lyons frowned. "Did they have demands or was it like the church—just bleed the news media for all the publicity they can and then kill everyone including themselves?"

"No, they actually had one demand this time," Brognola replied.

Lyons waited to hear it.

"They want every Muslim prisoner in county jails, state and federal penitentiaries all over the country released," he said.

"They aren't asking much, then," Lyons said sarcastically.

Brognola snorted over the line. "That's sort of the way the Man looked at it." He paused, then went on. "We know that they know that nothing of that sort is going to happen. Even if it did, they'd just wait and then carry on with what they've begun at the mall."

"What does the Iranian president say?" Lyons asked.

"Javid Azria isn't making any excuses. He openly admits that these are all official Iranian Revolutionary Guardsmen who've snuck into the country over the last few weeks and are now carrying out his specific orders."

"He's asking for war," Lyons said.

"No doubt about it," Brognola came back.

"That madman *can't* believe he's got a chance of winning against the U.S.," Lyons said.

"No," Brognola agreed. "But the joint chiefs are in session and they think they've figured out what Azria's large picture looks like."

"And?" Lyons urged.

"Azria has vowed to wipe Israel off the map," Brognola said. "That's a direct quote."

Lyons snorted sarcastically again. "Minor change from the old 'push them into the sea' threat we've been getting since the end of World War II," he said.

"Well," Brognola said, "this time it looks like they plan to carry through with the threat. Like I was about to say, the joint chiefs are all in agreement that Iran intends to force America's hand. They're prepared to take massive air strikes just like Afghanistan and Iraq did in order to draw us in, then bog us down on the ground like we already are in those two countries."

"Hundreds of thousands of Iranians who don't have a thing to do with this are going to die if that happens, Hal," the Able Team leader noted.

"I know that, the President knows that and so does Javid Azria. But he doesn't care about that." Brognola stopped talking long enough to take a breath, then went on. "Life's cheap to him. All life except his own."

"Okay," said the Able Team leader. "Anything else we need to know?" He glanced out the window at the clouds below the Concorde as he waited for an answer.

"Yeah," Brognola said. "Striker came across some interesting side intel in Bosnia. Evidently, there's a Russian connection somewhere inside this whole mess."

"A *what* connection?" Lyons wasn't sure he'd heard right.

"You heard me correctly. Some kind of Russian connection." The Stony Man director was chomping hard on the end of his stump of cigar. "Striker doesn't know any more, and it doesn't seem to have anything to do with his own mission there. It was just something he picked up along the way and passed back to us in case it helped."

"It helps confuse me even more than I already was," said Lyons.

"Me, too," Brognola said as Lyons felt the Concorde begin a rapid descent. "But it might start to make sense somewhere down the line."

"I'll keep it in mind," Lyons said. "Anything else we need to know?"

"Probably a lot. But that's all I have for now. I'm sure you'll find out yourself when you get to K.C."

"We'll keep you informed," Lyons said. "And thank Striker for me." He disconnected the call.

The flight from Oklahoma City to Kansas City, Missouri, was almost an up-and-down hop for the Concorde, and Lyons saw that it was only a little past 1500 hours on his wrist. As they deplaned to the runway, they saw the marked KCPD helicopter waiting for them on the ground, blades whirling as it warmed up for flight.

In a way, it felt like Oklahoma City all over again. But the mall was going to get a lot more complex than the church had been. It was far bigger, and there were thousands more places for men—or explosives—to hide.

Jack Grimaldi was the last one out of the Concorde but he raced past the men of Able Team as Lyons, Schwarz and Blancanales began pulling equipment bags out of the storage compartment. Lyons saw the air ace say a few words to the KCPD pilot inside the chopper, and then the uniformed man reluctantly stepped down.

Grimaldi patted him on the shoulder as he took the man's place at the controls.

It took a little less than four minutes for Grimaldi to get them over the tall downtown buildings of Kansas City, Missouri, to the Kansas border and then to Shawnee Mission, Kansas. Actually, Shawnee Mission was a region rather than a suburb, made up of several independent smaller towns that, if combined, would have taken over from Wichita as the state's largest city.

"There's the mall," Grimaldi said, nodding toward the bubble windshield in front of him. "Carpenters Square." He turned to glance at Lyons. "Want me to do a fly-over?"

Lyons nodded silently, frowning slightly as he looked out the side window of the chopper. Below, he saw what looked almost like a replay of the scene at the church they'd just come from. Blue-and-red lights whirled above both marked and unmarked squad cars, and the sirens were blasting so loud he could hear them all the way up in the helicopter. Most of the marked units were from Kansas, but some of the Missouri officers had crossed the state line as backup, too. Such was usually the case when a residential area spanned more than one jurisdiction—the cops on both sides knew each other and worked together frequently.

The mall itself appeared to be in a classic cross configuration, with two long hallways that intersected in the middle. At one end of the north-to-south hallway stood a large, three-story Dillard's store. At the other was a JC Penney.

Kohl's and Jan and Jeni's Sportwear made up the tips of the other long strip of stores.

"Take her down a little lower," Lyons told Grimaldi. "I want to get a look at the entrances and exits."

Grimaldi nodded and dropped the bird in the air, hovering a few feet off the ground and almost directly in front of one of the entrances into Dillard's. Through the glass, the Able Team leader could see several men with red scarves around their necks looking back at him. As he watched, one of them raised his AK-47 and fired.

But Jack Grimaldi had seen the man, too, and he twisted the chopper slightly in the air, not unlike a boxer sliding off a punch. The 7.62 mm bullet struck the windshield of the chopper and careened off, leaving only a tiny scratch in the glass to show where it had been.

That scratch was directly in front of Carl Lyons's nose.

The radio suddenly blasted with screeching and scratching. Grimaldi adjusted the squelch as a stern voice said, "KBI-1 to Missouri chopper—whatever your call name is!"

Lyons lifted the radio microphone from where it was clipped below the control panel and said, "Just call us AT," he said. "AT-1, 2 and 3. I'm 1."

"Well, whoever you are, get your ass out of there," said the same KBI voice. "They've just called and said if you don't land or fly away they'll ignite the whole mall right now!"

"Affirmative," Lyons said. He nodded at Grimaldi, who immediately raised the helicopter straight up in the air. He glanced down at the mike, as if it might actually be the man he'd just talked to. Whoever the guy was, he sounded as if he was used to being obeyed.

Carl Lyons's best guess was that KBI stood for Kansas Bureau of Investigation, a state investigative unit. And KBI-1 would undoubtedly be the director.

But he didn't sound as if he was going to be as easy to get along with as Dwayne Langford had been back at the church.

"AT-1 to KBI-1," Lyons said into the mike. "What's your 10-20?"

"We're set up at the edge of the parking lot, north side," the surly voice came back. "There's a place where you can land over here, and I'm ordering you to do just that right now!"

Grimaldi turned to the Able Team leader again. "Want me to land?" he asked.

Lyons nodded. "I'm not sure this clown's ego could take it if we didn't."

Grimaldi laughed and turned the chopper that way.

A few seconds later they were coming down on the asphalt parking lot next to one of the SWAT vans parked around the mall. Lyons saw the same hectic activity that he'd seen outside the church in Oklahoma City, with flashing lights and sirens blaring, with every SWAT team and other unit anxious to get started but not knowing how or where.

As the chopper's rails met the ground, a man in a dark blue shirt and bright red tie approached with a look of anger on his face. He reached out and opened Lyon's door with one hand, and would have grabbed the Able Team leader by the arm and dragged him out if Lyons hadn't intercepted his other hand first. Twisting the man's wrist into a classic jujitsu hold, the Able Team leader watched the anger on the man's face turn to a grimace of pain as he exited the chopper on his own.

"Well, we're certainly off to a great start, aren't we, Mr. KBI-1?" he said as he finally released the man's hand.

The Kansas Bureau of Investigation director was too proud to rub his wrist where it had come close to snapping, so he stood upright and at attention as he said, "Okay, you're under arrest for resisting an officer." He turned to look at Schwarz and Blancanales as they exited the helicopter behind Lyons. "What happens to you two remains to be seen." He ran his eyes up and down the blacksuits all three Able Team warriors wore, looking for any trace of a patch or insignia.

But, of course, he found none.

"What in the hell kind of dress-up is that?" he demanded. "Who do you represent, anyway? You're not Missouri cops. The chief would have called me himself."

Lyons had faced such irritating bureaucrats throughout his entire former career as a LAPD officer. He had never had any patience for pompous little jackasses like this man then, and if there had been any change in his attitude at all, he had even less now. "I get one phone call, don't I?" he said sarcastically, pulling the satellite phone from its case on his belt. Quickly he tapped in the number to Stony Man Farm. "Since you didn't get a call from the Missouri chief, I'll let you talk to our chief."

"Right," said the Kansas director with the same sarcastic tone the Able Team leader had used.

It took less than ten seconds for Lyons's call to be transferred to Hal Brognola.

The man in the red tie frowned in confusion as he took the phone from Lyons. It didn't take long for Brognola to read the riot act to the KBI director. "Yes, sir," was all he said before his face turned red and he handed the instrument back to Lyons.

"Thanks, Hal," the Able Team leader said, and then disconnected the line again.

"All right," said the man Lyons knew only as KB-1. "My name is Markham. Bill Markham. What are your plans and how can we help?" The words sounded as if they hurt coming out of his mouth.

"You can give us a rundown of exactly what's going on," Lyons said. "Then, unless one of my men or I tell you different, you can stay out of our way."

CHAPTER FOUR

Iranian president Javid Azria rolled up his prayer rug, nodded to the staff with whom he had shared afternoon prayers and returned to his office, closing the door behind him. Alone and out of sight, he tossed the rug carelessly onto a padded armchair as he moved behind his desk. As he dropped down into his chair, he felt a grin creeping across his face.

The entire United States, including their president, was still in shock. The Americans simply couldn't fathom the fact that a country such as his own was openly defying and attacking them at will.

And rather than denying the attacks or blaming them on terrorists, Iran was taking credit for them.

Azria opened the humidor on his desk and took out a long, thick, Cuban cigar. Snipping off the end with a tiny guillotinelike cutter, he stuck the cigar in his mouth and picked up the heavy marble lighter on his desk next to the phone. The cigars had been a gift from his most recent ally, and although smoking was forbidden by the

Koran, he liked the Cubans and indulged in one every afternoon and another in the evening. The rest of his staff studiously ignored this small transgression on his part.

As he circled the end of the cigar around the flame in front of him, Javid Azria's eyes caught sight of the painting on the wall to his left. It depicted Cyrus the Great in battle, a long scimitar in his right hand as he beheaded what was obviously a Jewish peasant. The painting was, of course, an artist's rendition. Photography had still been centuries away when Cyrus had ruled the Persian Empire, so no one really knew exactly what the man had looked like.

Azria was fairly sure he knew, however. He saw Cyrus's face every time he looked in a mirror.

He was in the process of starting the first real jihad the world had seen since the days of the Crusades. But this war was going to make those of the past look like an American Girl Scout meeting.

Turning the end of the cigar toward his eyes, Azria saw that it had lit evenly and set down the lighter. Contentedly, he puffed away as he awaited an eagerly anticipated phone call. His mind drifted back in time to his college days. He had been a dean's list student at Yale when the Shah had been dethroned and Ayatollah Khomeini had taken over Iran. And he had not returned until long after that initial regime had taken control of the country. For a while, the theocracy had ruled Iran with an iron fist, beheading offenders of even the smallest Islamic laws just like Cyrus the Great was doing in his painting. But with the Ayatollah's death, things had gradually loosened up. Students in favor of separating religion from government were now even allowed to demonstrate in the streets. The only thing that had not changed was what he perceived as an almost country-wide hatred of the Jews, and a certain amount of dependence on the United States and other countries in the Western world.

Azria leaned farther back in his chair. It was his mission in life to change all that. He could have felt it in his soul.

If he'd believed in souls.

He was halfway through the long Cuban when the buzzer on his phone finally sounded. "President Azria," the voice of his secretary said in Farsi. "I have President Gomez on the line for you."

Azria answered in the same language. "Put him on," he said.

The Iranian leader pressed the receiver closer to his ear as he heard a click. Then, an accent far different than his own spoke in English—the one language they had in common and therefore the one they always used. Ironically, he thought, it was the language of their common enemy.

"Good afternoon, Mr. President," said Raoul Gomez, the president of Venezuela.

"And the same to you," said Azria.

"We have not spoken since your American guests from Iraq arrived in your country," Gomez said in a lighthearted voice.

Azria laughed, knowing the other man meant the American hostages who'd been kidnapped near the border. "No, sir, we have not," he said into the receiver. "I believe they are resting at the moment."

"Yes," Gomez said. "I sometimes forget that night here is day in your country. An afternoon nap, no doubt?"

"Probably," Azria said. "They really have little to do but sleep and worry."

"Very good," Gomez stated. "I have a ship en route to your country even as we speak. And I trust that the shipment which is coming my way is on schedule, as well?"

"Yes," Azria continued. "It will arrive quite soon, in fact."

"Very good again," Gomez said. "Actually, that was the only reason for my call. Your other actions in America and Israel are having the desired effect, according to my intelligence operatives. The United States is focused on the Pasdarans you snuck across their borders and the hostage situation." He paused to cough, and Azria realized he, too, was smoking a cigar. Probably the same brand and size as the ones he had sent to the Iranian president.

When Gomez had quit coughing, he added, "The Israelis are being forced to rivet their attention on your increase in suicide bombings. And, in addition to the newsmen hostages, the Americans are focusing on the small strikes of your Pasdarans inside their very borders. These diversions are allowing our true objective to…" He paused for a second, searching for the right words. "To fly under the radar. Yes. I believe that is the slang term the *norteamericanos* use."

"If it means my shipment to you and yours to me is going unnoticed, then, yes, I believe you are correct."

"We must speak again when the ships have arrived," Gomez said.

"We will," Azria agreed, and then hung up the phone.

Javid Azria had to draw in hard on his cigar, which had almost gone out during the conversation. But after a couple of weak puffs of smoke, it returned to its former fully lighted state. Azria sat back in his chair again, stuck the cigar between his lips and smiled.

By either confusing or sometimes flat-out refusing to allow U.N. inspectors to do their job in his nuclear plants, he had successfully completed his program and now had several dozen nuclear warheads at his disposal. In addition to that, he was about to broker another deal for F-14 fighter plane parts from another source. There had been a time when his country still had many serviceable F-14s in their arsenal—purchased by the Shah before Iran and the United States became such bitter enemies. But now, the majority of these fighters had been grounded. And without the U.S. to provide new parts, they had been forced to cannibalize the few that remained to keep others running.

But that would change shortly, too. And the scope of suicide bombers would expand far beyond what the world had ever seen. He was even now shipping several of his nuclear warheads to Venezuela. President Gomez had promised to coordinate the timing with Iran's own attack, equipping his own airplanes with the nukes and having them flown the much shorter distance from Venezuela to the United States. Of course the Venezuelans were not Muslim, and the pilots could not be induced to kill themselves with the ridiculous and childish visions of gardens and virgins. So Azria had sent his own suicide men along with the nukes.

Javid Azria chuckled and his chest shook back and forth. At the same time, an Iranian aircraft carrier would fly the flag of some neutral nation, smuggling his newly restored F-14s within flying range of the U.S. Azria would send other nuclear-warhead-equipped F-14s directly into Tel Aviv, Jerusalem and other Israeli cities. He would concentrate particularly on Christian and Jewish religious sites.

It would be a three-pronged attack, Azria thought as he smiled and took another draw on the Koran-forbidden cigar. At almost the same exact second, the U.S. and Israel would find themselves the recipients of several dozen nuclear kamikaze strikes, and both nations would be crippled beyond comprehension.

Azria's grin slowly left his face and turned into a frown of determination. The timing was crucial. He had to make sure that the F-14s launched from the Iranian aircraft carrier coincided with those from Venezuela. And the F-14 strikes on Israel should come at almost the same instant, while both the Americans and Israelis were still in shock and their attention diverted.

The Iranian president drew deeply on the cigar, remembering Fidel Castro's words that the "second half of the cigar is always better." The Cuban dictator had meant it as a metaphor, he knew. But it was true in a literal sense, as well.

As he continued to smoke, Javid Azria's eyes fell on the copy of the Koran on the corner of his desk. All in all, Islam was the perfect religion for a man like Javid

Azria to use to control his people. He didn't have to believe in it himself, and he didn't. But it would keep the common Iranians in line during the inevitable retaliation the U.S. would heap upon his country, and keep public opinion on his side as thousands, or perhaps even millions, of his own people died.

Azria made a mental note to remind the people of Iran that they would go straight to Paradise if killed by U.S. or Israeli bombs. He'd have it written into his next televised speech.

Azria's smile turned into outright laughter as he thought about it. The masses were so easy to control. Just include the word "Allah" in every other sentence and you had them bowing and scraping at your feet. Personally, he believed in a god about as much as he believed in the Western ideas of Santa Claus and the Easter Bunny.

There was no Allah. And Muhammad had been dead for hundreds of years.

There was only Javid Azria.

As he glanced again at the painting on the wall, he wondered if he might not change his title from President to Cyrus the Second when the smoke cleared and he returned Iran to the Persian Empire it had once been.

He would have to ponder the idea.

It had merit.

SLOWLY, ALERTLY, the Kurds came down the mountain path toward the plateau. David McCarter and the other men of Phoenix Force had risen from behind the boulders. Still hesitant, a dark-skinned, broad-shouldered man of average height, wearing a soiled white turban and a much-patched-and-repaired robe, stepped forward. In a thick leather belt around his waist, McCarter saw what looked like a much-used Western bowie knife and an ancient ball-and-cap revolver.

The rest of the Kurds were similarly armed with a mixture of old and newer weapons that could have filled a museum.

"Name's Abbas," the Kurd leader finally said after carefully scrutinizing the men of Phoenix Force. His words were almost shocking, because instead of the Middle Eastern accent McCarter would have expected, they came out in a south-Texas drawl. But before the Phoenix Force leader could comment, the Kurdish leader transferred the battle-scarred bolt-action rifle he held to his left hand and extended his right. "I reckon this is the way you people in the West greet each other."

McCarter grasped the man's hand in a firm grip. "It is," he said. "And I'm McCarter. Your English is excellent, by the way. But curious. Where did you learn to speak the language?" Somehow he didn't think this Kurd who had taken to the mountains to escape the Iranian government had grown up in the American South.

Abbas shrugged his shoulders. "From an American I know," he said simply.

McCarter made a mental note to inquire about the man's accent later, if they had time. But now, he quickly introduced the rest of Phoenix Force. Only then did he notice that Adel Spengha seemed to have disappeared. "Where'd the Rat go?" he asked no one in particular.

"The Rat?" Abbas said. "You talking about Adel Spengha?"

McCarter turned back to the Kurd. "I am. You know him?" In his peripheral vision, he saw Spengha rise from where he had remained hiding within the rocks and walk timidly forward. "Hello, Abbas," he said uncertainly. "It is good to see you again."

The corners of Abbas's lips turned downward in what could only be called a sneer of contempt. "Where are my camels?" the Kurd demanded.

"I am sorry about that," the Rat said, looking at the ground and wringing his hands. "I needed one to ride out of the desert. The other, I am afraid, I was forced to eat in order to survive."

"I'm sure there's a fascinating story behind this little exchange," David McCarter said. "But if you don't mind, I'd like to save it for later and get on with the business at hand." He paused a moment, then said, "Whatever the Rat owes you, we'll compensate you double."

Abbas looked at the Phoenix Force leader now with piercing eyes. "My daddy taught me long ago that you don't get something for nothing," he said. "What are you looking for in return?"

"Help get us through these mountains," McCarter said. "And then you might be able to help further when we locate the American hostages."

"Ah," Abbas said, nodding. "So it is the hostages you're trailing." He wiped sweat off of his forehead below the turban. "We saw them pass below yesterday."

"You saw them?" McCarter said. "Where were they?"

"In the back of a pickup, escorted by several other cars," Abbas said.

"Are you certain they were the Americans?"

The Kurdish leader smiled, the prickly sticks of a five day growth of beard standing almost straight out from his face. "At least two had blond hair, they were trussed up both hand and foot, gagged and blindfolded," he said. "I'd guess there was a better than even chance that they were the Americans you're looking for."

"Any idea where they went?" McCarter's enthusiasm was picking up. It was the first lead they'd gotten since the mission had begun.

"They took the road toward Tehran," Abbas said. "But that means nothing. There's a lot of cities and villages between here and there." He paused for breath. "They could have gone anywhere."

McCarter's enthusiasm threatened to disappear but he forced his spirits to stay high. "Then I suppose the question is, are you willing to help us?" he said.

"Oh, I'm willing," Abbas said. He looked up at the sky, saw the sun dropping quickly in the west and said, "But we can't do anything at night. You can be guests at our encampment tonight," he continued. "Got plenty of room and food. We can start out as soon as the sun rises again."

McCarter remembered his earlier thoughts about the icy ridges near the tops of the peaks of the Zagros. He was anxious to be on their way now that they had some semblance of a trail to follow. But Abbas was right. It would be far smarter to wait until morning.

With Abbas and the rest of his Kurdish warriors

leading the way, it took less than half an hour to reach a valley somewhere in the middle of the Zagros. They were forced to descend in single file, moving crablike down the steep embankment to the bottom. But long before they got there, McCarter caught the smell of roasting meat and curry in the air. His stomach growled as he took the final steps to the flatter area, then stepped to the side and waited for the rest of his men.

Adel Spengha brought up the rear, and McCarter had to suppress a laugh. The man was still uncomfortable in the presence of Abbas, and the Phoenix Force leader couldn't help but wonder at the story behind the Kurd's two camels. Perhaps he'd find out that night.

Abbas led them through a narrow corridor in the rocks, and suddenly McCarter stepped out into a huge open cavern. In addition to the men he had already met, there were perhaps fifty more men, women and children, as well as several nursing babies. They had settled into this cavern as if it were home. But McCarter noticed that everything seemed already packed. The women roasting the meat over the fire even returned their utensils to a wide variety of backpacks and goatskins when they were not in use.

These Kurds were ready to flee again within a matter of minutes if they were discovered.

Abbas motioned the men of Phoenix Force to take a seat with the other Kurds around the campfire. The leader of the Kurds dropped to a cross-legged seat next to McCarter. A moment later, the women approached. Instead of eating out of one large communal pot as was the custom in many Arabic countries, they were handed clay mugs containing some kind of cloudy, yellowish liquid and steel plates filled with curried rice and roast mutton. McCarter could feel raised letters on the bottom of the plate, and lifted it high enough to read them.

"Property of the United States Army," the bottom of the steel plate read. He lowered the plate, chuckling to himself. The Kurds had ripped off at least one mess hall from one of the nearby U.S. bases.

McCarter began to eat. He and the rest of the men of Phoenix Force had been too busy for food since this mission had begun, and it just might have been the best meal any of them had ever had in their lives.

As darkness fell over the valley outside of the wide-mouthed cavern, the fire became their major source of light. As the flames flickered upward, casting ghostlike shadows on the rocks, a Kurd wearing a robe and turban and carrying an old scoped Enfield rifle hurried toward the circle of eating warriors. He spoke rapidly in the dialect McCarter couldn't understand, so the Phoenix Force leader looked to Abbas.

All the Kurdish chieftain did was nod his head, and the man with the rifle took off again.

After chewing the bite of mutton he'd just taken, then swallowing, the Kurd looked at McCarter. "We're about to have company it seems," he said.

The Phoenix Force man's hand moved toward the M-16 that, while still slung over his shoulder, now rested on the ground next to where he sat. "Any idea who?" he asked.

"I got my suspicions," Abbas said, taking another bite of the roast mutton. "They were still a far distance out

when my sentry spotted them. But if it's who I'm thinking it is, they're allies, not enemies. I sent the sentry
back to watch until he could make sure who they were."

"If they aren't your friends," McCarter said, "then
they'd have to be Iranian regulars or Revolutionary
Guards...." McCarter's voice inflection indicated that
what he'd just said was a question.

"If that's the case, and they know about this hideout,
then we will fight them to the death," said Abbas with
a shrug. "Like at the Alamo. But there'll be more than
enough time to get set for that after we know for sure
about their identity." He went on eating peacefully.

McCarter wondered briefly about the man's reference to the Alamo. It seemed a strange reference for a
Kurd in the Zagros Mountains to make. But it also
seemed that the best thing to do right now was to follow
Abbas's lead. And wait.

A few minutes later the same turbaned Kurd came
running back, a big smile on his face. Once again, he
spoke rapidly in the Kurdish dialect, and Abbas returned
the smile. "It's like I thought," he said, turning to
McCarter. "They're what you Yankees call 'friendlies,'
I think."

McCarter nodded. He saw no point in confusing
Abbas with the fact that he was not a Yankee himself,
or that the term actually didn't even apply to anyone
from the Southern part of the United States. But his hand
moved even closer to the pistol grip on his M-16.

It never hurt to be careful. And he wanted to see
these "visitors" himself before he fully accepted them
as allies.

Although it seemed like an eternity to the Phoenix Force leader, his watch told him it was not quite five minutes later when more people began appearing from the crack in the mountain wall and stepping into the clearing. Men, women and children again, dressed much the same as the Kurds with whom the men of Phoenix Force now ate dinner.

And the men were similarly armed.

"Another tribe of your people?" McCarter asked Abbas.

Abbas smiled. "Uh-uh," he said. "They're Iranians. Except for their leader who's the American I mentioned earlier. The man who taught me English."

"This American," McCarter said. "Who exactly is—?"

Abbas had anticipated the question and cut him off with two simple words. "Christian missionary," the Kurd said.

"A Christian missionary?" McCarter echoed in disbelief. "I thought they weren't allowed in Iran."

"They aren't," said Abbas. "But this man came anyway. Secretly. He had converted almost an entire village before he was found out and chased into hiding in these mountains. Most of his converts came with him, and they've had to adopt our nomadic way of life. They've been here even longer than we have, and we've helped each other out a passel of times."

A *passel*? McCarter thought. "These mountains just keep getting more mysterious by the minute," he said.

And he meant it.

As he finished eating the rice and meat on his plate, a tall, lanky figure stepped out of the shadows then took a seat next to Abbas. "Howdy, Abbo," the man said in a South Texas accent, and any question of where Abbas had learned English immediately evaporated from McCarter's mind. The lanky man wore a robe not unlike the Kurd's, but the legs revealed faded Wrangler jeans and a worn-out pair of cowboy boots mended with gray duct tape. On his head was a worn-out straw hat, repaired with the same tape. It could have started life as a cowboy hat. But it had lost any shape it might have once had far too long ago to tell. Perhaps the most prominent visual image about the man was the large Christian cross that hung around his neck on a chain. It looked as if it had been hurriedly cut out of steel, and rust spots were evident on both the front surfaces and sides.

"Howdy, Tex," Abbas said in reply.

McCarter shook his head in amazement. Looking down the line at his men, he could see that the rest of Phoenix Force was as surprised at this odd development as he was. On the other hand, the world was getting smaller all the time. And when warriors needed help, they took it from wherever they could get it.

Abbas called out, and the women began filling more plates for the missionary and his followers.

"Who're your new friends, Abbo?" the Christian missionary asked as he accepted a plate from one of the women. "They always dress up like ninjas?"

"Westerners," Abbas said. "Most of them American, I believe. Although the leader here is an Englishman. And one's Canadian if my memory doesn't fail me."

Rather than allow them to continue talking as if he weren't even there, McCarter extended his hand past

Abbas to the man called Tex. "McCarter is the name," he said as he shook the other calloused palm.

"Tex Karns," the lanky man drawled. Then he turned back to his plate, closed his eyes and bowed his head. "Thank you, Lord, for the food we are about to eat," he said quickly. "In Jesus's name I pray. Amen."

McCarter was slightly surprised when Abbas added his own "Amen" after the prayer. The mere mention of Jesus in a positive way of any kind in downtown Tehran could get your head cut off.

"Where exactly are you from?" McCarter asked as Tex scooped up a mouthful of rice with his spoon.

"San Antonio originally," Tex said.

T. J. Hawkins, who had been quietly listening to the exchange along with the other three members of Phoenix Force, suddenly leaned past his leader and extended his hand. "We're practically neighbors," he said, grinning. "I grew up mostly in El Paso."

Tex Karns shook his hand and returned the grin. "Well, there ain't no way the bad guys stand a chance long as there's *two* Texicans teamin' up," he said. "We'll have to get together and swap lies when we get a chance."

Hawkins laughed, finally pulling his hand back.

McCarter glanced at the Western bowie that Abbas wore and suddenly realized it must have been a present from Tex. "Then you come from a city of fighters," he said.

"Ever since 1836 and the Alamo," Tex said, and now McCarter knew where Abbas's knowledge about the Alamo had come from, too.

"Forgive my curiosity," McCarter said, "but how did a man like you end up here?"

"Long story," Tex said, taking a moment out of eating to adjust the tape on one of his boots. "I rodeoed for ten years out of high school," he said. "Lived the wild life, drinkin' and chasin' everything in a skirt. Finally, I got so busted up I wasn't good for much anymore. Took to drink pretty much full-time and got depressed. Nothin' left to live for. Had the barrel of my grandpa's old Colt .45 Single Action Army in my mouth when the Lord stopped me."

McCarter waited for him to take another bite, swallow and then go on.

"Don't get me wrong now," said the man from Texas. "I didn't hear no voice or nothing like that. It was just a feeling I got that God was saying 'Don't do it, Wilber. Sober up, and go to work for Me.'"

"So your real name is Wilber?" McCarter asked.

"Yep," said the other man. "But I prefer Tex. Don't let nobody call me Wilber except God. I figure bein' God, and all, I pretty much better let him call me anything he wants." He laughed as he continued eating, and it was obvious to the Phoenix Force leader that it was a joke he'd told many times in the past.

"We're trying to locate and free the American journalists who were kidnapped by the Iranians," McCarter said as a woman came and took his empty plate. "Abbas has told me you and your people have been hiding up here in the mountains even longer than they have." He paused, then took a drink from the clay mug. He didn't know exactly what he was drinking. But it wasn't bad, and certainly didn't taste as if it contained any alcohol that might cloud his judgment or slow his reflexes. "I don't know exactly where you stand on violence," he said as soon as he'd swallowed. "But we could use your help if you're willing."

Tex chuckled as he continued to eat. "Folks are always quoting Jesus about turning the other cheek," he said. But then he added, "They forget that the same Jesus also advised his disciples to expect attacks when they went throughout the world, spreading the Good News about Him and salvation. About that, Jesus said, 'He who hath no sword, let him sell his cloak and buy one.' That tells me that Jesus knew the difference between a slap—which is just an insult—and a real threat to life and limb."

"So you're willing to fight if you have to?" McCarter said.

Tex Karns chuckled under his breath. Then he squirmed back and forth while his right hand lifted his robe high enough that McCarter could see the pearl grip of a single-action Colt in the holster of a Buscadero rig. On the side of the grip he could see the carving of a long-horned steer.

"First-generation Colt .45," Tex said. "A little worn but still in great shape. And like I told you, it belonged to my mama's daddy. He was a deputy sheriff around the turn of the century—the nineteenth century—in Dennison, Texas. Name was Newt Lane." He paused for a moment, then added, "And yeah, it's the same gun I had in my mouth in between swigs from a tequila bottle when I quit rodeoin' and the Lord turned my life around."

McCarter smiled. He could tell he'd met not only a

friend and ally but a fellow warrior. "How about the rest of your people?" he asked. "Are they fighters or pacifists?"

Tex Karns laughed. "We're all pacifists," he said, "until it's time to fight. The Old Testament says, 'There's a time for peace and a time for war.' And I'm afraid we're in a time for war these days." He paused, cleared his throat, then went on. "They're all armed. They just keep their weapons concealed like I do."

McCarter turned his eyes from Karns and looked around the mass of newcomers who were now devouring the rice and mutton as if they hadn't eaten in a month. In addition to what he now knew they had hidden beneath their robes, he saw several long guns ranging from an old flintlock rifle to several M-16s and AK-47s—scavenged souvenirs of the wars that had been going on in Iran and Iraq for centuries. "You have a rifle, as well as your revolver?" he asked Tex Karns.

Karns nodded his head as he continued to eat. "Marlin 30-30 lever action," he said. "It was Grandpa's, too."

"If you're willing," the Phoenix Team leader said, "pick some of your men to go with us, and others to stay here and help secure the women and children at this site." He looked to Abbas. "I'm asking you to do the same."

"Already done it in my mind," Abbas said.

"And there's one more thing," McCarter said.

"What?" Abbas asked.

"Do you mind if I call you 'Abbo' like Tex does? It has a nice ring to it."

Abbas grinned and nodded.

CHAPTER FIVE

"They didn't think about the roof back at the church in Oklahoma City," Herman Schwarz said to Carl Lyons as they stared at the mall a few hundred feet away. It looked deceptively quiet now. No movement was visible, nor was there the sound of gunfire coming from any of the glass entrance and exit doors. "You suppose we might luck out and get in through the top again here?"

Lyons continued to stare at the bricks. "Maybe, Gadgets," he said after a long pause. "At least it's worth a try."

Grimaldi had joined them from the chopper and Lyons noted the pilot's trademark .357 Smith & Wesson wheel gun with its stubby barrel shoved into his belt. "Want me to drop you off up there?" he asked, glancing back at the Kansas City helicopter.

Lyons shook his head. "They made us the first time we flew over," he said. "They'll hear the whirlybird again if we use it, and that'll direct their attention upward. That's the last thing we want."

"I could keep her high and let you guys drop down on lines," the Stony Man Farm pilot said.

"Thanks, Jack," Lyons replied. "But I think it'd be faster and easier just to scale the walls." He looked to KBI Director Bill Markham. Several of the SWAT team leaders from various Kansas agencies had come to join the conference, and out of the corner of his eye, Lyons noted one wearing coveralls with sheriff's department patches on the sleeves. He had found, over the years, that county deputies were usually far more cooperative than city, state or federal cops. That was probably because the sheriff was elected rather than appointed, and good press meant more votes come election time.

"Deputy," the Able Team leader said, turning his back to Bill Markham and essentially cutting him out of the loop. "What's your name?"

"McFadden, sir," the man said. He had a well-trimmed blond mustache and blond curls stuck out of the side of his baseball-style SWAT cap. "Wes McFadden."

"Do your men have climbing gear in your vehicle, Wes?"

"We do," said the county officer, his head bobbing up and down.

"How about sound suppressors?" Lyons asked. Schwarz already carried a sound-suppressed 93-R like Mack Bolan's, and Lyons had twisted a suppressor onto the barrel of his .45. But the large-caliber weapons still made more noise than he wanted to be making once they were inside the mall.

McFadden nodded and patted the SIG-Sauer pistol

in his nylon thigh-drop rig. "These aren't suppressed," he said. "But we've got two dozen .22s, complete with suppressors, in the van."

"Go get them and the climbing gear," Lyons instructed the man. "And bring three of the .22s out for me and my men. I don't want a whole army on top of the roof, but if your team would like to join us they'd be welcome." He glanced over his shoulder at Bill Markham, whose red face looked as if it might burst an artery in his head at any moment.

Wes McFadden had already taken off at a jog when Lyons turned back. And now several other SWAT team leaders spoke up, asking Lyons what part he wanted them to play.

"Just secure all entrances and exits on the ground for now," the Able Team leader told them. "But stay out of sight." He took in a deep breath. "You've got to keep in mind that we're dealing with a whole different animal here. They aren't your typical criminals. Somehow, the Iranian president has brainwashed his own Pasdaran troops into becoming Islamic suicide bombers. The men inside this mall plan to die today, and even welcome the opportunity. The only question in their minds right now is how and when to blow the whole mall to smithereens."

"So you're saying we should shoot them as soon as we see them?" asked a short, stocky man with a sniper's rifle.

"Off the record, that's *exactly* what I'm saying," Lyons clarified. "But not until I give the order." He patted the satellite phone he'd dropped back into his pocket. "If you shoot one at this entrance," he said, pointing toward the closest glass doors in the mall, "they're likely to detonate the explosives in the rest of the mall. Wait until you hear from me." He paused again for air. "Somehow, my men and I have got to get inside and locate all of the explosives before we do anything else."

Suddenly a new armored van Lyons hadn't seen screeched to a halt on the street next to where the command post had been set up. The side door slid open and several men wearing steel-plated uniforms and helmets climbed stiffly from the vehicle. They walked awkwardly toward the men of Able Team and the others, and when they reached Lyons the man in the lead stuck out his hand. "Kansas Highway Patrol Bomb Squad," he said. "My name's Pepperdine. Can we be of help?"

Lyons smiled. "I think so," he said. "That is, if you can manage to get onto the roof in all that gear."

"No problem," Pepperdine said. "Van's got a five-story lift."

No sooner were the words out of his mouth than Wes McFadden and his team came running back up, carrying enough equipment to climb Mt. Everest. Lyons also noted that the larger-caliber SIG-Sauers they had worn earlier in their leg holsters had been replaced by what looked like Ruger .22 target pistols. The opening at the bottom of each holster allowed for the sound suppressors to slide through the ballistic nylon.

Which was nice but not very important. The sound-suppressed pistols were going to be out of the holsters more than inside them. And they would stay that way until the mission was complete.

Or the men wielding the quiet weapons were dead and the guns fell from their hands.

Wes McFadden had three more pistols stuffed into his waistband. Two were Rugers, which he handed to Schwarz and Blancanales. The third, which he offered to Carl Lyons, was a Colt Woodsman Match Target pistol. The square lines of the weapon had meant a longer, custom barrel had to have been installed and was threaded so the "whisper maker" could be screwed on.

When Lyons started to speak, McFadden said, "It's one from my personal armory. It's not approved by the department, and between you and me, it's not registered with the BATF, either." He stared into Lyons's eyes, and it was clear to the Able Team leader that he was wondering if he'd made a mistake in revealing that bit of information.

As Lyons accepted the Colt and a half-dozen extra magazines from the SWAT man, he said, "We're carrying full-autos that aren't registered, either, Wes. In fact, they couldn't be if we wanted them to—they have no serial numbers." He dragged in a breath as he watched McFadden's face relax.

Then it was time to change the subject.

"Sorry to make you carry all the climbing gear out here," Lyons said. "But I think we've found a quicker, easier way up to the rooftops." He indicated the bomb squad van with a nod of his head.

McFadden looked at the van, then nodded his understanding as he let the gear in his arms fall to the asphalt.

"We can still use you guys with us," Lyons said, and the deputy sheriff's grim look changed instantly to a grin.

Lyons felt a hand on his shoulder and turned to see Bill Markham, still red in the face and looking as if he might have a stroke at any time. "I want some of my men with you," he said in an authoritative voice.

The Able Team leader shook his head. "Too many," he said. "With the county and the bomb squad, we're already in danger of making enough noise to alert the men inside."

Markham's cheeks seemed to puff out, and Lyons wouldn't have been surprised if he'd seen them pop like balloons. "Well then, what exactly do you want us to do?" he said through clenched teeth.

Lyons took a perverse pleasure in smiling at the man while he said, "Stay out of our way. We'll call you once we're inside and have the site secured." Then he turned back to the deputies and state bomb squad. Pointing toward the mall, he spoke to Pepperdine and McFadden. "There's a couple hundred feet of solid brick there between Dillard's and the central entrances," he said. "That's about as good as it's going to get." He paused and felt his brows furrow in concentration. "I'm going to have all of the marked units start circling the mall with lights and sirens on Code 3. The vans—including yours, Pepperdine—will be somewhere in the group. On the second trip around, we'll wait until we hit that blind spot and cut away from the group to park next to the building."

Pepperdine nodded his understanding but had a question. "You don't think a parade of force like that'll make them go ahead and detonate?"

"I don't know," Lyons said. "We'll stay clear of the

entrances—the rest of the vehicles are just a distraction. But it still might make their bomb fingers start itching." He stopped speaking for a moment, then said, "It's a calculated risk, I admit. So if you've got a better idea, I'm willing to listen to it."

Pepperdine shook his head. "That's the problem," he said. "I don't."

"Then let's get everybody moving," Lyons finished. "Like George Patton used to say, a good plan now is better than a great plan thirty minutes from now."

Not sure if the Pasdarans inside the mall had police scanners, Lyons insisted that the orders be passed on by direct word of mouth to the hundreds of law-enforcement officers holding siege around the building. It took roughly five minutes for everyone to get the word, and another five for the patrol cars, SWAT vans and other police vehicles to assemble in a long line. Before he started them off, Lyons turned back to KBI Director Bill Markham. "I need the phone you've been using to communicate with the men inside," he said.

"No, you don't," Markham said, puffing out his chest. "I'll continue to negotiate—"

Lyons had no time, and was in no mood, to argue further with the KBI man. Grabbing the lapel of Markham's coat, he pulled it to the side and reached up, grabbing the cell phone in his shirt pocket.

Half of the pocket tore down the side as the Able Team leader ripped the phone from Markham's shirt.

Bill Markham stood there like a marble statue, a look of total bewilderment on his face.

"Thanks," Lyons said as he dropped the cell phone

into a pocket of his blacksuit. He, Schwarz and Blancanales joined Pepperdine, McFadden and their two teams at the bomb van. There was plenty of room inside the large vehicle, and after he'd given the word for the lead car to begin, Lyons slid the side door of the vehicle closed and took a seat on the floor. He could see through the windshield from the back, and noted that the driver followed his orders, entering the procession approximately halfway through, between two other vans where it could best blend in with the pandemonium.

"All right, gentlemen," the Able Team leader said. "The .22s have to serve as our primary weapons as long as we can keep things quiet. But somewhere along the line, maybe sooner, maybe later, we're going to be discovered. After that, the more noise and confusion, the better. So sling those assault rifles around to your backs for just as long as we're able to keep quiet." He paused a moment, frowning. "And continue to maintain walkie-talkie silence. They may have scanners inside."

With lights flashing and sirens blazing, the assemblage of law-enforcement vehicles began to circle the mall.

Keeping their speed down to roughly twenty miles per hour, the procession had almost completed its first trip around the mall when the KBI cell phone, now in Lyons's pocket, rang.

"Good afternoon," the Able Team leader said into the instrument.

There was a moment's pause as whoever was on the other end of the line realized it was a different voice he was talking to than he had before. Then a voice with a heavy Middle Eastern accent said, "Who is this?"

"I'm what they call a party pooper here in America," Lyons said. "Or, if you happen to be a Western movie fan, you might want to look at it this way—there's a new sheriff in town."

"Who are you?" the voice demanded again as the parade of flashing lights and raging sirens began its second circuit.

"Who are *you?*" Lyons returned.

"We are Iranian Pasdaran," said the voice on the other end. "The Iranian Revolutionary Guard. My name is Sergeant Bartovi."

There was a short silence, then Lyons said, "Well, since we're getting to know each other so well, you can just call me Carl."

"Why are your vehicles circling us, Carl?" Bartovi asked.

"Just to let you know we're still here," Lyons said.

"If any of them come within twenty feet of the doors," Bartovi said, "I will order my men to blow this shameless example of American imperialism—this godless, materialistic mall—off the face of the planet."

"So *that's* what you're doing all the way here from Iran," Lyons said. "What happened? You accidentally buy a pair of jeans you need to return to the Gap?"

"I do not understand that comment."

"There are a lot of things you don't understand," Lyons said. "Like the fact that we're either going to kill you or capture you alive and extract a lot more intelligence information from you than even you know you have." He cleared his throat. "Can you read between the lines, there, Sergeant Bartovi? Surely your puny, little, ass-backward, twelfth-century country hasn't declared war on the U.S., has it?" He paused, hoping the insults were fully understood by this man for whom English was obviously a second language. His words had been designed to anger the man. At least enough to adversely affect his decision-making.

The trick was to do so without angering him to the point where he went ahead with his threat to blow the mall down to its foundation.

"I am a soldier in the army of Allah, Carl," the man calling himself Bartovi said. "And I am following orders."

"Oh, yeah," Lyons said sarcastically. "Allah tells his followers to murder innocent women and children all the time."

"It is for a greater cause," Bartovi replied in a tone of voice that made it sound like a recording.

"Sure, sure, sure," Lyons said. "The end justifies the means and all that."

"That is another way to put it," Bartovi said.

They were halfway around the second lap of the mall when Lyons spoke again. He was about to hit the blind spot in the building, and he wanted to keep Bartovi's mind off of what was about to happen outside. "Are you telling me that gerbil-like little president of yours, who looks like he needs to shave about six times a day, ordered you to invade this country and blow up this mall?" he asked.

"Yes," said Bartovi. "More or less. Not this mall in particular. But we were ordered to pick a mall and destroy it. Malls are symbolic of your godless American materialism and consumerism."

"I think you already covered that part," Lyons said. "It is indeed symbolic, and everybody seems to be more concerned with symbolism than substance these days. So, tell me. Are you *really* planning to destroy yourselves at the same time?" He let his voice sound incredulous.

"We will be Islamic martyrs," the sergeant said. "We will awaken in Paradise with twenty-seven virgins—"

"Only twenty-seven?" Lyons interrupted as he tapped the driver of the van on the shoulder and pointed toward the long line of windowless bricks to their side. "Last I heard, your kamikaze idiots were getting over forty virgins for a mere suicide bombing. Surely a sacrifice this big is worth more than twenty-seven." He paused to let his words sink in, then closed with, "Sounds like your virgins go up and down like the price of gas. I guess this global recession has even affected Allah."

The van driver suddenly pulled out of the parade and accelerated toward the brick wall of the mall. He twisted the wheel slightly and then came to a halt parallel to the wall and no more than a foot away.

"You will burn in the fires of Hell for all eternity," Bartovi said angrily.

"Somehow, I doubt that," said Lyons. He took a quick look around him. Schwarz, Blancanales and the bomb squad and sheriff's office SWAT teams were all ready to go. And he didn't want Sergeant Bartovi listening to him issuing orders. "Sorry, Sarge," he said into the cell phone as he held his other hand up so the rest of the warriors would remain quiet. "I've gotta run now. But why don't you call me back in about fifteen minutes or so?"

Without waiting for an answer, he pressed the button to end the call.

Before dropping the phone back into his pocket, Lyons switched the incoming call alert from Sound to Vibrate. Then he looked past the driver and saw that the van that had been trailing them had hurried to fill the gap they'd left when they pulled away.

The procession continued, virtually unchanged to the observers inside the mall.

"Pepperdine," Lyons said, "get your lift moving and get us up top. My men first. Then the SWAT deputies and bomb experts." He frowned again, looking at the men of the bomb squad. Although they each wore pistols, they were so covered in armor that they could barely walk, let alone fight. "You guys," he said to the SWAT deputies. "Pair up with a bomber and take him on as your own. You're responsible for his safety until we can get things under control and start defusing."

The deputies all nodded their heads in understanding. So did the heavily weighted bomb squad warriors.

Outside the van, Lyons heard several metallic clanks and then a hydraulic lift hissed back at him.

Two minutes later they were all on the roof of Dillard's. And wondering if they were about to be suddenly vaporized, along with the building they now stood on.

DAVID MCCARTER AWOKE inside his sleeping bag to the sight of the campfire being stomped out and a hand on his shoulder. Turning his eyes toward that shoulder, he saw Abbas holding a finger to his lips with the other hand. "Be real quiet," the Kurd whispered. "We've been discovered."

"By who?" the Phoenix Force leader whispered back.

"Iranians," said Abbas.

"Pasdarans?" McCarter asked.

Abbas shook his head in the light that kept dimming as the Kurds' boots stamped out the fire. "Regular army," he said. "Not as well-trained or as good as the Pasdarans. But they're dangerous in their recklessness."

McCarter climbed out of the sleeping bag as quickly as he could, then began rousing the other members of Phoenix Force. None of the other four members of his team had been very deep in sleep, and they came awake and began immediately preparing to leave the opening in the mountains.

Tex Karns had joined Abbas in awakening his people, and he now joined the Kurdish leader and McCarter near where the campfire had been. "Their point man saw one of our sentries," Abbas said simply. "Then he disappeared before our man could take him out." He shook his head in disgust. "He's undoubtedly gone back to his squadron and told them where we are by now." He stopped talking long enough to adjust the bowie knife and .45 on his belt. "This place is blown for good. And it was the best camp we had."

McCarter looked up into the dark rocks surrounding the vast opening between the mountains. "Maybe," he said. "And maybe not."

"What does that mean?" Abbas twanged.

"I assume there are other ways in, and out, of this encampment," McCarter's voice inflection turned the statement into a question.

"Of course," said Abbas. "On both sides of this open area. But they're harder climbing. So we always use that passage you came through."

"Depending on how far ahead the scout was, and how fast these Iranian regulars can get here, we may still have time to evacuate the women and children and send them on to another one of your hideouts. And if we and the other men can get hidden up in the rocks before they arrive, we may be able to trap them right here where we are now."

The swooshing sound of steel leaving Kydex sounded in the night and McCarter turned to see that Calvin James had drawn his Crossada. "You've read my mind," he told James.

James nodded. "Unless they find some of these other entrances, they'll have to come into this clearing one at a time, just like we did," the black Phoenix Force operative said. "I can take several of them out, one by one, before the men behind them realize it's a death trap." He paused to grin, his lips stretching the well-trimmed mustache on his upper lip. "We've been comparing this to the Alamo," he added. "But it's going to really be more like Thermopylae."

The men of Phoenix Force nodded. They were all familiar with the ancient battle in which a handful of Greek warriors had stalled thousands of Persians at a narrow mountain pass not too different from this one.

McCarter nodded. "It'll work—at least for a while." He turned toward Abbas. "Abbo, pick a few leaders to guide the women and kids on to your nearest hiding place and tell the rest of the men to set up in the darkness of the rocks above and around this clearing. Tex, you do the same. Get your men who are armed hidden. But first, there's one important thing we need to do." He quit speaking and looked up at the dark sky.

Tex and Abbas waited for him to speak again.

"You've got a number of AK-47s in your men's hands," the Phoenix Force leader said. "I don't want them used if a firefight breaks out before we can all get out of here."

"Why not?" Tex said, frowning.

"I don't have time to explain," McCarter came back. "Just trust me on this one, okay?"

Tex and Abbas both nodded. But the frowns stayed on their faces.

"We can send the AKs out with the men guiding the women and children," Tex said.

"There should still be enough M-16s to go around," Abbas said. "Hardly anyone else knows it, but every so often, we get a CIA care package dropped on us from a plane. We've got plenty of ammo to go with them. But why—?"

"I told you, there's not enough time to explain," McCarter cut in. Then, turning to Gary Manning, the barrel-chested Canadian explosives expert who was also the strongest man on the team, he said, "Calvin's going to stick 'em. You flip 'em. Just as soon as they've had a taste of James's Crossada, I want you to throw the bodies to the side—out of vision to the others coming through the passageway." He glanced at the crack in the rocks. "Like James said, it won't work forever. But it should confuse and stall them for a little while." Then, staring both men in the eyes, he said, "Just as soon as they catch on to what you're doing, I want you to climb up into these rocks with the rest of us."

"Even after they know," James started to say, "we might—"

"There's no time to argue, Calvin," McCarter said. "Once they're on to you, they'll start finding those other ways into this place like Abbo said. I'm just hopeful that'll give those of us in the rocks overhead time to spread out. Now, like I said, no argument. You're both too valuable to lose on what would amount to its own suicide mission once you're discovered."

Both James and Manning nodded their understanding.

By now both Abbas and Tex Karns had picked men to lead their noncombatants out of the clearing to one of the other hiding places both the Kurds and Christian Iranians used. As he had noted earlier, they had kept packed and were ready to move out at a moment's notice.

And they did, disappearing around the side of the cavern into another crack in the boulders that McCarter hadn't even noticed until now.

In less than five minutes the women and children were all gone. And the Iranian Christian soldiers, as well as the Kurdish fighters and the men of Phoenix Force, were all hidden away in the shadowy rocks surrounding the clearing. McCarter stayed where he was for the time being to make sure some surprise didn't come along that would call for sniper fire from above. He sent Schwarz and Blancanales on to lead the Kurds and Christian warriors back over the rocks above the narrow passageway.

David McCarter reached up and wiped a thin layer of sweat off his forehead with the sleeve of his black-suit. Resting the barrel of his M-16 on the boulder behind which he crouched, he dropped to both knees. But as soon as he did, he felt the sharp pain of a muscle cramp in his right hamstring.

It was a sure sign that he was low on electrolytes, most likely potassium or sodium or both. So, as he straightened again, he lifted the canteen from his belt and downed several swallows of the energy drink he'd filled it with. Then he dropped to his knees once more. This time he was careful to keep his right leg as relaxed as he could as the knee touched down on the ground.

Five minutes went by. Then ten. Under the moonlight, all he could make out of James and Manning were black, shadowy blobs. James held his Crossada down at his side, lifting it ever so slightly when McCarter suspected he heard something inside the narrow passageway.

In the distance, high in the rocks, he heard the spooky, mournful call of an owl.

But it wasn't an owl—it was T. J. Hawkins. Hawk was signaling that the armed Christians and Kurds were in place—scattered above the fissure through which the Iranian regulars were walking.

Fifteen minutes after James and Manning had set up, a man wearing worn Iranian BDUs stepped out of the passageway into the clearing and stopped. Under the light of the moon, McCarter saw him sniff the air, taking in the odor of the recent campfire.

It was the last thing he would ever smell in this world.

Calvin James's Crossada fighting knife shot out

from the side and drove upward through the man's ribs, slicing through the left lung before piercing his heart. The lung collapsed, and the scream that had been about to come out was reduced to nothing more than a quiet hiss.

Twisting the blade vigorously, James withdrew the razor-edged steel. Satisfied that the man had only seconds left to live, he pushed him toward Manning, who stood just to his side.

Manning grabbed the man by both shoulders and pulled him forward, executing a simple judo hip throw and sending the corpse flying behind him.

Manning turned back to James and nodded just as the second Iranian stepped out of the passageway.

CARL LYONS USED SILENT hand signals to direct each pair of men—one armed SWAT deputy and one armor-covered bomb expert—to the different air shafts and return air vents leading from the mall roof down into the structure itself. By the time he had finished, a good five minutes had passed. But as he rejoined the other two Able Team warriors, he looked back and saw that he now had almost fifty mini-strike teams poised and ready.

Lyons stared back at the men he had just positioned. Somehow he had to get them into the mall to check every nook and cranny where explosives might have already been set up. It would be next to impossible to accomplish that feat without the Pasdarans discovering them.

Some of the men he now saw were going to die. There was simply no way around it. And that was if they were lucky. If worse came to worst, the terrorists might set off the explosives all over the mall and kill the hostages, themselves and the SWAT and bomb experts.

Not to mention Schwarz, Blancanales and himself.

Nevertheless, it was a job that had to be done.

With the exception of the JC Penney store, at the far end from the Dillard's on which Able Team now stood, the roofs covering the various stores were only two stories high. Which meant Lyons could easily be seen by the SWAT men and their bomb-squad partners. Now he motioned for the men to begin removing the screens, trapdoors and corrugated-metal air shafts and proceed on down into the building.

Although they were entering the mall through the roof just as they had the church in Oklahoma City, Lyons knew this entry was far more dangerous. At the church, all of the hostages had been centralized, and they'd had a guide who knew in advance that they'd be dropping down into the water of the baptistry.

Exactly where each two-man team would emerge in the mall was anybody's guess. They might find that they had to drop a full story to the floor of the outer mall, or come down on top of a rack of T-shirts in Journey's. All they could really count on was that somewhere, close by, there would be men wearing red scarves around their necks who would do their best to kill them.

The biggest advantage the enemy had, Carl Lyons knew, was that they intended to die that day themselves. Once a warrior had been brainwashed into that state of mind, all bets were off.

Schwarz and Blancanales had pulled the sheet-metal cover from an opening and now Lyons looked down to see the third story of the Dillard's store. Even with his limited view it looked like the top floor of most other stores in the chain, and he caught glimpses of furniture, kitchen china and other home furnishings rather than men's and women's clothing, which would be found on the first two floors.

The Able Team leader had started to lower himself down when he suddenly saw the flat, circular top of a khaki Pasdaran cap walk into view and stop directly beneath the hole in the ceiling.

Lyons lined the sight of the Match Target Colt up on the center of the cap as if it was a bull's-eye target. Slowly, he squeezed the trigger.

A tiny hissing noise came out of the sound suppressor as the .22 Long Rifle hollowpoint drilled down through the cap into the Pasdaran's brain. The man collapsed on the floor almost as silently as the Woodsman had coughed.

The Able Team leader waited a moment. Where there was one of the enemy, there were likely to be more.

And he wasn't disappointed.

The second Iranian Revolutionary Guardsman suddenly appeared below him and knelt on one knee next to the man Lyons had just shot. "Omar?" he said. "Omar?" The small entrance wound made by the .22, combined with the thick canvas crown of the cap, had kept blood down to a minimum.

But finally, after he'd shaken the downed man's shoulder, Lyons saw the Pasdaran stop and stare at the top of the cap, which was now turning red. For a second, he looked confused.

Then the awareness of the direction from which the bullet had to have come dawned on him, and, still on one knee, he looked up as he fumbled for the AK-47 slung over his shoulder.

The Colt Woodsman Match Target pistol's magazine held ten rounds. Lyons had topped it off by chambering a round, then adding one more to the mag. Which meant he had carried a full load of eleven rounds in the sound-suppressed weapon.

He had used the first .22 on the head shot down through the Pasdaran's cap and into his brain. Now he fired two more quick hollowpoints into the second man's face. The first round drilled through the man's neatly trimmed mustache and sent yellowed teeth and blood blowing back into his throat, as well as out the front of his mouth. The second .22 hollowpoint caught him squarely in the left eye.

The Pasdaran's eyes looked puzzled as the life drained abruptly out of them and he fell on top of his comrade.

Once again, Lyons waited. But this time, no one came to check on the downed men. Waving Schwarz and Blancanales toward other rooftop entryways, the Able Team leader finally lowered himself through the ventilation shaft, then released his grip on the side of the roof.

The two dead bodies on top of which he fell served to cushion the impact, and a second later Lyons had rolled off them and up on one knee, the Colt Woodsman gripped in both hands and ready to fire again at anything wearing a red scarf.

But there were no more Pasdarans to be seen.

Lyons stood cautiously, looking up at the ceiling after doing a quick 360-degree check of the grounds. The top floor was much smaller than the first two, and he saw Blancanales dropping—Ruger in hand—onto a mattress and box springs held in place by brass head and footboards.

Schwarz was not as lucky, being forced to swing back and forth several times to gain enough momentum to clear a display stand of knickknacks that would produce extra noise if he crashed down on them. He finally let go, dropping to a semisquat position as his black leather-and-nylon combat boots hit the recently waxed floor.

Satisfied that the other two members of his team were okay, Lyons turned his thoughts toward the SWAT team and bomb squad men as they made their way toward the escalator and steps. He had listened carefully, but had heard no other gunfire besides his own coughing .22s.

So far, so good.

But Carl Lyons was far too seasoned a warrior to think the rest of this operation would go as easily as the first encounter. "Check this floor for explosives," he ordered Schwarz and Blancanales. "Especially around any load-bearing walls and—"

The Able Team leader cut himself off in midsentence, then said, "Well, look no further."

There, in plain sight against one of the central walls, he saw a contraption far beyond his own experience with bombs.

"They haven't gone to any trouble to hide it," Blancanales, the former U.S. Army psychological-operations expert and Stony Man Farm's resident psychologist, said. "That means they planned for it to blow before police even entered the building."

Lyons nodded as he stared at the confusing conglomeration of wires and glass tubes filled with a nearly clear liquid. "Nitro?" he asked Schwarz.

Schwarz nodded. "And pretty simply constructed unless I miss my guess. Shouldn't be too hard to defuse."

"Well, don't miss your guess, Gadgets," said Lyons sharply. "And neutralize it is quickly as you can. Pol and I'll search the rest of this top floor for anything else that could go boom, but for the most part, it looks like they just sent a couple of men up here to guard the floor."

Schwarz glanced at the two dead Pasdarans on the floor as he pulled a small pair of red-rubber-handled wire cutters out of a pouch on his gun belt. "They didn't do a very good job, did they," he said as he turned back to the bomb.

Lyons and Blancanales took off in different directions, silently making their way through the various products for sale on Dillard's top floor. They looked beneath beds, reclining chairs and within luggage displays. It was not uncommon for the terrorists of today to set two levels of bomb in place. If the Pasdarans had done that here, then the first wave of explosives stashed throughout the mall would be triggered when the man, or men, with the igniting mechanisms pushed the button. The first bombs were designed to kill the hostage shoppers in the mall. But there could very well be a second set of bombs set to explode ten to fifteen minutes later.

The second round was intended to take out the police, firefighters and other rescue workers.

Looking over his shoulder as he rose to his feet after checking beneath a fancy-laced canopy bed, Lyons saw that Schwarz knelt next to the bomb against the wall. The electronics expert frowned for a moment, then a smile covered his face as his chest moved in and out in a long series of chuckles.

Lyons hurried back that way. "Something funny?" he asked.

"Either funny or pathetic," Schwarz said. "Depends on how you look at it, I guess. Whoever rigged this tried to set a trap wire for people like us who might come along and try to defuse it." He paused and pointed to the explosive device. "You see that green wire?" he asked the Able Team leader.

Lyons nodded.

"To defuse this thing without it blowing, that wire has to be cut first. Otherwise, it's set to explode the moment any of the other wires are snapped."

"And there's something about this that's making you laugh, Gadgets?" Lyons said as his eyebrows furrowed in concentration.

"Yep," Schwarz said. "There is. Watch this." Without bothering to even touch the green wire, Schwarz went through the other plastic-coated conductor lines and severed them all first.

Lyons had felt his heart jump up into his throat the second before Schwarz cut first a red, then a blue, then a yellow line, then snipped all the rest of the wires except for the green one he'd pointed out as the trap wire.

"Okay," Blancanales said. "I'll bite. How come you didn't cut the green wire first? And how come it didn't explode?"

Schwarz used the wire cutters as a pointer, following the green strand from where it was connected to the glass tubes, through a maze of connecting wires and then finally to the end, which showed where the plastic had been cut away and the brass-colored wire stuck out.

The end had curled up and rested on the violet plastic sheathing the yellow wire.

"Because whoever the idiot was who set this bomb, he forgot to ground it," Schwarz explained. He reached out and finally severed the violet wire up near the glass tubing. "Just for good measure," he said. "In case somebody comes along after we're gone, sees what happened and decides to rerig things. Unlikely but possible."

Blancanales turned to Lyons, and with a poker face said, "I knew if we kept him around long enough he'd find a way to be useful," he said.

Lyons just nodded his head at the joke. "Wait a minute," he said, looking at Schwarz, who was still on the floor. "Can you rerig that thing in a more complex way that the Iranian bomb man can't figure out if he sees it?"

Schwarz turned his head slightly. "A first-semester electrical student at a vocational school could do that, Ironman," he said. "But excuse me if I sound a little confused. Obviously, I was under the false impression that we were trying *not* to blow up this mall."

"We are," said Lyons. "But once we get downstairs we may need a diversion. The only people up here were the two Pasdarans—"

Blancanales looked down the aisle to the men Lyons had shot. "I really don't think they're going to give us much trouble, Ironman," he said with his tongue in his cheek.

"Cut the wisecracks for a minute. Close your mouths and open your ears. I'm not talking about these dead guys." Turning back to Schwarz, he said, "If you can reset this thing and attach it to a wireless remote control, we could make it look as if the bombings had begun if we needed to. And it would be up here where they're obviously not keeping hostages."

"I can do that," Schwarz said.

"Then do it." Lyons and Blancanales took off again, circling the top floor of Dillard's in opposite directions. They found no more Iranian troops.

Rejoining Schwarz, Lyons looked back down at the two dead men on the floor. Both had been shot in the head with .22 long rifle hollowpoints, and the tiny bullets had made only small entrance holes. Kneeling next to the two men, the Able Team leader rolled them over.

He could find no exit wounds at all. Which meant the fragments of the hollowpoints were still inside their heads. And that, in turn, meant that with the exception of the cap still on the head of the first man Lyons had shot, there was very little blood on the Pasdaran uniforms.

"Are you thinking what we're thinking, Ironman?" Schwarz asked.

Lyons nodded his head. "Their BDUs will fit you two better than me," he said. "Which means I'll have to go down as your prisoner."

Blancanales shook his head as he began unbuttoning the uniform shirt of the man with the bloody cap. "Nothing I like better than putting on some other man's bloody clothes," he said in disgust.

"Count yourself lucky they weren't shot with a larger caliber," Lyons said. "These uniforms should fit over your blacksuits. If what little red there is contains any blood-borne pathogens, your suits will block it from getting on you and reaching any open wounds."

"I'm glad you're so confident," Schwarz said as he unbuckled the belt on the other corpse. "Particularly since you aren't going to have to wear these things yourself."

"I'd say the odds pretty much even out," Lyons responded. "I'm going to be dressed in this blacksuit combat gear, which will be taken for an American SWAT uniform, and it'll be obvious that I was captured entering the mall." He paused for a moment as he handed his Colt Woodsman, then his .357 Python, sound-suppressed .45 and finally his Randall fighting knife to Schwarz. "And I won't even be able to carry a weapon of any kind."

A few minutes later Schwarz and Blancanales had donned the BDUs. Blancanales left the bloody cap where it was. "Okay," he said as he finished buttoning the cuff on his Pasdaran uniform. "As I see it, we've only got two major problems."

"And they are?" Lyons asked.

"None of us speak Farsi," Blancanales said. "And now the good guys are going to be shooting at us."

"Points taken," said Lyons. "But sometimes you've just got to go with what you have."

The other two men nodded. It was hardly the first time they'd stood up against long odds.

Putting his hands behind his back to make it look as if he'd been handcuffed, Lyons led the other two Able Team warriors to the steps between the escalators and started down. They had descended only three steps when a Pasdaran wearing another bright red scarf around his neck appeared at the bottom of the stairs and called something up to them in Farsi.

Without answering, the Stony Man trio kept walking toward him. The man repeated his words—whatever they were—and when he got no answer again he started to raise the barrel of the AK-47 slung over his shoulder.

Blancanales put a .22 long rifle round between his eyes and he sank to his knees, then fell to his side.

The men from Stony Man Farm picked up their pace, racing to the bottom of the steps to see if any other of the enemy had observed what had just happened. They saw no one.

The trio of warriors dragged the body from the center of the second floor and dropped it behind a tall stand of men's shoes.

Lyons stared at the body. The man was tall for an Iranian, and had a muscular build. The only blood on his uniform was a thin spray of blow-back mist that had settled on the collar.

"There you go, Ironman," Schwarz said, smiling. "Just your size, too." He paused to chuckle.

Lyons didn't answer him. He just began unbuttoning the man's shirt.

Two minutes later the three Stony Man warriors—all

of whom were now disguised as Iranian Revolutionary Guardsmen—began searching the second floor of Dillard's for any sign of hostages, more bombs or men wearing red scarves around their necks.

CHAPTER SIX

The Pasdaran camouflage uniform was too tight across the chest, and the pants were an inch too short. But with the cuffs bloused inside the man's light tan combat boots—which, luckily, fit reasonably well—Carl Lyons had no doubt he could pass for an Iranian rifleman. At least from a distance.

Unless he was forced to speak.

Lyons tied the dead soldier's red scarf around his neck, and as he did his face must have taken on a scowl because Schwarz—who was already wearing the scarlet symbol of the Iranian Revolutionary Guard—said, "I know, Ironman. No matter how loosely you tie these things, they still feel like they're choking you."

Blancanales grunted his agreement at the deeper meaning in Schwarz's words, and Lyons just nodded as he tucked the tails of the scarf inside his shirt collar.

Now that they were all dressed as Pasdarans, there was no need to pretend that Carl Lyons had been taken prisoner. But the Able Team leader still wanted to keep a low profile, lest one of the Revolutionary Guardsmen see them and begin speaking in Farsi. Playing the strong, silent type and just nodding your head every once in a while could get you a long way in this business.

But it couldn't get you all the way home.

A search of the second floor left them still without hostages or Pasdarans, but when they finally descended to the ground floor of Dillard's they heard murmurings coming from the back of the store. Lyons led the way cautiously through the children's clothing department. Instinctively crouching lower behind a rack of pajamas, he heard a louder, authoritative voice shout, "No speak!"

The murmurings instantly ceased, and although he couldn't yet see them, the Able Team leader pictured women and toddlers being threatened with AK-47s and other firearms, as well as knives and explosives.

The Able Team leader could sense Schwarz and Blancanales behind him as he dropped to his knees. Moving slowly and carefully through the hanging pajamas—which was little different than crawling through a thick path of primary jungle—he did his best to ensure that the clothes over his head didn't move enough to give him away.

Lyons stopped to risk a peek beyond the pajamas and determine the exact location of the hostages and their captors. Cautiously and silently Lyons pulled his hands off the floor and let his head begin to rise. With a backward wave of his hand he told the other two men of his team to keep their positions. And as his eyes finally cleared the top of the clothes rack, he saw three Iranian

Revolutionary Guardsmen strutting back and forth, their red scarves tucked into their shirts at the neck.

He also saw at least fifty people huddled in a mass on the floor against the wall. Their wrists were bound together behind their backs with gray duct tape, and the garment racks to their sides were pure wreckage from the Pasdarans throwing them out of the way to make more room for their hostages.

Just as Lyons had predicted, the vast percentage of hostages were women with toddlers and babies. Here and there was a male face. But, like most fathers around the world, he guessed that the male members of these families had come up with some excuse to do something other than shop at the mall.

A split second before he dropped out of sight again, Lyons caught a quick flash picture of an old man in a wheelchair. There was something odd about the man, but he could not put his finger on exactly what had caught his attention.

Out of sight again amid the pajamas, Lyons turned around to see Schwarz's and Blancanales's heads sticking out from clothes racks behind him. Even though he knew it wasn't necessary, the Able Team leader raised one hand to his lips for silence. Then he held up both hands as if gripping an AK-47 and, so low that the other two team members could barely hear, whispered, "Put-put-put-put-put."

The men of Able Team nodded their understanding. The enemy had full-auto weapons. Still holding the invisible rifle, Lyons left it in the air as he stuck both hands out, palms away from him. Opening and closing his hands once, then keeping his left hand in a fist and extending only two more fingers from his right hand, he passed along the knowledge that there were roughly a dozen Pasdarans.

Then, grabbing the invisible rifle from the air again, the Able Team leader tossed it to the side before crossing his arms and hugging them tightly over his chest. Blancanales and Schwarz both realized that the gesture symbolized being tied up, which in turn meant the hostages.

This time, the Able Team leader opened and closed both fists five times.

Schwarz and Blancanales now knew there were around fifty hostages.

But Lyons's silent instructions didn't stop there. Pulling a felt marking pen from his blacksuit, he drew a rough map on the tile beneath their knees. For the hostages, just around the corner of the glass entryway from the outside, he scribbled zigzags back and forth, then wrote, "50." Using small circles with arrows pointing back and forth in front of the hostages, he put a small "P" inside each circle.

The Pasdarans.

Again, the other two Able Team men knew what it meant and nodded.

Now, Lyons finally drew several straight lines and then wrote "pajamas" next to it. Both men nodded yet again as he created circles with an *S* a *B* and then an *L* inside.

The diagram on the tile was not unlike what a football coach might draw on a chalkboard in the locker room to introduce a new play to his team.

The Able Team leader looked upward and mimicked a man about to rise above their concealment. Holding the marking pen between his thumb and forefinger to simulate a gun barrel, he squeezed the nonexistent trigger three times, then brought the thick-tipped marking pen back down. Next to each of their circles, the Able Team leader wrote "3+" and then drew a curved arrow that led out of the pajama racks and into the aisle in front of the hostages.

Neither Schwarz nor Blancanales had any trouble understanding Lyons's orders. On command, they would rise and fire three rounds of .22s. The plus sign meant that if they saw more opportunities to slay these red-scarfed dragons they should take advantage of them. But eventually they were to make their way out into the aisle in front of the hostages to set them free.

There was one catch in this trick.

They had to do all this before any of the Pasdarans fired their own nonsuppressed firearms and alerted the rest of their brethren scattered around the mall that they were under attack.

Carl Lyons gripped the Colt Woodsman Match Target .22 in his right hand as he extended his left behind his back so Schwarz and Blancanales could see it. Taking a deep breath, then letting it out, he extended his index finger.

One.

The Able Team leader took another breath. Then his middle finger shot out to join the index finger.

Two.

Another breath, and Lyons's ring finger joined the

others as he began to rise up out of the children's sleep-wear rack.

Three.

Blancanales and Schwarz followed him, mimicking his movements.

As Lyons's finger found the trigger of the Colt Woodsman, he thought of the old man in the wheelchair again. Something had seemed odd about the man, but Lyons's quick visual recon had prevented him from identifying just what that was until now.

As he rose to his feet and extended the .22 in front of him, Lyons suddenly saw the old man again. He had a terrified look on his face.

And what had made him look odd was the bomb in his lap, strapped down to the arms of the wheelchair.

Carl Lyons was the first to fire, sending a double tap of .22s into the chest of the Iranian closest to the wheelchair. Both bullets struck home in center mass. But the Able Team leader followed his own instructions to his men, adding a third round to the head in what was some-times called the "Mozambique technique."

Almost at the same time, the sound of Schwarz's and Blancanales's .22 Rugers puffed quietly behind him. And the two other Pasdarans fell to the tile.

A remote-control detonator fell out of the hand of one of the men wearing a red scarf.

Lyons wasted no time. "Get the bodies out of sight," he whispered sharply, then held a finger to his lips before the hostages could begin cheering. As the other two Able Team members dragged the dead men into the cover of the children's pajamas where they had hidden themselves, he went around the group, slicing through the duct tape with his Randall knife and whispering, "You've got to act like you're still hostages. There are other rescue teams all over the mall."

Even though their hands were now free, the hostages kept them behind their backs as they nodded their understanding.

Schwarz had grabbed the remote detonator from the floor and returned to where Lyons stood. There was no reason for the Able Team leader to give him any further commands.

The Able Team electronics expert knew what had to be done.

Grabbing the back of the wheelchair, Schwarz pushed the disabled man past the pajamas to a spot behind a display of little girls' jumpers. There, the man and bomb would be hidden from the hallway while he went to work disarming the explosive.

Lyons and Blancanales turned their backs to the hallway and jammed their sound-suppressed .22s into the front of their belts. Lifting the AK-47s that had fallen from two of the men, they aimed them at the hostages and pulled the red scarves up high at the nape of their necks so they'd be easily seen.

With any luck, any of the Iranians who passed behind them would think they were Pasdarans themselves, just guarding the hostages as they had been all afternoon.

It took Herman "Gadgets" Schwarz only a few minutes to disarm the bomb and return to the front entrance of the store. "All clear, Ironman," he whispered to Lyons.

The Able Team leader nodded. He had been looking the hostages over while they waited, and his eyes had fallen on two men with short haircuts who were sitting cross-legged in the center of the mass of people. He stepped forward and bent over slightly. "Army or Marine?" he asked.

"Army, sir," one of the young men said. "We're still in college. ROTC."

"Then you two are in charge of getting these people out of here," Lyons said. "One of you'll have to push the wheelchair." He took time to drag in a breath and glance around him. Things were still quiet, and none of the Pasdarans—whom the Able Team leader could see at the front of several other stores in this wing of the mall—seemed to have noticed the change in command at Dillard's. Returning his eyes to the two ROTC soldiers, he said. "Take them out the back of this store. Through the loading docks. There's none of the enemy between you and them. At least none who are going to protest."

"Yes, sir," both men said almost in unison. "How do we know where the back exit is?"

Lyons looked the questioner squarely in the eye. "Turn left at the first dead bodies you come to," he said. "Now, move out quickly."

The three Able Team warriors kept their backs to the main hallway of the mall as the former hostages stood and started back into the store. They even moved in, prodding them along with the AK-47s. If there turned out to be any curious eyes on them, Lyons wanted to make sure it looked as if the change came from Pasdaran orders rather than a rescue.

As they walked swiftly away from the entrance to the store, Lyons suddenly felt the hair on the back of his neck stand up. There was something behind him. He could feel it. And that something was dangerous.

A moment later a voice called out sharply in Farsi. Carl Lyons had no idea what the man had said. Regardless, it meant he had to turn around and face the voice if he wanted to continue the charade.

So he did. But as he turned, he pulled his right hand off of the AK-47's pistol grip and drew the Colt Woodsman from his belt.

What he saw as he turned around was a swarthy man wearing sergeant's stripes with a curious look on his face.

Bartovi? Maybe. But somehow, he didn't think so.

The curiosity left almost as fast as it had come as Lyons pumped out a double-tap of sound-suppressed .22 hollowpoints—one into each eye socket.

The Pasdaran who had spoken was blind, then dead before he even started to fall.

Blancanales stepped forward and caught the body before it could hit the floor. Without needing to be told, he dragged it into the store and back to where the other dead Pasdarans now lay.

Led by the two young ROTC men, the hostages rounded a corner deeper in the Dillard's store and disappeared from sight. Lyons's jaw was firmly clenched as he nodded to himself. At least those men, women and children were going to get out of the mall alive.

But what of the rest of the people spread out all over the mall? There were so many of the two-man teams of shooters and explosives experts that at least one was going to draw fire. So far, they had been lucky, and Lyons had to figure that meant other groups had successfully taken out Pasdaran guards as they had. As his eyes skirted down the hallway, he saw another group of hostages near the front of a Victoria's Secret store. Much smaller than Dillard's, there appeared to be only about a half-dozen men and women sitting on the floor.

And there was only one Pasdaran guard.

The shot was long, but the guard was facing away from Carl Lyons. Which meant Lyons was able to take time to line up the adjustable sights on the Colt. But just as he was about to squeeze the trigger, a soft, barely audible coughing sound came from inside the store and the man fell on his own.

Not completely on his own, Lyons thought to himself. The man in the sheriff's department SWAT uniform who stepped quickly forward and pulled the Iranian into the store had had something to do with it.

Which made Lyons break out in a rare smile.

Turning in the opposite direction, Lyons saw the silhouettes of a man and woman on a sign just above the words *Rest Rooms*. But what caught his attention was the sign beyond. It read General Office.

When he turned to the other two men of Able Team he saw that they had both followed his line of sight, and undoubtedly had the same thing in mind.

With the hostages and explosives so spread out, it was a million-to-one chance that every rescue team would be successful. And at the first sound of gunfire, or the first explosion, the remaining Pasdarans would detonate their own suicide bombs.

Able Team needed some way to centralize the situation and get all of the Pasdarans in one place.

And suddenly, as if it had been a flash of thought sent straight from heaven, Carl Lyons knew exactly how to accomplish that task. He turned to Schwarz and Blancanales. "We're going to the office," he said, and the two men nodded.

"There'll be Pasdarans and maybe hostages inside," Blancanales warned.

"I know," Lyons said. "So we'll have to be quick and accurate. We need to immediately ascertain just who it is in charge in there and take him down without killing him."

Schwarz frowned. "How about the others?" he asked.

Lyons looked down at the sound-suppressed Woodsman in his hand. "Kill 'em," he said bluntly.

As the three Able Team warriors started off down the hall toward the general mall offices, Lyons whispered, "We should have a second or two in which they think we're part of their team," he said, pulling the front of his Iranian BDU blouse out of his pants to cover his pistol. "But that's all the time we'll get."

When they had drawn near the glass door, Lyons whispered again. "Keep your .22s out of sight and make sure the AKs are visible. But as we pass the door, use your peripheral vision to glance inside." Silently, the three warriors marched past the door as if headed toward some important task.

When they had moved ten feet beyond the field of vision from inside the office, Lyons said, "I saw a lot of camouflage in there."

"So did I," Blancanales concurred. "But I didn't see any hostages."

"Me, either," Schwarz said, shaking his head. "But they might have taken them into some rear office."

"That's possible," Lyons said in a low voice. "But everywhere else we've been and seen, they had their prisoners at the front of the store. They've got men at all of the exits, and I think they still believe they own the whole place at this point. The storefronts provide better photo ops if they plan to film or take pictures before they massacre themselves and everyone else."

"Well, let's hit 'em before they have the chance," Schwarz said.

Blancanales nodded.

Lyons said, "Pol, you open the door wide and stand back. I'm going in first with Gadgets right behind me. You'll join us as quickly as you can."

Blancanales nodded in agreement.

Silently the three Stony Man Farm warriors crept back to the glass door. Blancanales inched up as close to the door as he could without being seen. As soon as he heard Lyons say "Let's go," he reached out, grabbed the steel handrail across the glass and jerked it back.

A second later Lyons and Schwarz both entered the mall offices, .22s in hand.

A moment later, Blancanales joined them.

And the gunfire began.

CALVIN JAMES, like all of the other Stony Man warriors, had gone through extensive physical testing before being accepted into Phoenix Force. Two things about that final phase of Stony Man training still stuck out in his mind. First, it had made the Navy SEAL Hell Week he'd undergone a few years prior seem like a game of shuffleboard. Second, he had scored in the top one percent in the nation when it came to quick reflexes.

God, James suspected, had gifted him with his speed and tremendous hand-eye coordination. And he always had, and intended to continue, using his lightning-like reactions to combat evil in whatever form it came at him.

James knew he was fast with a blade and gun. And his reaction time, as well as his cognitive thinking, got even faster when his life, or the lives of his comrades, was on the line.

But there was a limit even to what he could accomplish with his speed.

And after the fifth Iranian regular had tasted the hilt of his Crossada, the black Phoenix Force warrior realized that he was quickly running out of luck.

Through the narrow passageway, he could hear loud, excited voices. The Iranians had sensed something was going on at the end of the line into the huge cavern. And the sixth man to step out of the stone passage did so hesitantly, with his AK-47 stock against his shoulder and ready to fire.

James stepped forward and thrust the Crossada up and into the man's lung and then heart. But instead of twisting it this time, he immediately withdrew the twelve-inch blade and slashed downward, severing the enemy soldier's right hand from its wrist a thousandth of a second before the man could pull the trigger. And this tiny variation of the sequence of attack, which had worked so well up until now, gave the dying man time to scream out.

As Manning grabbed the man's other arm, twisted it into a solid jujitsu shoulder hold and threw him on top of the other five bodies piled up behind him, the Farsi chatter in the passageway increased tenfold.

James didn't even take the time to wipe the blade off the Crossada before shoving it back into its Kydex sheath and swinging his M-16 around from his back into a firing position. When he looked across the tight opening to Manning, he saw that his fellow Stony Man warrior had done the same.

Calvin James waited a moment but no one else appeared through the opening. Now the Iranians knew something bad was happening at the end of the passageway. They just weren't clear on exactly what it was. So they waited.

With the fire quenched, the only light in the clearing came from the fingernail-clipping crescent moon above. It looked almost like the sign of Islam—like the cross was to Christianity—and had he been a superstitious man, that might have bothered him. But as things were, James found the comparison only ironic.

It was a crescent moon in the sky. And that was all it was.

But in the dim shadows over his head, James could see dark forms appearing from what had to be the other entrances Abbas had warned about. Quickly scanning the rocks, the black Phoenix warrior guessed that roughly a dozen of the Iranians had found other paths into the clearing.

And they had passed the word back to the rest of their men.

The main entrance was a death trap. And now they knew why.

"Time to hit the rocks," James whispered to Manning. The burly Phoenix Force fighter nodded, then turned his back and began climbing up the side of a boulder.

James kept his M-16 ready as he pulled a fragmentation grenade from his blacksuit and jerked the pin. Then, stepping into the opening just far enough to shoot, he sent a 3-round burst of 5.56 mm hollowpoints into the passageway.

The rounds ricocheted off the rocks as they made their way into the twisting tunnel, and gave him time to toss the grenade in as far as he could.

James had turned in the opposite direction from the passage, and found a short walkway that led up into the side of the clearing. He was ten feet above the passage when the grenade exploded.

The detonation caused a domino effect, and the ground beneath his feet began to close as the rocks around the path changed positions. James leaped up onto a large boulder before he could be crushed by the shifting stones, and waited for them to settle. He doubted that the explosion had delivered much of a change to the other men—both allies and enemies—who were higher up than he was.

But the gunfire had already begun.

James caught quick flash of a shadowy form in his peripheral vision and turned his M-16 that way. He saw a dark shadow aiming an assault rifle at him, preparing to fire.

His finger had already taken up the slack before firing when he realized the man with the rifle was McCarter himself. James lowered his weapon at the same time the Phoenix Force leader did the same.

But almost immediately, the telltale roar of an AK-47 erupted just above them and both men turned as the 7.62 mm rounds chipped at the rock around them. James and McCarter responded almost simultaneously, sending six well-aimed 5.56 mm rounds back up at the muzzle-flash. James would never know exactly how many rounds had hit the Iranian. But it didn't matter.

Enough hollowpoints had struck the man that his lifeless body came tumbling down between them with a flurry of blood and pebbles flying out to the sides to spot the dim moonlight.

James started to press his fingers into the man's throat to make sure he was dead. But there was no need.

Half of the Iranian's head was gone. The top half.

All around them now, James could see the muzzle-flashes as men on both sides of the battle fired. Suddenly he realized why McCarter had given out the strange order banning AK-47s. John "Cowboy" Kissinger, Stony Man Farm's chief armorer, had fitted all of Phoenix Force's M-16s with flash suppressors. Without them, the men from Stony Man Farm might accidentally start killing each other.

That still didn't take care of most of the M-16s in the hands of Abbas's and Tex's men. But at least the muzzle-flashes that shot out the barrel of the M-16s looked significantly different from those of the Kalishnikovs.

James turned his weapon toward the nearest bright flash and cut loose with another deadly triburst. The man holding the AK-47 didn't fall as his companion had. He just dropped his rifle and leaned back over a boulder. And didn't move again.

The passageway James had defended with his Crossada had closed with the grenade. But now the Phoenix Force man saw an Iranian regular climbing out of the rubble below. The man had an AK-47 slung over his shoulder. But he was cradling what looked like a broken wrist in his other hand.

Which also held a Russian Tokarev pistol.

James aimed downward and cut loose with another three rifle rounds.

The man who had climbed out of the rubble with the broken wrist forgot all about the pain as the hollowpoints jerked him back and forth like a rag doll.

He fell forward onto his face.

McCarter had moved from his last position and was now firing in the opposite direction. James spotted him perhaps twenty feet away in the darkness. At almost the same instant, from the corner of his eye, he saw a man appear from some hidden entrance high in the rocks. Silhouetted in the dim luster of the moonlight, James made out the shape of a rocket launcher over his shoulder.

Without hesitation, and almost without realizing what he was doing, James raised the barrel of his assault rifle and pulled the trigger. The man with the rocket launcher shook for a moment, then started to fall backward.

The launcher fired as he fell, sending its rocket harmlessly out at a forty-five-degree angle. For a brief moment the combatants up and down the rocky sides of the clearing were blinded by the light.

All except Calvin James, who had known what was coming and closed his eyes tight as soon as the third round of his volley had fired.

The Phoenix Force warrior waited until he could see the light dim again through his eyelids. Then, opening them wide, he took advantage of the enemy's temporary loss of vision, at the same time praying that his fellow Phoenix Force warriors—whose vision had no doubt been compromised, too—were safely covered behind boulders.

James ran the rest of his 30-round magazine dry, sending 3-round bursts at every spot where he'd seen bright muzzle-flash before the rocket went off. He heard men moan, groan and scream as his hollowpoints found permanent resting places in their hearts, lungs, throats and heads. When a full-auto burst of 7.62 mm lead hit three feet to his side, he knew the Iranians were recovering their vision. And he moved higher in the rocks, taking up a position behind another huge boulder.

Now James was beginning to see the tiny spots of fire that came out of the other Phoenix Force warriors' flash suppressors. He counted four and breathed out a sigh of relief—the rest of his team were still alive and combat able. Their vision might not be one hundred percent but they were seeing well enough that every few seconds another Iranian regular tumbled down the mountainside to the ground of the clearing.

With the smile still on his face, James continued to fire.

PHOENIX FORCE LEADER David McCarter knew his men. And he knew that Calvin James must have seen the man with the rocket launcher while he was busy taking out other Iranians who had crept into the clearing through various routes. He scanned the stone walls around him for other soldiers who might also have rockets at their disposal.

He saw none against the dark sky.

McCarter had moved away from the spot where Calvin James had stopped after fragging the main entrance tunnel, climbing higher in the rocks. And even though he hadn't seen it, he had recognized the sound of the rocket being launched and closed his eyes immediately, before the pupils could contract against the sudden burst of light.

Now the Phoenix Force leader could see the flashes of at least two dozen AK-47s spotting the rock wall across the clearing from him. The Iranians were firing blindly into the night, truly living up to the adage of "spraying and praying." But the tiny fires he saw occasionally from his own men counted four. Which meant that they were all still alive.

Several bursts of fire came in a group almost directly across from him. McCarter fired into the mass, then moved ten feet to his side. A few return rounds came in his general direction. But none was particularly close, and told him the men with the AK-47s were still suffering from the sudden light.

McCarter pulled a frag grenade from his belt and transferred his M-16 to his left hand. Rolling his shoulder in circles to warm it up, he continued to stare at the spot from which the multiple AK bursts had come. Then, pulling the pin, he reared back much as he'd done in his younger days as a cricket bowler, and let the explosive fly.

He lost all sight of the sphere as it sailed off into the darkness. But a second or so later, he saw the burst as it exploded in the center of the area he had concentrated on. As the roar died down in his ear, he heard several loud moans, as well as a wailing that sounded more like a wounded dog than a human.

But all firing from that area ceased.

McCarter kept moving, knowing that sooner or later the Iranians' eyes would readjust to the darkness. He would take out as many of them as he could before that happened. The smart ones would be behind cover, keeping silent until their pupils dilated once more. But, in contrast to Iran's Pasdarans, their regular forces were not particularly well trained or smart. The Iran-Iraq war during the '80s had been a long time ago, and the men who had fought it were old and retired now. It was their sons who were doing this fighting, and few of them would have seen much combat, if any at all.

It seemed that the men McCarter and his allies now faced had all entered the clearing through passages on the other side from the Phoenix Force leader. As he raised his rifle and fired again, he realized that three of his men were on that side. They had to look behind them, as well as in front.

And being in that situation was a great way to get killed.

McCarter moved in safely behind a boulder with a

stumpy tree next to it. Lowering his weapon, he stared across the clearing as the battle continued.

It was time to get this whole thing over with.

But he didn't want to kill his own men in the process.

McCarter squinted into the darkness as the battle continued. He knew Calvin James was on the same side of the clearing as he was. But Manning had taken off after James had blown the tunnel and joined Hawkins and Encizo on the other side of the clearing. The AK fire had dwindled somewhat now, telling the Phoenix Force leader that many of the Iranian regulars had either been killed or had retreated back through the entrances into the clearing. So he waited until he spotted a tiny, cigarette-ash-size glow come from a Phoenix Force M-16 across the clearing and just to his left, near the ground. It was followed almost immediately by three more tiny flashes perhaps fifty feet directly above it. A moment later McCarter watched three more tiny lights appear briefly to his right, not far from the passageway they had come through.

That would be Manning. Hawkins and Encizo were the tiny lights to his left. And the majority of the great, flashing fire was coming from in between them.

McCarter had five fragmentation grenades left. James would have the same number after blowing the passageway.

It was time they ended this fight. With a bang.

Pulling his remaining five hand grenades from his belt, McCarter set four of them on the ground to his side behind the boulder. Then, clamping his fist down hard around the handle of the one he still held, he pulled the pin with the other hand.

A moment later the grenade was sailing across the clearing toward another cluster of AK-47 flashes. And a second later, it exploded.

But before the grenade had even reached its target, McCarter had reached down and pulled another from the ground next to his feet. He threw again as the first grenade exploded, sending the second projectile to the left of where he'd thrown the first. Again, he pulled another hand-launched bomb from the dirt, pulled the pin and let it fly.

The third grenade landed a little to the right of the first one. Just before he reached down again, McCarter saw two tiny red spots across the clearing. The sight made him smile as he rose once more.

The red spots had moved farther away from where the grenades were landing. Which meant Hawkins and Encizo were safely out of the way. But he wondered about Manning as he reached for another frag grenade.

As he stood again, two things caught his eye at the same time. First, Calvin James had caught on to his solution to the problem and was lobbing his own hand grenades across the clearing just as fast as he could. And another tiny red spot appeared briefly roughly fifty feet from where the tunnel had once been.

Manning was safely out of the way and firing away, too.

McCarter heard screams and what he suspected were curses in Farsi as he threw again. The explosion coincided almost exactly with the detonation of one of James's grenades, and the explosion on the other side of the clearing rivaled the rocket launcher for both light and power.

It caught McCarter by surprise, and his pupils contracted just as those of the other men had done earlier. But this new strategy didn't require the precision that bullets needed, and he threw the next grenade using muscle memory alone. He saw something move near the spot where Manning had been, and then yet another grenade exploded.

McCarter smiled. His men were so familiar with each other that he rarely had to shout out orders. They knew what to do, and now he, James and Manning were all fragging the clusters of Iranian soldiers who had entered the clearing.

McCarter suddenly saw a new kind of light on the other side of the clearing and recognized it as a flashlight. Then, as his eyes cleared again, he saw other flashlights flash on. In their beams, he saw the remaining Iranian regulars making their way toward the spots where they must have entered earlier.

The Phoenix Force leader started to throw his last grenade, then stopped. They were taking themselves out of the fight anyway. There was no reason to use the final grenade, which he might need later.

Instead he lifted his rifle once more and aimed it toward the area in the mountain where the men were disappearing. Switching to full-auto, he blew out an entire magazine at the spot. At least two of the men fell to his onslaught. The rest disappeared.

And suddenly the entire mountain clearing went eerily silent.

With his M-16 still up and leading the way, McCarter joined James at the bottom of the rocks and started warily across the clearing. But there were no more explosions from either guns or grenades. The fight was over, and the only Iranians who had survived had turned tail and fled.

McCarter and James were joined by the rest of the men from Stony Man Farm, as well as the Kurds and Christian Iranians, as they reached the other side. Tex and one of his men came down the side of the mountain dragging what looked like a half-dead Iranian soldier by the arms.

McCarter looked down at the Iranian captive as Tex and his man dropped him. He didn't appear to have been shot. But before McCarter could ask what had happened, Tex stated, "This guy just jumped up out of nowhere like a jackrabbit in the dark. He was so close to me I didn't even have time to shoot him. So I busted his face with the butt of my M-16." He held up his assault rifle as he finished talking.

Looking at the captive man, McCarter pulled his own flashlight out of his blacksuit. The beam showed the face of a man who looked as if he'd been hit by a bowling ball.

"Bring him with us," McCarter said. He had kept one eye on the area where the soldiers had exited, and seen no sign of any of them coming back. But it was too soon to start patting each other on the back. "Let's get moving," he said. "There's always the chance of reinforcements coming back."

A moment later the men of Phoenix Force were following Tex, Abbas and their respective men into yet another fissure in the huge mountains around them.

CHAPTER SEVEN

The mall office was so filled with Pasdaran terrorists that it was like shooting fish in a barrel.

Carl Lyons began firing the second he was through the door, emptying his eleven rounds of near-silent .22s into the mass of Iranian camouflage uniforms as fast as he could pull the trigger.

Schwarz who had dived in behind him and was lying on his side, was doing the same thing from the tile floor with his sound-suppressed Ruger.

As the Able Team leader deftly flipped down the European-style magazine lock at the butt of the Colt and switched magazines, he saw Blancanales come through the door in his peripheral vision. Blancanales now entered the engagement, firing his own quiet Ruger at the surprised men who had stood around a desk, looking at what appeared to be the blueprints of the mall.

In less than three seconds all of the Pasdarans in the front office were on the ground, having fallen to the .22 long rifle hollowpoints loaded in all of the borrowed weapons. But the small-caliber rounds had not killed them all, and as Lyons hit the Woodsman's slide release to chamber the first round from the new magazine, one of them struggled to clear a Russian Tokarev pistol from the flap holster on his belt.

The former LAPD cop shot a hole through the hand grappling with the leather, and the man screamed at the top of his lungs. Lyons glanced at the door. It had closed. But there was no way of knowing if the quiet shots or the scream had been heard outside by any of the other Iranians scattered around the mall.

There was nothing to do at this point but wait and see.

While Blancanales separated the wounded Iranians from the dead bodies, Schwarz moved through the door into the rear offices. Lyons could hear excited voices and cheers coming from somewhere in the back, and he motioned Blancanales to cover the wounded men while he hurried after the Able Team electronics expert.

A second later he saw roughly twenty people—men, women and children—crammed into one office, hands bound behind their backs and sitting on the floor. "Quiet!" the Able Team leader ordered. "We're still not out of this thing."

The congratulatory voices immediately fell silent.

As quickly as they could, Lyons and Schwarz cut the gray duct tape around the hostages' wrists with their knives. Then Schwarz took off to check the last mall office, farther back within the complex.

As he left, Lyons turned to address the captives. "I know you all want out of here," he said. "And I don't blame you. But there are other hostages scattered around the mall, as well as an undetermined number of these scumbags. And if we all parade out of here, they'll turn this whole place into a Fourth of July celebration." He paused to clear his throat. "And I'm talking about the fireworks part, not the picnic."

The frightened heads—who were staring anxiously at him and hanging on every word—seemed to understand. Many of them nodded.

When Lyons had let it sink in, he went on. "As for now, I need all of you to just stay right where you are and keep quiet. We'll let you know when it's time to move out." He paused again. "Does everybody understand?"

Again they nodded.

Lyons took a moment to clear his mind. He had been forced to concentrate on the mall offices first. Now it was time to consider the bigger picture.

Scanning the frightened faces in front of him, he finally said, "Does anybody here speak Farsi?"

Slowly and hesitantly, a hand at the rear of the seated hostages rose into the air. "I do," said a heavily accented voice.

Lyons looked from the hand down the arm to see a face only a shade or two darker than his own. The man's blue eyes reminded the Able Team leader that ancient Persia had come into being from migrating Aryans.

"You're Iranian?" he asked, staring at the young man.

"Yes," the man said hesitantly as he stood. "I am sorry that my people—"

"They aren't your people," said Lyons. "The fact that you're here now pretty much proves that."

Lyons was about to speak again when Schwarz suddenly returned.

"Find anything, Gadgets?" the ex-cop asked.

Schwarz nodded his head. "No more hostages," he said. "But there was one big-ass bomb back there. I've neutralized it."

Turning his attention back toward the standing Iranian, the Able Team leader said, "Come with me," then turned and headed back into the hall toward the front office where Blancanales was still covering the wounded Pasdarans with his sound-suppressed Ruger. Looking around the office, he saw a large microphone on a small side table next to the desk. Turning back to the young man who had followed him, he said, "I'm going to need you to interpret, communicate with these animals who are still alive and announce what I tell you throughout the mall." He nodded toward the three men who were still alive. One had a shoulder wound. Another had been hit in the thigh, and the third had an ear partially shot off.

"Do you understand?" the Able Team leader asked.

"Yes," the young man said. Lyons noted for the first time that he was wearing blue jeans and a Kansas State University hooded sweatshirt. Undoubtedly an exchange student.

Whether he could be trusted or not remained to be seen.

The Able Team leader walked over to the desk and looked at the blueprints rolled out over the top. Finding the Dillard's store at one end, he saw the numeral "2" and an *X* written in by hand on the third floor. The "2," he reasoned, stood for the two men they had already encountered and neutralized. The *X* had to mean the first bomb Schwarz had defused.

Looking over the rest of the map, he found more numbers and *X*s. At least two dozen bombs had been set in the various stores, and roughly the same number of Pasdarans appeared to be guarding them and whatever hostages they had managed to nab when they first took over the mall.

"We're never going to get these clowns with them spread out like this," Lyons said. "Even with all of the SWAT guys and bomb squads, who by now are hidden around the place, it'd be a miracle for us to get to each and every one before someone detonated a bomb. And we've already used up our miracle for this strike, taking this office before any return fire could give us away."

He turned back to the young Iranian college student. "What's your name, young man?" he asked.

"Ali," the boy answered.

"Well, Ali," Lyons said as his eyes fell on the man whose ear was still bleeding. "I need you to ask them if all of the bombs are tied into one central detonator." He paused, then nodded. "Go ahead."

The young Iranian spoke quickly, addressing the man who was holding the side of his face where his ear had once been. The Pasdaran's lips turned down into a snarl as he answered.

Ali looked back to Lyons. "He says he will not help you infidels in any way. And he also suggested, in the most vulgar way possible, that you have sexual relations with a camel."

Lyons nodded, then turned back to the man holding his ear. With a wide smile on his face, the Able Team leader reached into a pocket of his blacksuit and pulled out a pair of rubber gloves. Sliding his hands into the latex gloves, he grabbed the hand covering the Pasdaran's ear and pulled it away from the bloody injury. Then, with his other hand, he clenched what was left of the earlobe between his thumb and index finger and twisted.

The Iranian Revolutionary Guardsman screamed like a banshee.

Lyons wondered how much the other Iranian Revolutionary Guardsmen could hear through the glass door in the front office.

"Tell him if he doesn't shut up I'm gonna pull the rest of the ear off," Lyons told Ali.

Ali passed that information along in Farsi, and the man covered his mouth with his bloody hand. He began shivering as if he was cold.

But he made no sound.

Looking at the man with the .22 in his shoulder, the Able Team leader said, "Ask him if he'll be more cooperative or if he'd like a .22 in his foot to go with the one in his shoulder. I'll make sure it hits a part of his foot that'll ensure that he limps for the rest of his life. Of course that life probably won't be all that long."

Ali spoke, then translated the answer into English. "He says he would be more than happy to help."

"Ask him again if there's one central place where all the bombs can be detonated at once," Lyons demanded.

Ali spoke again, listened to the answer, then said,

"The only place where that can happen is right here in this office." He paused to take a breath. "And the detonator is in the pocket of one of the dead men."

"Which one?" Schwarz broke in.

Ali asked the man in camouflage, and he pointed to one of the corpses on the floor.

Blancanales began shaking him down, and came up with a digital remote-control device in one of the breast pockets of the man's camo BDU blouse. He dropped it on the tile floor and was about to stomp on it when the man with the bloody ear shouted frantically. Then he spoke directly to Ali again.

"Don't break it!' Ali said quickly. "It's set so if you do, it'll automatically detonate all of the bombs."

Blancanales set his foot down to the side and said, "It would've been nice for you to tell us a little earlier," he said.

"Ask him what the combination is to defuse that thing," Lyons told Ali.

After a brief exchange Ali said, "He doesn't know. And according to him, neither do any of the others. The guy who was carrying it was the only one trusted with the numbers. And he, of course, is dead." The exchange student glanced toward one of the bodies on the floor.

Lyons felt his teeth grind in both disgust and anger. But he went on, using Ali as his interpreter, watching the young man closely for any signs that he might actually be on the other side of this miniwar inside the mall. There were no rules in the terror game—which was hardly a game at all— and nowhere was it written that just because he wasn't wearing camouflage he couldn't be one of the enemy.

The Pasdaran might easily have put one of their men in plainclothes to pretend to be a hostage for just this very type of situation. On the other hand, Carl Lyons knew that Iranians in general were no different from any other group of people. Some were extremely good and kindhearted while others could pass for Satan's meaner brother.

And, as with all races, the majority fell somewhere in between.

But Ali showed no signs of deception as Lyons, Schwarz and Blancanales learned that there were twenty-nine Pasdarans still alive and scattered throughout the mall. And there was no way to get an estimate on how many hostages were with them. But even one man, woman or child meant they had to shut this operation down before the Revolutionary Guardsmen had time to react. And the only way to do that was to get them all centralized.

"Ask him about their backup plan," Lyons told Ali. "Surely they had a plan B in case something like this went wrong."

Ali did as ordered. And the man on the floor answered.

Ali turned toward Lyons. "He says that the emergency plan was for the lieutenant—one of the other men who's dead on the floor now—to announce over the loudspeaker that all of the men were to herd the hostages to the food court at the center of the mall. Where the four hallways intersect."

Lyons felt his eyebrows lower as he stared at the man on the floor. There was more to this than met the eye.

He could sense it, almost smell it burning in his nostrils. Glaring at the Pasdaran with the shoulder wound, he said, "Tell him I want the code word or number that makes the announcement official," he said. "And make your voice sound like you *know* there is one."

Ali now glared at the man on the floor himself, and Lyons could feel the bitterness within the young man as he spoke. His instincts told him this was a good kid whose own country of birth was embarrassing him before the world. He sounded as genuine as anyone the Able Team leader had ever heard.

But that didn't mean Lyons wouldn't still have to keep a close eye on him.

The man with the wounded shoulder listened to Ali, then looked down at the floor as he mumbled an answer.

Ali looked back at Lyons and said, "It is a word— the Farsi word for *tiger.*"

"Well, tell our injured friend there that he'd better use it when he gets on the microphone and calls everyone to the food court," Lyons said.

Ali translated. But the man on the floor shook his head when he spoke.

"He is not afraid to die," Ali said. "It's the usual story about Paradise and a bunch of virgins waiting on him there."

Carl Lyons looked down at the man as he suddenly remembered an old story about General Blackjack Pershing and a group of renegade Islamic Arabs over a century ago. The memory brought a smile to his face.

It had worked for Pershing. And he saw no reason it wouldn't work here.

"Ali, tell him to listen very closely to what I'm about to say."

Ali did.

"Here's what I'm going to do with him after I kill him," Lyons said through clenched teeth. "First, I'm going to take his body out to a pig farm where I'm going to buy a pig. Then, I'm going to gut both him and the pig and switch their insides—heart, liver, lungs, intestines, everything. Then I'm going to bury them side by side in the same unmarked grave."

Even Ali looked frightened as he translated Lyons's words into Farsi.

And the man with the shoulder wound looked suddenly petrified. He answered, but in a mumbling, frantic voice.

Ali looked back at Lyons. "He says that would mean eternal Hell for him," the college student said. "I think he'll agree to do whatever you want now."

Lyons stepped forward, grabbed the microphone from the stand and dropped it into the wounded Pasdaran's lap. Then he pressed the barrel of the Woodsman against the man's temple and said, "Make sure he knows that if this doesn't come off right—for any reason—he's going to be the first to die. And remind him about the pig."

Ali spoke, and the man's head bobbed vigorously up and down. He keyed the mike and began speaking into it.

"He has used the code word," Ali whispered as the wounded man continued to speak into the microphone. "And now he is calling them all to the food court, telling them to bring their hostages…."

"Let me know if he says anything that seems even remotely out of place," the Able Team leader said. "There could always be another code word that cancels out the first and puts them on alert."

Ali frowned as he listened. "I cannot be sure," he told Lyons. "But I do not think there was any secret meaning to anything he said."

Carl Lyons nodded. A plan was already formulating in his brain, and he needed very badly to get word to the two-man teams of SWAT officers and bomb experts. But, still worried that the Pasdaran might be equipped with police scanners, he had ordered radio silence throughout this mission.

Which meant there was only one way to get word to the other men. Taking the satellite phone out of one of his pockets, he tapped in the number he'd gotten from KBI Director Bill Markham.

"Tell the SWAT and bomb men inside the mall to stay hidden and hold off until they hear gunfire," Lyons told Markham. "Then tell the bomb boys to begin defusing whatever bombs they've found, and the SWAT men to join the party in the food court." He paused a moment, then said, "We've got all of the Pasdaran getting ready to assemble there, so the bomb experts can come in behind them. I need the SWAT men sniping from the railing around the second floor."

"All right," Markham said. The tone of his voice said he'd do it. But it also said he still didn't like the idea of someone else running the show.

Carl Lyons didn't care. All he and the other two men from Stony Man Farm wanted was to get the hostages out alive and to see the Pasdaran carried out horizontally in body bags. He moved closer to the glass door where he could see out into the food court.

"What do we do now?" Ali asked him.

"The hardest thing you ever do in any battle," Lyons answered. "Wait."

DAVID MCCARTER WALKED directly behind Adel Spengha as Phoenix Force, the Kurds and the Christian Iranians made their way down out of the Zagros Mountains to the plateau where Isfahan was located. Although he spoke no Farsi, the Phoenix Force leader remembered an old expression that had been around for centuries.

"Isfahan nesfe jahan."

"Isfahan is the center of the world."

It came from the days of the Persian Empire, when Isfahan was a major trade center. But today, at least for the Christian Iranians, Kurds and the men of Phoenix Force, the old saying was once again accurate.

McCarter continued to follow the Rat. Ever since they'd encountered the Kurds and Tex's Christian followers, Adel Spengha had done his best to fade into the background. And Tex and Abbas—both of whom knew the mountains even better than the Rat—had taken over as guides. They had even known of a shorter and lower route into Iran, a route that would keep them below the snow and ice so they didn't have to worry about sliding off the side of a cliff to their deaths.

McCarter squinted through the night, his eyes piercing a hole through Spengha's back. He had considered paying the man, then letting him go. But Spengha was like most snitches—he was likely to take the money, thank McCarter, then slip out and try to sell the information he had about them to the remaining Iranian soldiers back at the clearing.

It was less risky to keep the man tagging along with the group.

McCarter waited until they were a good two miles from the clearing where the battle had taken place before he called for a rest stop. The sun was just coming up and the mountains began breaking out in a kaleidoscope of blue, red and violet. The Iranian soldier who Tex had taken alive had been helped along by the American cowboy-missionary and Abbas until he'd regained his senses enough to walk by himself. McCarter had then assigned the two men to guard him while he moved along by his own volition. He was in no shape to run.

But the Phoenix Force leader was taking no chances.

Now the men from Stony Man Farm had dropped to the ground on the trail to rest, and McCarter saw that Tex, Abbas and the Iranian Revolutionary Guardsman had taken seats on the flat limestone overlooking a steep drop-off. He joined them, sitting next to the Iranian with Tex on his other side. "Either of you talk to him yet?" he asked Abbas.

The Kurd nodded his head. "He speaks pretty good English," he said. "But if he gets stuck, I can always translate."

McCarter nodded, pulled the canteen from his belt, took a long drink and then handed it to the Iranian. The man had carried no water or overnight equipment, so it appeared the forces who had attacked them in the clearing had not planned to be away from camp all night.

The Iranian regular drank as if he'd been in the desert for a week.

"Slow down," McCarter told him as he reached up and took his canteen back. "We're not going up to where the snow is, which means this water has to last us."

The Iranian nodded his head. "Thank you," he said.

"What's your name?" McCarter asked the man.

"They call me Mani," the bearded soldier said.

"Well, Mani," McCarter said. "What can you tell me about the American newsmen who were kidnapped a few days ago?"

Mani shook his head back and forth almost animatedly. "I had nothing to do with that," he said as the sun rose higher.

"I'm not saying you did," McCarter answered. "I just want to know what you've heard about their location."

"I am not allowed to tell you that," Mani said. His words were coming out accompanied by a thin mist of red blood from the teeth that had been crushed with the M-16 butt.

McCarter took an OD green do-rag out of his blacksuit and held it in both hands, twirling the center until only a tiny corner remained flapping between his hands. Then, holding one of the ends, he snapped it out like a whip into the center of the blood covering Mani's already split lips.

Mani cried out in pain and the scream echoed down the mountains.

With both hands shielding his face, Mani said, "You are not allowed to do that! The Geneva Convention does not allow torture!"

"You're right," McCarter said. "And Iran has always led the pack in the human rights department, haven't it?" He paused. But when Mani didn't respond to his obvious sarcasm, he said, "Sorry about that. Actually, I meant to blow my nose and the rag just slipped."

Mani dropped his hands from in front of his face, and McCarter snapped the makeshift whip into his mutilated mouth again.

"Bloody hell," McCarter said, shaking his head in mock surprise. "There it goes again. Got to watch these things all the time. They seem to have a mind of their own, don't they?"

Mani had screamed again. But now he kept his hands up in front of his face.

McCarter leaned back slightly, peering down into the valley below them. It was a shallow valley compared with many they had passed earlier. But it was deep enough that no man was going to survive a fall into it.

"Let's retrace our tracks a little and start over," the Phoenix Force leader said. "What can you tell me about the American newsmen?"

"Nothing," Mani mumbled from behind his hands. "I know nothing."

"Okay." McCarter shrugged, standing. He turned to Tex and said, "Give me a hand, will you?" Both men grabbed Mani by an arm. Stepping onto the limestone on which they'd been sitting, they dragged Mani up between them.

"What…what are you doing?" the Iranian soldier asked in a trembling voice.

"Well," said McCarter as he and Tex began to drag Mani toward the edge of the cliff. "Since you've cited the Geneva Convention, I can't torture you. So we're just going to toss you off this cliff and be done with you."

"No!" Mani yelled. "No! No! No! No! No!"

"Yes, yes, yes, yes, yes," Tex said.

"No, please!" the Iranian regular shouted. "What can I do for you? What can I do to keep you from killing me?"

"You can stop acting like a total wanker and answer my questions," McCarter said. But they kept dragging the man closer to the drop-off as he spoke.

"Stop! I will talk!" Mani cried.

They were only a foot or so from the edge when McCarter quit pulling on the man's arm. Tex took the cue and did the same. With Mani lying on his back against the greenish rock, McCarter and Tex looked down at him. "This is your last chance," the Phoenix Force leader said. "Tell us what you know about the whereabouts of the hostages or you're going to find out you can't fly like a bird."

Mani was panting from fear rather than exertion as he said, "They keep moving them around. The last I heard, they were in Arak but getting ready to leave for Isfahan."

McCarter and Tex pulled the man to his feet and shoved him back away from the drop-off. He fell off of the flat limestone onto the trail, landing in a seated position.

"Looks like we're headed for Isfahan," McCarter told the rest of his team, Abbas, Tex and Adel Spengha.

All of the men nodded.

Looking from Tex to Abbas, McCarter asked, "Are you going to draw any unwanted attention in the city?"

Abbas's laugh was friendly. "No," he said. "We Kurds often go into town for supplies. And even the Iranian military is reluctant to murder us in front of witnesses." He paused a moment, then went on. "I'm afraid it's you who's going to draw all the attention." He glanced up and down McCarter's blacksuit from head to boot. "You look like…" He paused, searching his mind for the right words.

"They all look like Batman," Tex said for him.

"Yes, that is the name I was trying to think of." Abbas laughed. "Batman!"

The men of Phoenix Force all laughed as one.

The sun was high enough now that they had good vision as they prepared to continue through the mountains. When they all looked ready, McCarter turned to Calvin James. "Robin," he said. "Why don't you run point for any target of opportunity?"

"Okay, Batman." James chuckled as he turned and started on along the trail.

YURI KOVACH WATCHED as his men loaded the last of the F-14 fighter plane parts into the semi-trailer. When they were finished, there was still a good two feet of empty storage room right in front of the rear doors.

Wasted space? Kovach thought. Hardly. He continued to watch as the men began stacking boxes of food and medical supplies marked CARE behind the airplane parts to cover the real cargo. To the casual observer, each of the even dozen trucks making its way from Russia to Iran would look like part of a truly humanitarian effort.

They would encounter inspection sites along the way—not just at the borders but "surprise" inspections set up arbitrarily along the roads. But between his contacts and those of Javid Azria, the president of Iran, the guards at each location would give the trucks no more than a cursory glance. And should they run into a snafu anywhere along the way, the two men in each truck, who would take turns driving and sleeping, were armed to the teeth with Kalashnikov rifles and a variety of pistols.

Of course the news of an incident that involved gunfire—even if the border guards were all killed—would spread like wildfire across an open prairie. Which was why near each border Kovach had planted a dozen other empty trucks.

He figured the transfer from the original vehicles to those waiting would take less than one hour. Then his men would be off again with different trucks and license tags while the authorities looked for the original big rigs.

Kovach smiled as he stuck an unlit filterless cigarette into his mouth and let it hang from the corner. He had been trying to quit smoking for over two years now but had been unsuccessful. And he knew that before the day was out he would give in to the cry of his body for nicotine. It was only a matter of time.

Kovach cursed silently under his breath. He despised weakness, and weakness was exactly what kept him from stopping this habit that threatened his life. Was he self-destructive? No, he didn't think so. If he had been, he would have taken one of the many opportunities that life had presented to him in which he could have just not done anything, and died. Hundreds of rounds had been fired at him when he had been in the Soviet army in Afghanistan. All he would have had to do was charge out from behind cover.

The Afghans would have done the rest, and he would have been awarded the coveted Hero of the Soviet Union medal posthumously. And there were dozens of other situations in which he'd found himself since the fall of the Soviet Union where all he would have needed to do was simply not put up resistance and he'd have been dead.

So, as the trucks carrying enough spare parts to completely outfit at least three dozen F-14s left the parking area of his heavy-equipment lot on the outskirts of Moscow, he used his hands to scratch at his opposite arms. Then he finally bit down hard on the cigarette, feeling a tiny amount of nicotine rush through his body.

For a second, he found relief. Then the short high disappeared and his body screamed for more! The taste of the unfiltered tobacco was almost enough to get him to light the end so he could drag two full lungs' worth of smoke into his body. In a way, it was not unlike meeting a woman who was not willing to let you go any further than playing with her breasts.

Frustrating. Infuriating.

Deciding that the unlit cigarette was doing more harm than good, Kovach spit it out, then ground it into the damp earth with his heel. As the trucks heading for Iran disappeared out of his lot, he glanced at the other heavy equipment around him. Bulldozers, tractors, wheat combines and ditch diggers were everywhere, some lying stripped of parts while others were in mint condition. Kovach forgot all about cigarettes and nicotine for a moment and smiled. He had built the business up from scrap soon after the hammer and sickle fell, and he was proud of it. It could stand alone, making him money without ever stepping outside the law. But even as successful as it was, an entire year's profit was mere pocket change compared to the money he'd receive for the jet-fighter parts he was shipping to Iran.

Kovach turned and started back toward the office building, his boots slushing slightly in the damp soil between row after row of machines and parts. He sometimes tired of buying and selling tractors. But the legitimate business provided the perfect money-laundering front. Kovach Investments and Heavy Equipment was also an ideal place to hide stolen equipment or other machinery—including the F-14 parts—until he could find a buyer.

Yuri Kovach had not even bothered to throw a tarp over the airplane parts he had purchased from one of the many groups of former KGB agents and Soviet military personnel who were collectively, and ignorantly, referred to as Russian Mafia by the Americans these days.

Yuri Kovach's smile turned into an audible laugh as he neared the building. The Americans seemed to think that all of the former Soviets knew each other and had formed a single, united criminal enterprise.

Nothing could be further from the truth. There were dozens of smaller groups, and they did indeed call for each other's help from time to time. But there was no central authority—no godfather system, so to speak. And these smaller criminal groups spent as much time fighting each other as they did scamming, stealing and murdering Americans and other non-Russians.

Entering the office, Kovach heard the phone ringing. A moment later the pudgy paw of an enormous black-haired woman reached out and answered, "Kovach Investments and Heavy Equipment."

The huge woman listened for a moment, then turned to Kovach and nodded her head. "He has just returned," she said in Russian. "I will transfer you."

Kovach nodded as he stepped onto the carpet just inside his office door. The phone on his desk began to buzz as the door closed behind him. Lifting the receiver, he said, "Hello?" in the same language that the secretary had used.

"Let us speak English," said the voice on the other end. "My Russian is not so good. I could barely understand or answer your secretary. And I have heard your Farsi. It is even worse than my Russian."

Kovach laughed out loud at the joke, then said, "English it is, then." He paused to clear his throat. "If you have called about your shipment, it just left."

"Were you able to find all of the parts I required?" the voice asked.

"Yes, and duplicates in many cases. I have thrown them in for free as a show of good faith."

"Excellent!" said the excited voice on the other end of the crackling line. "Perhaps I should do the same by tipping your drivers when we take possession of the goods."

"A splendid idea, Mr. President. But please inform me by phone exactly how much and who you give it to."

There was a silence over the phone. Then Iranian President Javid Azria asked, "Why do you need to know that?"

"Because my men are supposed to turn over *all* of the money they receive. I have already paid them for their driving services."

"And you want to know who is holding out on you?" Azria said.

"Precisely," Kovach answered. "I want to know who to kill and who to let live."

"A most excellent method for testing loyalty," Azria agreed. "I shall have to remember to use similar ways to trap any of my own men who appear to be getting greedy." He coughed for a second, then said, "Is there anything else?"

"Only one thing," Kovach said. "I am assuming you were successful at bribing the truck checkpoints and the border patrol agents my men will encounter during their journey."

"I was," said the Iranian president. "None of the trucks will be inspected. And everyone's papers will be—how do they say it?—rubber-stamped."

"That is the way they say it," confirmed Kovach.

"Then we will not speak again until my men meet yours inside our border near Mashhad," Azria said.

"Unless something unexpected comes up," Kovach said.

"Nothing like that will happen," Azria said. "It has been written. And I have prayed to Allah, and he has promised to protect us all in this jihad."

"Yeah, well, whatever," Kovach said disinterestedly. Although the words had never been spoken, he had gotten the distinct impression over the past few weeks that President Azria didn't believe in an Allah any more than he did.

"Goodbye for now," Javid Azria said.

"Yes, goodbye," Kovach answered and hung up.

The former Soviet military officer sat back in his desk chair and automatically reached into the breast pocket of his shirt. But the gold cigarette case that he had carried there for years was absent. He glanced to the bottom right-hand drawer of his desk where he had locked it at the beginning of this latest attempt to quit.

He had the key that would open it on his key ring, in his pocket. All he would have to do was reach into his pants, pull it out and twist it into the lock.

Kovach's hand was already moving toward the pocket of his slacks when he forced himself to stand. Without speaking to his secretary, he left the building and began walking down one of the pathways between the heavy equipment and scattered parts.

He would defeat this nicotine habit if it killed him.

But in the back of his mind, Kovach suspected that he might just be doomed to die long before the desire for cigarettes went away.

CHAPTER EIGHT

The other two men of Able Team waited as Carl Lyons moved into position just to the side of the glass door. He had forced the wounded Pasdaran to his feet and positioned him in front of the door, facing inward to hide the shoulder wound. The Pasdaran now blocked the view of anyone trying to peek inside the offices from the mall's hallway.

The Able Team leader reached out and separated the venetian blinds covering the large picture window next to the door with his fingers. He looked out into the hallway.

Lyons had debated whether or not the men of Able Team should enter what he knew would be the final battle at the mall wearing the Iranian BDUs they'd used to cover their blacksuits or go back to wearing the blacksuits alone. There were advantages and disadvantages to both options. In the end, he had decided to go with the Stony Man Farm battle suit. The camouflage might give them an extra half second of confusion once they rushed out the door and began shooting Pasdarans. On the other hand, it might get them killed by any of the SWAT men who entered the foray behind the enemy. Those sharpshooters wouldn't have time to pick and choose before they shot; they would open up with their rifles on anything in a Pasdaran uniform.

As he watched, still peering between the blinds, Lyons saw several groups of hostages—their hands duct-taped behind their backs—hurry past the office, prodded on by the barrels of AK-47s in the hands of other camouflaged men. Directly across the hall he could see a Foot Locker athletic store next to a tobacco shop.

Ten minutes later the parade had ended. Lyons sat the Pasdaran with the shoulder wound down in a chair facing the front office desk and dropped the microphone in his lap once more. "Okay," he said to the other two Able Team warriors. "No matter how we do this, it's going to be sloppy." He paused for a deep breath, then turned to Ali and went on. "Tell our friend here to order all of his men to get the hostages seated at the tables in the middle of the food court, then break off and assemble in front of the Foot Locker. Tell him to use the code word again if necessary. And remind him about the pig funeral waiting for him if anything goes wrong."

Schwarz butted quickly in. "Not trying to tell you how to run the show, Ironman," he said. "But if you don't leave a few of the men to guard the hostages, don't you think it's going to look kind of suspicious?" He cleared his throat. "Why not leave a few in the food court? The SWAT guys on the second floor can take them out easy enough."

Lyons nodded his head. "That's why we keep you around, Gadgets," the Able Team leader said. "Good idea." He turned to Ali. "You get that?"

"Yes, sir," the young Arabic student said. "I will include it in my instructions." He looked down at the wounded man now seated facing the rest of the men in the front office, then reeled off a paragraph or two that no one but he and the Pasdaran could understand.

"Get this guy's name, too," Blancanales added.

Ali spoke a few more words. Then the man in the chair looked up at Lyons and said, "Moe."

Without further prodding, the man who had identified himself as Moe keyed the microphone and began speaking. Lyons turned back to the window and spread the blinds slightly once more.

In the hall just outside the office, the Able Team leader saw the Pasdarans assembling in front of the Foot Locker store. He could hear a low rumbling of voices as the men talked among themselves. He couldn't understand the words but he could tell by the tone of their voices that they were suspicious.

They had met no resistance so far. So why were they being ordered to switch to plan B?

Lyons felt himself grinning as another adage popped into his mind. This one was particularly suited for the occasion.

"If Muhammad can't go to the mountain, bring the mountain to Muhammad."

Lyons gave the Pasdarans another three minutes, then moved toward the door. "Lock and load," he told the men of Able Team. He checked to make sure the Colt

Woodsman's safety was on, then jammed the sound-suppressed .22 into his belt and watched the other two Able Team warriors do the same with their Rugers.

The time for silence was over.

It was time to replace it with thunder.

The clicking and clanging of rifle bolts sliding home echoed throughout the offices as Lyons lifted his M-16 in his right hand and continued to peer through the window. When he saw one of the Pasdarans break away from the group and start toward the door, he knew that time had run out.

This Pasdaran who walked toward him had been chosen by his brethren to go into the office to find out just exactly what was going on.

Which meant he was going to be the first to die.

Lyons stepped back from the large picture window and said, "Ali, take Moe and go back to the farthest office and drop down on the floor." Turning to Schwarz, he said, "Gadgets, grab the cord for this thing."

Schwarz closed a fist around the cord to the venetian blinds.

The Able Team leader waited until he saw the camo-clad hand reach out and push against the door rail, then yelled, "Pull!"

Schwarz jerked on the cord and the blinds suddenly shot upward, leaving nothing but clear glass between the office and the hallway outside.

On the other side of the glass, Lyons saw the Pasdarans—who had carelessly let their weapons fall to the end of their slings—turn toward him. The glass was going to get broken anyway, so the Able Team leader aimed through it at an angle, pointing the muzzle of his rifle at the man about to push open the door and cutting loose with a steady stream of 5.56 mm firepower. The hail of lead shattered the glass, and the target began dancing like some crazed marionette.

A split second later the thunder the Able Team leader had known would come arrived as their enemies began returning fire.

But many of them were already dead in the first few seconds of the fight.

BY THE TIME they saw the uniformed men in the distance, the men from Stony Man Farm had covered their black-suits with extra robes and headgear provided by Abbas and the other Kurds. Tex had already been in traditional attire except for his hat and boots. McCarter had talked him into exchanging his straw hat for a turban. But the Phoenix Force leader had come up against a brick wall when he'd suggested that the leader of the Iranian Christians get rid of his worn-out cowboy footwear.

"If I get killed," Tex had said firmly, "I fully intend for it to be doing the Lord's work, and with my boots *on.*"

So McCarter had let it pass. Modern Kurds and Iranians wore whatever they could find anyway, and several of them wore soccer T-shirts from European teams, American-made athletic shoes and other clothing that was distinctly Western in origin mixed in with their more conventional wear.

The fact was, to dress completely as either an Iranian or Kurd might draw more suspicion than even their blacksuits would.

The soldiers continued to approach them as they came down out of the mountains onto the flat plain. McCarter, who had been leading the way except for James, who was running point, called over his shoulder for Abbas and Tex to join him.

The two warriors came jogging up on both of his sides.

"Abbas," McCarter told the Kurdish leader, "you'd better be the one who handles this." He pulled out the same OD-green rag he'd flipped into Mani's face and wiped sweat from his brow. "Tex, I suggest you do your best to fade into the background like my men and I plan to do."

"They're out hunting the Christians," Abbas said in the same Texas twang that still amused McCarter. "And they're gonna see real fast that at least half of our party are them. We aren't getting out of here without a fight."

McCarter nodded. As the camouflaged figures continued to grow larger in the distance, he counted eleven jeeps and what looked like two American Hummers. The Hummers made him grind his teeth together.

They had to have come from American troops in Iraq. Which meant good guys had been killed by the bad guys to obtain them.

It made the warrior inside McCarter want to begin pulling the trigger of his M-16 immediately.

But his brain told him to wait. The Iranian soldiers were too far away. And if they could get out of this confrontation without a battle, so much the better. There was a good chance that if the bullets started flying an Iranian radioman would contact their base and distribute the information that this strange conglomeration of men was heading into Isfahan.

That would mean an even larger welcoming party down the line.

McCarter ordered everyone to hide their weapons beneath the bulky robes they wore. Then he and Tex dropped back into the group, letting Abbas take the lead as the Iranians continued to near. McCarter maneuvered his way next to the Rat so the man could keep him apprised of what was being said when the two groups finally encountered each other. When they were roughly twenty feet apart, the Iranians—McCarter could tell by their shoulder patches that they were regulars rather than Pasdarans—ground their vehicles to a halt.

A man wearing the rank of colonel stepped down out of one of the Hummers and walked directly to Abbas. He carried no rifle, just a lone .45-caliber Colt 1911. Like the Hummers, it had probably come off of the dead body of an American GI. McCarter scanned the rest of the Iranians and saw the usual mixture of American M-16s and Russian AK-47s, as well as a spattering of other .45s, 9 mm Berettas and Russian Tokarevs and Makarovs.

The Iranian army had been weapons scavengers ever since the Iran-Iraq war. They immediately made use of everything they could beg, borrow or steal. With heavy emphasis on the *stealing* part.

As the men of Phoenix Force waited, Abbas and the colonel began to speak in a strange mixture of dialects. "What are they saying?" he whispered to the Rat. "And in what language?"

"It's what they call 'border talk,'" Spengha whispered so low that McCarter could barely hear him. "A mixture of Arabic, Farsi and Kurdish."

"What are they saying?" McCarter asked. The men had been frowning at each other, and their voices were gradually rising in tone. The former British SAS officer knew that Middle Easterners frequently argued among themselves, and when they did they seemed to think whoever could shout the loudest had won the argument. They also displayed another trait that most Westerners found odd—they could yell and scream at each other as if they were both about to thrust daggers into each other's heart, then suddenly quiet down and go eat dinner together as if no disagreement had ever taken place.

In any case, Abbas and the colonel obviously disagreed about something and their voices had begun to rise.

This time, McCarter didn't have to ask the Rat what they were saying—the man volunteered it. "I can't keep up with it all," he whispered. "But the gist of things is that the Iranians are out hunting Tex and his fellow Christians. The colonel thinks they're mixed in with this group, and Abbas is insisting that we are all Kurds." He paused to draw in a breath. "Abbas is risking his life, and those of his men, to protect the rest of us."

"I wish him all the luck in the world," McCarter said dryly.

The Phoenix Force leader turned his attention to the rest of the Iranian regulars as the conversation continued to grow louder. The men in the jeeps and Hummers were all used to such arguments, and had begun relaxing as the argument continued to heat up. Some had even lit hand-rolled cigarettes while they waited.

The bottom line was that they had decided the chance meeting was not going to end in any kind of battle.

McCarter slowly moved away from Spengha and began walking through the crowd. He spoke to his men and Tex first, then the other men he knew had rifles or pistols tucked under their robes. Even the men who spoke no English understood what he was telling them all, which was to spread out and get ready.

The Phoenix Force leader kept one eye on the colonel and the rest of his men as he moved. The Christians and Kurds had mixed in together to camouflage Tex and his followers. "Move them back as far as you can," McCarter said in a quiet voice when he'd returned to Tex's side.

"Will do, amigo," Tex said. Slowly and carefully the men began to move toward advantage points in case gunfire broke out.

Abbas and the colonel were yelling at each other now, and the men in the jeeps and Hummers seemed to be enjoying the show. Most of them were smiling, and a few were trying to suppress laughter at this unexpected entertainment.

McCarter knew this was the only advantage he was going to get. Seeing no sense in shouting out an order in English that many of the armed men in the group wouldn't understand and that would also be heard by the Iranians, he suddenly pulled his M-16 from under his robe and pointed it at the colonel as the man continued screaming his lungs out. McCarter pulled the trigger, letting the automatic explosions be the cue for the rest of the men.

All at once, the shouting voices of Abbas and the colonel were drowned out by gunfire. All of the other members of Phoenix Force had responded a half second behind their leader, and the armed Kurds and Christians were only a brief moment slower. Bullets of all sizes, shapes, calibers and vintages flew through the air like hives of angry bees, striking the Hummers and jeeps and destroying their windshields, as well as penetrating the glass to drive on through to the men inside the vehicles.

The Iranians, caught completely off guard, danced and jerked as the metal and lead struck their bodies. Only one man, hanging out of the side of one of the Hummers, even got off a round. And it sailed harmlessly into the sky to fall somewhere in the mountains behind them before a combination of rifle and pistol fire caused him to drop his AK-47 and fall out of the vehicle onto the ground.

McCarter swung his M-16 away from the colonel as the man fell out of the giant transport vehicle. But by then, the fight had ended.

The entire battle had taken less than five seconds.

"Check for wounded," McCarter yelled out, and the armed men moved on to the jeeps and Hummers, looking for any of the Iranian soldiers who might have survived the unexpected onslaught. But it was McCarter himself who found the prize.

A young man in his late teens, wearing the insignia of a corporal, had hidden beneath one of the jeeps. The Phoenix Force leader might have missed him altogether had it not been for the sniffles and sobs floating out from under the vehicle.

The former SAS man looked down and saw the heels of a pair of well-worn black leather combat boots barely visible beneath the jeep. Letting his rifle fall to the end of its sling, he reached down and grasped the man by the ankles.

"Out you come, mate," McCarter said as he pulled the crying man from cover.

The sobs grew louder as McCarter dropped the man's legs and grabbed an arm, jerking him to his feet. "Please!" the young man pleaded. "Do not kill me!"

McCarter was slightly surprised that the young man spoke English. But the world grew smaller by the minute as new technology, especially communication devices, was invented and perfected.

By now he had been joined by the rest of the Phoenix Force crew, Tex, Abbas, the Rat and several of the other men—both Kurds and Christians—who had searched the vehicles. "Anybody else left alive?" he asked the group in general as he reached into his captive's holster and pulled out an old and worn Makarov.

All of the men either shook their heads or muttered, "No."

"Then we'll have to make do with this little crybaby," the Phoenix Force leader said, then waited as Abbas translated. Several of the men laughed out loud at whatever word the Kurd leader had used in place of "crybaby."

McCarter turned to Calvin James, who had done his best to cover up his black skin with a kaffiyeh and bulky robe. It had not been because men of African heritage were unknown to this part of the world. It was simply the fact that they were more unusual than the caramel-colored faces of most Arabs.

And there were already more than enough aspects of this situation that were beyond the control of Phoenix Force. They couldn't afford to let any facet within their grasp to go uncorrected.

"So," McCarter said out of the side of his mouth to James at his side, "what's the preferred method of torture in the depths of the African jungle where you come from?" He had turned away from the young man as he spoke so his grin wouldn't give him away. But he made sure his words were still loud enough to be heard behind him.

In actuality, David McCarter had no intention of torturing this kid. Torture was not only distasteful but it was also unreliable. Enough pain could get a man to say anything. All men could be broken—it was simply a matter of degree. And once they were, they'd say anything they thought would curtail the pain.

Which was not necessarily the truth.

James knew the game McCarter was now playing every bit as well as the Phoenix Force leader. Torture was one thing. But the threat of torture—that was something else.

Since their young captive spoke English, there was no need for a translator, and out of the corner of his eye McCarter saw the young man cringe.

James smiled widely as he drew the bladed Crossada from its Kydex sheath. "My tribe has always been big on cutting," he said, the smile evaporating and turning into a scowl as he stared at the young Iranian regular. "Just little cuts here and there. Over a long period of time." He paused, cleared his throat and then extended the Crossada until only the very tip of the point touched the young Iranian's forearm. Slowly, he drew the blade down the man's arm, barely breaking the skin but producing a tiny line of red as it also shaved off several hairs. Then he pointed the Crossada downward and said, "I can start with the testicles and—"

"No! Please!" the young soldier screamed in a high-pitched, childish voice. "I will tell you whatever you want to know!"

"Well, let's begin with your name," McCarter said. "What is it?"

"Hamid," the young man said, and the word came out as frightened as those he had spoken previously.

"Okay, Hamid. What was your mission out here?" McCarter again had to work hard to keep from smiling. James was holding the Crossada's spear-point blade up in the air, occasionally pointing down at the man's crotch as he went through a grip-changing drill that consisted of both forward- and reverse-grip techniques.

"It was a routine patrol," Hamid said, his voice still quavering with horror. "But we were to specifically look for the American missionary and the followers he had turned into infidels, as well."

"Well, boy," Tex said, stepping forward. "You found him." He chuckled softly. "But now you're like that dog who likes to chase cars—what you gonna do with me now that you've got me?"

"Nothing!" Hamid screamed. "I am sorry!" His eyes shot back and forth between Tex and Calvin James. "I will become a Christian if you want me to be one! I love Jesus! I love him a lot!"

Tex smiled again. "That ain't how it works," he said. "I'm more than delighted to help you get on the right path to God. But you don't get there by saying you accept Jesus because you're afraid somebody's gonna change you from a bull to a steer."

Tex's colloquialism was obviously beyond Hamid's frame of reference. Instead of answering, he just stared in confusion at the man in the duct-taped cowboy boots.

"We'll talk about that later," Tex said. "When you aren't so upset and scared."

"When you tell him you'll talk to him later, Tex," McCarter said, "we're assuming he lives that long. And that depends on how well he answers our questions." He looked the frightened young man squarely in the eyes. "What do you know about the American journalists being held hostage by your Pasdaran troops?" he asked.

Hamid's face suddenly brightened with the knowledge that he might indeed have some intel that would keep his nether regions intact. "They are on their way to Isfahan!" he shouted.

McCarter was getting really tired of Hamid's high-pitched, girl-like voice. It was every bit as irritating as fingernails scratching down a blackboard. "Okay," the Phoenix Force leader said. "Quiet down. We're not going to hurt you—as long as you cooperate."

The young man suddenly fell forward on his knees, then leaned over and began kissing McCarter's boots.

"Thank you," he said in a lower voice. "Thank you, thank you, thank—"

The former SAS warrior actually felt embarrassed for the boy. He reached down, grabbed the epaulets on the shoulders of his BDU blouse and yanked him to his feet. "None of that, mate," he said in a stern voice. "If you're a man, then act like one."

The boy came back to his feet. But he still bowed his head.

"Man," Calvin James said, shaking his head in awe. "And here I was thinking Chicago's South Side culture I grew up in was weird. These folks have no self-respect at all." He continued to shake his head. "Boot-kissing. Makes me feel like regurgitating."

McCarter reached out and grabbed the Iranian regular's chin, lifting his eyes until they were even with his own. The time for frightening this kid was over. Now he had to find a way for the young man to relax enough to be of intelligence value. "Do you know exactly where they're being held?" he demanded.

"Maybe," Hamid said, wiping the tears from under his eyes with the back of his BDU cuff. "They spent the night at our camp last night. But they aren't there anymore. When we left on patrol this morning, the rumor was that they were heading toward a safehouse in the basement of a metalworker's shop in Isfahan's bazaar area."

"A metalworker's shop?" McCarter frowned.

Hamid's head bobbed up and down. "Yes. I know the shop. This man—the metalworker—hammers out copper pitchers and trays. It provides enough noise to cover any sounds coming from his basement."

The story sounded fishy to McCarter. "This man can't pound his hammer nonstop twenty-four hours a day," he said. "What about the noises after he quits working for the day?"

"They—the hostages, I mean—are gagged at the end of his shift. And they are closely guarded and warned that even a whisper will bring about instant death from one of the Pasdarans' scimitars."

The story still seemed unlikely to the Phoenix Force leader. After all, the journalists had been captured by official state soldiers, not some local terrorist group who'd have to keep the hostages hidden from both the American and Iranian governments. Why didn't they just take the prisoners to one of the Pasdaran bases where tight security would be easy?

McCarter voiced the question to Hamid.

"Because President Azria expects the United States to start bombing Tehran and Isfahan and some other large cities within the next few days," Hamid said. "And he holds no illusions about American intelligence operatives. Your country will know of every military base in the nation, and the first bombs will fall there."

"I can correct you on two errors in what you just said," said McCarter. "And perhaps I'll find more as we go along."

"What are my errors?" Hamid asked.

"First, you said my country when referring to the U.S. I'm British by birth. The United States is my adopted country. So, actually, we represent not just the United States but the entire free world."

"I understand," said Hamid. "What is the second mistake?"

"You said the first bombs would fall on military bases," McCarter said. "That implies civilian targets later. The U.S., Great Britain—all of the free Western nations—simply don't do that." He paused for a breath of air, then went on. "Of course that little rodent of a president of yours will start spouting out the usual dribble about 'baby-formula-manufacturing' sites being hit, and bombed-out mosques. But the truth is, that simply won't happen."

McCarter had evidently struck a sensitive chord in Hamid's brain. For the first time since he'd come out from beneath the jeep, Hamid seemed to lose his fear and actually became a little surly. "Americans, British," he nearly snarled. "You are all the same. And you do murder innocents."

McCarter couldn't keep from laughing out loud. "And the world accuses the West of being racist?" He shook his head in disbelief. He had not been brought up to think of any race being "better" than another, and he viewed different groups of people as equal. But that kind of attitude wasn't going to get him far with Hamid. So finally he said, "All right. If we can both put our pre-conceived notions about race aside for a moment, maybe we'll both live through the night."

Where he was, what he was doing and the increased danger he'd just invited with his words, came back to Hamid in a flash. "What else do you need to know?" he asked, his voice shaking slightly again.

"You say you know this metalworker well?" McCarter asked.

"No, I said I know his shop," Hamid said. "I have purchased items from him several times in the past."

Tex, still standing next to McCarter, said "What— you trying to tell us you collect pitchers and trays and other sweet little copper things?"

Hamid turned toward the man. "No," he said, his voice sounding slightly offended. "I purchased gifts for girlfriends there."

"Did I just hear you use the plural, Hamid?' McCarter asked. "*Girlfriends* rather than *girlfriend?*"

"Yes," Hamid said. "There are several young women with whom I consort."

Calvin James had finally sheathed his Crossada. But now he said, "No wonder you didn't want to lose your *cojones.*"

"So you can lead us to the metalworker's shop, then," McCarter said before Hamid could reply to James.

"I would rather not," Hamid said.

All of the men within hearing distance chuckled.

"That's what war is all about, Hamid," McCarter said. "Doing one thing right after another that you'd rather not be doing."

"But if my superiors find out I helped you, I will be beheaded," Hamid whined.

McCarter looked up and scanned the dead bodies in and around the jeeps and Hummers. "It appears that your superiors aren't going to have much to say about what you do either way."

"Not them," Hamid said. His voice had begun to sound as if his tongue had swollen. "My superiors back at the base. It will be hard enough to explain why everyone else was killed but I survived. If I take you to the metalworker's, they will behead me."

Abbas had stayed at the back of the group during most of the interrogation. But now, it appeared he had heard all he could stomach. Making his way through the rest of the armed warriors, he suddenly drew a long scimitar which he'd kept hidden along with his other weapons inside his robe, and unsheathed its wickedly-curved blade.

McCarter had not seen the sword before. But now he noted speckles and splotches of brownish-red blood that had permanently stained the blade.

"Hamid," Abbas said. "You must decide this very moment. Will you help us or your army?"

"If I say that I will help you, and the army learns of it, they will cut my head off," Hamid sniffled, reverting to his irritating girlish voice. "But if I choose to go with the army over you, you will behead me here and now."

"Well, that's right perceptive of you," Abbas said sarcastically. "So, do you want me to slice and dice you now, or would you rather take the chance of losing your head later?"

Hamid smiled nervously. "I believe I will hang on to my head a little longer, if possible," he said.

"Then take us into Isfahan, to the metalworker's shop," said McCarter. "We can use the jeeps and Hummers until we're close enough to the city to be seen, then ditch them and hump the rest of the way on foot."

"Your wish is my command," Hamid said, as if quoting a line out of *1001 Arabian Nights*. But he was rubbing the shallow blood line on his forearm, trying to get it to stop bleeding, as he said it.

"So," McCarter said, turning toward Tex and Abbas. "This isn't really your fight anymore. If some of you want to go back and accompany the women and children, there's no disgrace in that. But those who choose to stay with us—you're welcome and appreciated."

Both Abbas and Tex looked around at their various followers. All of the heads—both Kurdish and Iranian Christian—nodded.

"We all want to come with you," Abbas said. "As you yourself said, this ain't just the United States's war. It's the responsibility of all free nations."

Tex nodded his head. "We've been getting chased through these mountains by the Iranian regulars long enough," he drawled. "It'll be nice to be on the other side of the hunt for a while."

"Then let's get to it," McCarter said. "First we need to find out which of these vehicles are still operable."

As the strange alliance of Christian Iranians, Kurds and the men from Stony Man Farm began inspecting the damage to the jeeps and Hummers, David McCarter heard Hamid's trembling voice one more time.

"What should I do?" the young man asked.

"Change into that colonel's uniform," the Phoenix Force leader ordered him, pointing down at the dead man on the ground. "You've just been promoted."

SEATED IN HIS WHEELCHAIR in front of a long bank of computers, Aaron "the Bear" Kurtzman frowned at the satellite photos on the screen. Each time he clicked the mouse on the pad next to the computer, he saw a slightly different image of a convoy of trucks leaving Moscow, heading southeast. Clicking the back icon on the screen, he retraced the tractor-trailers back into the city, then began clicking the icon to zoom in more closely to the point where the trucks had originated.

Finally, a clear view of what appeared to be a heavy-equipment lot came into view. He could see the trucks parked in a line, and a sign at the edge of the screen that read Kovach Heavy Equipment. Going back a few more frames, it became clear that the trucks were being loaded, one by one, by a small group of six or seven men.

Kurtzman was a computer genius rather than an aircraft mechanic. But the parts he saw didn't look as if they belonged on a ditch digger or a bulldozer. Frowning again, the computer wizard lifted the phone receiver at his side and tapped Barbara Price's extension into the instrument.

"Hello, Bear," he heard the Stony Man Farm mission controller say in his ear.

"Hey, Barb," he returned. "Is Grimaldi on the ground?"

"Uh-uh," Price answered. "He took off a little while ago to pick up Striker in Bosnia. Mott's here, though. You need him?"

"Yeah," the man in the wheelchair confirmed. "Send him in, will you?"

"Sure thing," Price said. "He's catching a few Zs upstairs in one of the rooms. But he's been up there for almost two hours. That's a good night's rest for you guys."

Kurtzman laughed. "I've gotten to the point where I sleep with my eyes open and operate these machines at the same time," he said.

"Hang on a moment," Price said, and Kurtzman heard a click in his ear. A moment later the mission controller came back. "I've got Charlie on the other line," she said. "He wants to know who's going where."

Kurtzman smiled. Charlie Mott was only human, and although he'd act professionally and not complain about this intrusion into his well-earned sleep, the computer man knew he'd be slightly unhappy about it. Charlie wasn't alone on this. Nobody would like it.

"Tell him I just need him in the Computer Room for a minute, then it's back to the Land of Nod for him. That ought to make him happy."

Price clicked in his ear, then a moment later came back on and said, "He's on his way and you're right. He's delighted."

A few minutes later a tussle-haired Charlie Mott entered the Computer Room and walked wearily up the wheelchair ramp to Kurtzman's side. The number-two Stony Man Farm pilot—just like everyone else at the Farm—had fallen asleep in his clothing, ready to be awakened for an emergency. Now Mott was dressed in a blue plaid flannel shirt, blue jeans and a well-worn pair of boots with rings and leather straps on the sides. Jammed in his right front pocket, the top of the grip visible and ready to be drawn, was Mott's North American Arms .380 automatic. Roughly the same size as most .25-caliber pistols, but packing the stopping power of a 9 mm Kurz, it was as much of a trademark for the number-two Stony Man pilot as Grimaldi's snubby .357 was for him.

The pilot still looked sleepy. But he smiled as he

stopped next to Kurtzman and said, "What can I do for you, Bear?"

"Take a look at what they're loading onto these trucks," Kurtzman said. He wheeled to the side, giving Mott access to the mouse. The pilot knew how this program for downloading satellite photos worked, and he began clicking away at the pictures.

After a few clicks Mott said, "They're loading all sorts of aircraft parts, then hiding them with the CARE packages." He clicked several times more. "They look like..." His voice trailed off as he continued to click the mouse. "Yeah, they are. All of these parts go to F-14 fighter jets."

Kurtzman wheeled back into his place. "Thanks, Charlie. That's all I needed to know. Go back to sleep now."

"I don't think that's going to happen," Mott said, walking to a small table between the computers where a half-full coffee carafe stood. He poured himself a cup. "You've got my curiosity up now."

Having gleaned all of the intel he could from this set of photos, Kurtzman had switched programs and was now poring over a listing of bills of lading issued the day before in Moscow.

"Well," he said as Mott returned with a cup for him. "If you're really interested, here's the paperwork on the trucks. According to this, they're all packed to the hilt with CARE packages bound for Tehran."

"Unless the Iranians have started eating stick controls and passenger seats," Mott said, "they've been mismarked."

"Bingo for you, Charlie," Kurtzman said. "Now, refresh my memory. Way back when, didn't the Shah of Iran equip his air force with American-made F-14s?"

"He did," Mott said as he took a sip from his steaming cup. "And by now, most of them have at least one broken part that they can't get from us because they aren't on our Christmas card list anymore."

Kurtzman chuckled at Mott's understatement, then said, "They've had to cannibalize different planes to keep even a few in the air," he said. "But this big shipment is going to solve that problem if it reaches its destination. How many F-14s would be your estimate from looking at these pictures?"

"Hard to say for sure," Mott stated. "But a conservative guess would be around forty or so."

The man in the wheelchair nodded. "Hang with me for a second," he said. He went through a long series of keystrokes as he hacked his way into the computers of America's Central Intelligence Agency.

When he was finally in, Mott shook his head. "That just flat scares me," he said. "If you can gain access to the spooks, who else can?"

"Nobody," Kurtzman declared. "I hate to brag, but I don't think there's anyone else in the world—including my own staff—who knows the secret." He quit tapping for a minute, then said, "Let's see what intel is coming out of the Russian and Iranian desks these days."

Together, the two men began poring over CIA reports from field agents who acted as controls for the agency's informants.

One of the reports immediately caught Kurtzman's

eyes. "Huh," he said, chuckling again. "It appears that an Iranian patrol stationed in Isfahan went out this morning and never came back," he said. He clicked the mouse again and came to another report. "Here's an update. A CIA snitch says a search party found their dead bodies at the foot of the Zagros Mountains, and there were footprints and other evidence that a large party had confronted them. Whoever it was also stole their jeeps and two Hummers."

Mott laughed and took another drink of his coffee. "That's got Phoenix Force's signature all over it," he said. "McCarter's an absolute wizard at forming alliances with indigenous people who have common enemies."

"That he is, Charlie," Kurtzman said. "That he is."

"Anything else you need from me?" the Stony Man pilot asked.

"Not for the moment," Kurtzman said. "But thanks."

"Well, sooner or later somebody from around here is going to need a pilot," Mott said. "So I guess I really will try to catch up on my beauty sleep." He set his coffee cup down on the table.

"The good Lord knows you can use all of the beauty sleep you can get," Kurtzman quipped.

"Hey, have *you* looked in a mirror lately?" Mott retorted.

"Touché, and let's call it even," said the man in the wheelchair.

Charlie Mott just smiled and walked down the ramp as Kurtzman turned his attention back to the screen in front of him.

CHAPTER NINE

Schwarz aimed his M-16 through the broken window glass and began firing at the Pasdarans between the mall office and the Foot Locker store.

As the Iranian who had tried to push through the door to find out what was going on jerked and jiggled under Lyons's steady fire, Schwarz aimed his own M-16 at the far left of his field of vision through the window. He and Blancanales had discussed it ahead of time, and his partner had agreed to start at the right. Both men would then work their way toward the middle, where they'd meet.

That way, they took out the farthest Pasdarans—the ones with the best chance of escaping—first, before they could get away. Even though they had taken possession of what Mani assured them was the only central detonation device, any and all of the bombs could be activated individually at their various locations.

The men who now began returning Able Team's fire had come prepared to die. It would be no problem in their brainwashed minds to run to the nearest bomb and set it off. Such action would not do nearly the damage that the Pasdarans had planned. But the men of Able Team didn't intend to allow even one innocent American to die.

As he pulled the trigger on his rifle, in the corner of his eye, Schwarz watched Lyons and Blancanales both run their magazines dry. He switched to a broader attack, cutting figure eights back and forth into the mass of Iranians as his teammates threw their backs against the side walls of the office to reload. With his weapon on full-auto, Schwarz watched a half-dozen of the Pasdarans fall to the floor under his fire. Then the bolt locked open, empty.

By now, however, Lyons and Blancanales had dropped their empty magazines and inserted loaded ones in their place. Both bolts slid home with a clank, not a second apart, and another second after that, the two Able Team warriors were back in the game.

Schwarz had been standing directly in front of the reception desk, and now return fire missed him by millimeters, drilling through the thin steel at the back of his thighs. The desk would provide little to no cover. But at least it offered a bit of concealment while he reloaded.

So, sitting back on the desktop, the Able Team warrior flipped his knees up to his face in a backward somersault, landing behind the desk on both feet before dropping down beneath the desk.

A moment later his M-16 was operational again and he aimed it out of the shattered window and pulled the trigger.

Some of the Iranians had donned traditional Islamic headwear after entering the mall, and Schwarz's first 3-round burst of fire caught a man in a kaffiyeh who had worked his way almost to the window. He screamed something in Farsi as the 5.56 mm hollowpoints struck him in the chest.

Schwarz couldn't resist the temptation to scream back at him. "Have fun with your virgins!" he shouted at the top of his lungs as he swung the assault rifle toward a new target.

This time, it was a man wearing a BDU cap bearing the Pasdaran emblem who caught the Able Team man's bullets. The first of the trio caught him in the throat, taking out his jugular vein and sending a fire-hose spray of crimson straight back at Schwarz. The other two rounds caught him in both eyes, creating great caverns where the now pulverized eyeballs had once rested in their sockets.

In his peripheral vision, Schwarz could see that Lyons and Blancanales were doing their part. Both men from Stony Man Farm were mowing down Iranians like a threshing machine slashing its way through a field of ripened wheat. So far, Schwarz had not seen any of the Pasdarans escape Able Team's sudden explosive resistance.

But the men who had been left in the food court to guard the hostages were a problem, a problem that Schwarz knew wasn't going to take care of itself.

Someone was going to have to take the responsibility on as his own.

And that someone was him.

Herman "Gadgets" Schwarz had found over the

years that sometimes the safest thing to do during a firefight was what appeared on the surface to be the most dangerous. Only true warriors understood this line of thought, let alone practiced the philosophy. But those who did knew its value; it was unexpected and gave the man brave enough to attempt it a split second of confusion on the enemy's part.

And a split second to a Stony Man Farm operative was like a half hour to the average man on the street.

So, instead of continuing to fire from behind the desk, Schwarz suddenly rose, jumped over the barrier and dashed directly toward the window. Behind him, he heard Lyons order Blancanales to halt his fire for a moment.

And during that moment, everyone on both sides of the firefight quit firing. The Pasdarans stared at what looked like an insane American in a weird black costume of some sort, their trigger fingers frozen.

Schwarz flipped his selector switch to semiauto and took advantage of their shock, taking out three more men with a single shot each. He cut to his left toward the food court. As soon as he was out of the field of fire, he heard Lyons and Blancanales resume their assaults.

A few scattered shots came Schwarz's way. But the Pasdarans in front of the Foot Locker were tied up with the other two men of Able Team. And as he raced down the hall toward the food court, Schwarz noted that the rounds flying past him ceased.

The Able Team warrior saw the SWAT men on the second floor before they saw him. They had already begun firing at the Pasdarans guarding the hostages who had been duct-taped to the tables and chairs. There were four of them in all, and all were dressed in the same camouflage BDUs with the same insignias of the Iranian government. One had taken a bullet from one of the snipers above and dropped his AK-47 and staggered drunkenly before collapsing to the floor.

Schwarz took careful aim, superimposing the red dot inside his scope over another enemy's center mass. The Pasdaran had come to the mall prepared to die in an explosion. But now, he died far sooner than he'd expected as another lone 5.56 mm round exploded from Schwarz's rifle and cored through his heart.

The roar of Schwarz's M-16 drew the attention of the SWAT snipers circling the railing above him. Several rifle barrels turned toward him, some emitting Crimson Trace red laser dots from their front grips. The Able Team warrior saw the small red spots light up against the black of his chest. Both of his hands shot out to his sides, making sure the men aiming at him took note of the fact that he was clad in the blacksuit they'd all seen earlier.

The red dots disappeared.

Not so the firing, however.

Behind him, Schwarz could still hear the gunfire as the battle between the Foot Locker and mall offices went on. He looked briefly over his shoulder and saw that several more of the Pasdarans had fallen onto the tile of the hallway. Turning back to the situation at hand, the Able Team man caught sight of an Iranian with his arm wrapped around the throat of a young blond woman as he backed away from the tables and chairs. His other hand held one of the familiar AK-47s.

The cowardly Iranian had not seen the Able Team warrior's approach from the side hall, and had positioned the screaming and crying young woman as a human shield between him and the SWAT snipers above.

Which meant his entire right side was exposed to Schwarz.

With his weapon already on semiauto, Schwarz placed the red dot in the center of his scope just above the man's ear and gently squeezed the trigger.

The sound of the primer igniting the gun powder was lost somewhere beneath the roars of other weapons. But Schwarz felt the light recoil of his M-16, and saw a tiny hole appear in the side of the Iranian's temple. A split second later, residual blood sprayed out of the hole, hiding it again, and even more blood, brain tissue and tiny fragments of skull exited the man's head as the hollowpoint blossomed open before exiting the Pasdaran's head on the other side.

Blood covered the chest and hair of the blond girl as the man who had been dragging her went limp. She turned as he fell, then went as limp as her torturer had gone.

But Schwarz had no doubt that the scream that came out of her mouth could have been heard on the third floor of the Dillard's through which Able Team had entered the mall.

To his side, Schwarz caught a glimpse of camouflage running toward the corpse of the first terrorist the Able Team warrior had dropped at the food court. Schwarz swung the M-16 that way, dropping the bright red dot on the man's chest.

He took up the slack in the trigger and was perhaps

a half-pound away from feeling it snap, when something he couldn't identify suddenly told him not to shoot. Frowning, he let up on the trigger and looked up and over the scope.

The young man who was running toward the dead Pasdaran had blond hair in curly ringlets that reached all the way down to his shoulders. A plain blue T-shirt fell over the waistline of his camo cargo pants, and on his feet were glittering gold-and-red athletic shoes atop white socks.

The kid wasn't a Pasdaran. He was just a kid. And the camouflage pants were a fashion statement on his part rather than a practical item of military clothing.

Schwarz had already started running toward him as the teenager reached the body and bent to retrieve the dead man's AK-47. Schwarz could see the lines of adhesive still on his wrists where duct tape had bound him before he'd somehow managed to free himself.

The young man was going after the AK-47 to assist in eliminating the Pasdarans. But the pants he had chosen to wear this Sunday afternoon had almost gotten him killed.

And they still could.

The young man had taken several seconds to get the Russian rifle's sling untangled from around the dead man's chest, and that split second was all that Schwarz needed. Slamming into the boy like a red-dogging line-backer sacking a quarterback, Schwarz tackled and then threw him into a corner where he'd be out of sight from the mall.

The kid's face was ashen when he looked up and saw

Schwarz wearing the distinctive blacksuit. "Who are—?" he asked.

"I don't have time to explain it right now," Schwarz told him. He had grabbed the AK-47 away from the kid and held it in his left hand. "Just stay here until this is all over."

The boy looked at the Russian assault rifle that he had held so briefly. "Can't I keep that weapon, sir?" he said as some of the color returned to his face.

"You know how to use it?" the Able Team warrior asked.

"Yes, sir," said the kid. "My dad's a retired Marine gunny sergeant. It's an AK-47. Thirty-shot mag. Fires from a closed bolt and—"

"Enough," Schwarz interrupted. "You've convinced me." He handed the Kalashnikov back to the boy and said, "But you stay here until this is all over. Those pants are gonna get you killed. In fact, if I catch you outside of here again I'll shoot you myself. You got it?"

"I got it, sir," the kid said.

Schwarz stood and turned to rejoin the ongoing gun battle.

CARL LYONS COULD HEAR both screams and gunfire from the food court down the hall as the last of the Pasdarans outside the Foot Locker fell to his and Blancanales's fire. As the explosions died down around him, the gunfire from the distant food court grew louder and more distinct.

"Any idea where Gadgets went?" Blancanales shouted over the noise.

"Food court," Lyons said. "Toward the fight still going on."

Lyons looked at Blancanales. No further words needed to be spoken.

The two men from Stony Man Farm took off running, their rubber-soled combat boots squeaking against the tile floor of the hallway with each step. If the circumstances had been different, that might have been a dead giveaway that they were approaching the gunfight in the distance. But the rapid bursts of the firefight easily covered the annoying squeaks.

As Lyons and Blancanales emerged from the side hall Lyons saw Schwarz leaning out around the corner a few fast-food outlets down. Seated on the floor to his side, safely ensconced behind the short walls at the entrance, was a teenage boy wearing camouflage pants and a blue T-shirt and holding an AK-47.

There had to be quite a story behind that, Lyons thought as he dropped low and hustled on toward the hostages taped to the chairs and tables of the food court. But this was no time to find out. There'd be plenty of time for Schwarz to explain once this firefight was over.

Assuming all three of the men of Able Team survived it.

Looking up, Lyons saw a SWAT man aiming his AR-15 downward into the mass of hostages and Pasdarans. There appeared to be only two of the enemy still alive and shooting. But they were using the hostages as cover, and they had come here to die, which more than evened the odds in their favor.

The Pasdarans were vastly outnumbered. But they

had the welfare of the men, women and children all around them as an advantage. The SWAT shooters ringing the entire second-floor guard rail were being forced to slowly pick and choose their shots on semi-auto, careful not to hit any of the innocents.

As the Able Team leader swung the M-16 around to his back and drew the sound-suppressed Colt Woodsman from his belt, he watched as a SWAT man leaned low over the railing to fire almost straight down. This angle proved a perfect target to the top of his head and shoulders, and one of the Pasdarans took advantage of it, sputtering out a 3-round burst that struck the Kansas lawman just to the side of the head on the top of his left shoulder.

But Carl Lyons saw no blood as the SWAT man fell forward over the railing, performing an aerial somersault before crashing down onto one of the tables. That meant he wore a ballistic bullet-resistant vest.

But it didn't mean the fall couldn't have killed him.

As Lyons dropped to all fours, the SWAT man who had fallen remained motionless, flat on his back. The men and women taped to the chairs around the table looked at him with terror in their eyes. They had already been screaming.

Now all they could do was scream louder.

Using a three-point stance not unlike the one he had used as a high school football player years ago, the Able Team leader held the Woodsman in his right hand and entered the nearest row of tables. Dropping even lower onto the tile, he could see through the legs of the hostages, and spotted a pair of black boots connected to camo-covered calves. He paused a moment. Could this be another kid wearing the camouflage BDU pants like the one who had been with Schwarz? Or was it a Pasdaran?

His thought process lasted well under a second. If it had been another innocent who had just chosen to wear the wrong kind of pants on this particular day, he'd have been taped to a chair like the rest of the hostages. Not standing and moving around.

Taking careful aim between several of the hostages' legs between him and his target, Carl Lyons squeezed gently on the trigger. A poof came out of the end of the sound-suppressor along with a .22-caliber hollowpoint bullet, and the Able Team leader heard a shriek a couple of rows over.

The Pasdaran who had taken the shot to the middle of his calf fell to the tile, facing the Able Team leader. For a moment the two men's eyes locked and Carl Lyons could feel the hatred emanating from the other man's scowl.

Lyons face remained deadpan as he pulled the Woodsman's trigger once more. And it stayed non-committal as another hollowpoint erased the scowl from the face of the enemy.

For the Pasdaran, the bullet had meant the end of his part in the jihad.

For Carl Lyons, it was all in a day's work.

The occasional explosion from the second floor still echoed off the walls and ceiling of the two-story mall as Lyons resumed his three-point pursuit down the row. When he reached the end, he had still not seen any trace of the last remaining Pasdaran. But he had seen Blancanales enter the mass of tables and chairs a few rows over, and now, between the reports from the second-story rail, he heard the soft cough of a sound-suppressed pistol as he rounded the corner of the row of tables and moved to the next group of hostages.

"Got him, Ironman!" Blancanales called out from somewhere within the mass of screaming, moaning and praying people taped to their chairs.

It took a few seconds for the explosions to quit echoing off the walls. But when they did, the entire mall fell into a silence not unlike what could be found in a mausoleum.

And for the Pasdarans, that was exactly what the mall had become.

Lyons and Blancanales rose to their feet and began cutting the hostages free with their knives. But as his Randall Model 1 knife slashed through the tape binding a crying woman's wrists, Lyons looked down the hallway toward the Foot Locker and the mall's general offices, and saw a man dressed in Pasdaran camouflage rise to his feet.

There had not been time to check each man in the gunfight before Lyons and Blancanales left the scene to help Schwarz and the SWAT teams. And now it was evident that at least one of the men had been playing possum.

"We've got one still alive!" Lyons called as he slid his knife back into its Kydex sheath. Without further words, he took off after the man in the distance.

Now, the squeaking of his boots did present a problem, Lyons knew, as each footstep squealed down the hall. The Pasdaran was about to enter Dillard's through which Able Team had come when he twisted around and stared hard at the approaching Able Team warrior.

Lyons fired a wild shot on the run and missed his target. It served only to make him turn back and increase his pace. The Iranian had been cradling one arm with the other, and it became obvious now that his limp was to keep the injured upper limb from hurting—not from a leg wound of any kind.

And now survival took over from pain relief as he sprinted out of sight into Dillard's.

The Able Team leader followed, hurdling the dead bodies outside the Foot Locker as he came to them. But he scrutinized each one carefully as he leaped to make sure there were no more of the men faking death. Satisfied that they were all dead, he ran on into Dillard's, reasoning that the man who had disappeared would try to make it to one of the upper two floors.

The exits from the store to the outside were all being covered, and this man knew it. There was going to be no escape for him.

But escape was not what the brainwashed zealot was looking for, anyway.

Ahead, Lyons could see the escalator running upward. But the fleeing Iranian was not on it. Just beyond the moving steps, however, was an elevator for people with disabilities who couldn't take the escalator. The light was on, meaning someone had pushed the button to call the car down to the ground floor.

But the man Lyons sought was no fool. He had hidden somewhere in the clothing racks to wait for the doors to open.

As Lyons cut back and forth between a seemingly endless number of circular clothes racks, he saw the elevator doors open and the man with the wounded arm step inside and push a button. The Able Team leader fired off another snap-round, barely missing the man and causing him to duck as the doors began to close again.

Lyons arrived just in time to see a flicker of the Pasdaran's snarling face as the doors locked together in the center.

The Able Team leader looked up at the lights above the elevator. The "2" was bright with a yellow-gold light that illuminated the round button. He turned to the escalator and sprinted upward, letting the moving steps make him run faster than he could have on his own. But by the time he reached the second floor, the elevator stood open.

And empty.

Lyons had stuck the Woodsman back in his belt while running up the escalator and now he let the barrel of the M-16 lead the way. In a hurry to get to the hostages, he and his men had not checked this second floor of Dillard's as closely for bombs as they had the third.

So the injured man might be anywhere on the floor. About to detonate an explosion that would not only take out that floor but also create a ripple effect that could set off other hidden bombs and injure or even kill the people still below.

Not to mention Lyons himself.

The Able Team leader paused for a moment, his eyes

making a quick 360-degree scan of what stood in front of him. Much of the second floor was taken up by cases full of jewelry, watches and women's perfume. Against the wall, he could see rack after rack of ladies' shoes— everything from high stiletto-heel boots to puffy house shoes. Also spaced throughout the floor were female mannequins, displaying everything from skirts and blouses to lingerie.

What that all meant to Lyons was that bombs could be planted in any of a thousand different places.

The warrior frowned. So far, the explosive devices they had come across had all been located intelligently against weight-bearing pillars or walls. And Lyons saw no reason why the Pasdarans would have changed their strategy on the second floor of Dillard's.

So, glancing quickly around again, the Able Team leader spotted a huge square column almost in the center of the floor. Slowly, wondering now how much time he actually had before the injured Pasdaran blew up Dillard's, himself and Lyons, the Able Team leader began making his way toward the column.

Lyons used every bit of instinct and training he had as he walked slowly down the aisles of jewelry display cases toward the column. As he neared, he stopped altogether and turned an ear that way. Nodding to himself, he confirmed what he thought he had heard.

Heavy breathing. The kind that might come from an injured man who still had a task to perform and was trying to work through the pain.

The Able Team leader hunched over as he made his way directly toward the column. A moment later, he stepped out from behind the last display case and saw the injured Pasdaran holding two wires.

A yellow wire was in his left hand. A red one in his right. He was staring down at them, his eyes closed tightly as he prepared for his own death.

"Drop the wires and step back," Lyons ordered as he trained the barrel of his M-16 on the man.

The Pasdaran's eyes opened in surprise and he turned toward the sound of Lyons's voice. He spoke in broken English as he said, "No. We die together. I go Paradise. You go Hell." He started to bring his two hands together.

"I think you're a little mixed up on which tickets we both have," the Able Team leader said as he pulled the trigger. A triburst of 5.56 mm hollowpoints almost completely obliterated the man's head above the neck.

Silence once again fell over the room. Lyons walked back to the escalator and rode it down, not bothering to move his legs this time. Below, the SWAT teams would have descended and finished freeing the hostages. Detectives and other investigators would be taking statements.

And none of those duties required the specialized abilities of Able Team.

Lyons had just reached the ground floor and stepped off the escalator when the satellite phone in a pocket of his blacksuit began to vibrate. He pulled it out and flipped it open. "Lyons," he said into the instrument.

The voice on the other end of the line was Barbara Price's. "We just got word that you were successful at the mall," the Stony Man mission controller said. "Good job, Ironman."

"Thanks," Lyons said. "But I'm guessing that wasn't the only reason for your call."

"And you're guessing right," Price confirmed. "Hang on. Hal wants to talk to you."

Lyons waited while Price connected them. A moment later he heard Hal Brognola's voice say, "Ironman?"

"Present and accounted for," said Lyons.

"Nice job at the mall. But the locals can take care of the rest of it. I need you and your boys back here on the East Coast as soon as you can get here. Mott's on his way to pick you up."

Lyons felt his eyebrows furrowing. "What's up?" he asked.

"We don't have time to go into it now," said the Stony Man Farm Director of Sensitive Operations. "I'll brief you once you're on the plane."

"Affirmative," Lyons said. "I'll grab Gadgets and Pol and get to the Concorde ASAP."

"Thanks," Brognola said before disconnecting the call.

WILSON "PAT" PATRICK had learned a lot about himself during the past day and a half. First, he was human and that meant he could die. He'd already known that in his brain, of course. But now he felt it in his soul. He had already watched death come to two of his compatriots, and that underscored his own mortality.

Second, the Geneva Convention rules weren't worth the paper they'd been printed on. In Iran, the military and the rest of the government was quite simply above the law. It could do anything it damn well pleased, and justify it by saying it was all in the name of Allah.

And third, he didn't like watching his fellow newsmen die or get tortured.

Patrick looked across the dark room and saw Court
Hough, Roger Stehr and the man he knew only as Wilkens facing his way. But the men weren't looking at
him. They seemed to be looking at nothing, in fact.
Their eyes had a sheen covering them, as if their brains
had pulled some mental survival switch that took them
to a better place and time, and away from the horror
they'd experienced since becoming hostages to the Pasdarans. Regardless of what imaginary world their brains
might have taken them to, the dried blood and swelling
on their heads and faces reminded Patrick that they were
really here, right now, being held captive by one of the
most murderous terrorist groups on the planet.

And they might be killed at any moment with no
more emotion on the parts of the Pasdarans than could
be expected out of a man stepping on an insect.

The *Newsweek* reporter couldn't reach his head with
his hands cuffed behind his back. But he knew that his
face and head couldn't have looked any better than those
of his colleagues. He could feel the throbbing all over
his head, beneath his close-cropped hair. In fact, he
could probably just use those lumps as an outline for the
story he'd write if he survived all this. Along with the
painful swellings, he felt the encrusted blood covering
his scalp. It crinkled every time he raised his eyebrows.
The bump on the right side of his head, in particular, had
broken the skin, and the abrasion had dripped blood
down over the top of his ear.

Patrick sighed softly. That particular bump had come

from an old-fashioned wooden police nightstick that some of the guards carried. He'd received the blow because he'd asked for water. Just to the side was another lump that had been the result of him whispering something to the newsman—who had sat next to him in the back of the pickup that had transported them. And he had one whopper of a swelling atop the center of his head that had come when he'd managed to get one hand out of the handcuffs behind his back. He had done so more to stop the aching in his shoulders—the natural result of keeping his arms behind his back in such an unnatural position for so long. But his Iranian captors had looked at it as an escape attempt and beaten him soundly.

If it hadn't hurt so much, Patrick would have shaken his head in wonder. Escape? Right. Supposing he actually could get his hands free, and then untie his feet. Where was he to go then? The Iranians watching over them always had a man in this cold, musky room or at least a pair of eyes looking through the bars covering the small window in the ancient wooden door. Patrick had no idea what lay on the other side of the door other than the staircase they'd been brought down.

They could be in Tehran or Isfahan or Tabriz or any other Iranian city. Or they might be in some smaller village, or in the basement of a house in the Iranian countryside, or not even in Iran anymore. All he knew was that they had been taken down a flight of steps that smelled of a curious blend of mold and copper, and seated against the wall on a cold stone floor before their blindfolds were finally removed.

The bottom line was that even if he and the others miraculously got away from wherever it was they had been dumped this time, it would be only a matter of minutes before the elite Iranian soldiers found them again. None of them spoke Farsi, and the Iranian citizens who had seen them when they'd stopped for gas last night—Patrick had smelled the fuel being pumped—had done nothing but jeer at them.

There was going to be no escape on their own. Their only hope was a rescue team like Delta Force or SEAL Team 6. And Patrick wasn't at all certain that even those highly skilled professionals would be able to get them out alive. They were being moved around too much. On the other hand, unless he got caught, Patrick was leaving anyone trying to find them a fairly decent trail. His multipocketed photojournalist's vest had been so crammed with other items when he'd put it on the other morning, he'd jammed a couple dozen business cards in his back pocket. Had he carried them in the vest as he usually did, he'd never have been able to reach them with his hands cuffed behind his back. But as it was, he had been able to work one out of his back pocket and left it on the bed of the pickup.

There was various other debris like dried leaves, tangled twine and a stick or two in the pickup bed, too. The card didn't stand out as much as it might have had it been alone. Since the writing on the card was raised, he had been able to ascertain which side it was on and dropped the card facedown. When they'd been taken out of the pickup, the card seemed to go unnoticed.

Now, Patrick worked his left hand into the same back

pocket and felt his index and middle fingers clamp the sides of another business card atop the crumpled stack. He pulled it out, felt the raised writing again, then dropped it against the wall and slid slightly forward so it would settle on the floor beneath him.

He wondered again if this trail of cards he was leaving was all in vain. Maybe. But even if no one ever found them, and knew he and the other hostages had been there, it made him feel better to think that he was at least doing something to assist in their rescue.

The card trail was worth it—even if it was only for morale.

The *Newsweek* reporter closed his eyes, reminding himself that he wasn't alone in his injuries. The Pasdarans had taken out their anger on the other captives, too, using nightsticks and lead-filled saps. One of the men had even carried an African weapon called a *sjambok*. The *sjambok* was a semiflexible whip made from rhinoceros hide and could slice a man open almost as neatly as a knife. And it carried with it far more pain than any blade could ever hope to produce.

Opening his eyes once more, Patrick's gaze fell on the man named Wilkens. He had been beaten less than the others because he had been as compliant as possible. But even though his wounds were less apparent he was sniffling softly in the corner of the truck next to the cab.

Every man had his own threshold of pain—both physical and mental—Patrick knew as he watched the man cry. But Wilkens's limit seemed to be an ingrown toe or fingernail.

Every so often, the face of the man who had recuffed

Patrick after he'd slipped out of his restraints appeared in the window, and when it did, Patrick was reminded that his right hand had swollen and lost all sensitivity. That was because when this man had recuffed him, he had squeezed the ratchets as tightly as he could with both hands.

It felt as if someone had twisted a giant steel tourniquet around his wrist and, although he couldn't see it, Patrick was sure that he was well on his way to losing that hand due to a lack of blood flow.

It was this man whose snarling face was keeping watch on them now while Patrick contemplated his options. They had been taken out of the pickup after entering some kind of closed area. The smell of steel being tempered, and the constant, near deafening pound of metal being hit with hammers had made his ears ring. There had been many people around—he could both smell and sense their presence. So he had determined, finally, that they were in a city.

Which city? That was impossible to know. They had made far too many twists and turns in the pickup last night to keep track of their path.

Patrick waited until the man watching through the window glanced at the men across from him, then turned to Buford Davis and whispered, "Any idea where we are?" He kept his eyes on the thickly bearded Pasdaran in the window as he spoke.

"I think it's Isfahan," Davis whispered back so quietly that Patrick could barely make out the words. "My blindfold slipped a little when we were in the truck. I think I recognized a couple of places driving in."

Patrick frowned. "Isfahan's the biggest city next to Tehran, isn't it?" he said.

"Something like that I think. I—" Davis quit whispering in midsentence as the eyes of the man in the window suddenly shot to him.

The bearded face looked at Patrick and Davis for only a moment, then turned around. Through the iron bars, Patrick could see him place a hand on the shoulder of the man whom he remembered seeing driving the pickup before the blindfolds went on. They spoke briefly, then the ancient wooden door suddenly opened and four of the Pasdarans burst into the room carrying blindfolds.

"On your feet!" ordered the man who was responsible for Patrick's numb hand.

The hostages all struggled to their feet, and allowed themselves to be blindfolded without protest, which they knew would have been fruitless and accomplish nothing but the receipt of more bumps on their heads. Then unseen arms guided them through the door and up the steps again. A moment later, they were thrown back into the bed of the pickup.

Patrick heard the sound of a garage door rolling upward and a few rays of dim sunlight penetrated his blindfold. He had lost all sense of time in the sensory-deprived cell below. But now it seemed like early evening. Regardless, the same plastic cover was being tied down over all of their heads. He could feel it.

The truck moved slowly through honking traffic and then picked up speed as the lanes cleared out. But then, suddenly, they slowed, then pulled off the road onto the shoulder and stopped.

Patrick had been using his shoulder to try to move his blindfold to the side, and praying none of the Pasdarans could see him beneath the cover. Finally he had worked the rag far enough up that if he tilted his head slightly backward, he could see a sliver of light to his side. He saw that they had stopped in front of a butcher's stand on the outskirts of the city. Twisting a little farther, he could see the skinned carcasses of several goats hanging from hooks at the front of the stand.

A moment later the man who would be responsible for the loss of his right hand was out of the pickup's cab and pulling what Patrick could now see was a blue plastic tarp up at the tailgate. The man climbed into the back of the pickup on his knees.

In his hand was one of the flat, lead-filled saps.

"Well," Buford Davis whispered. "I don't like this development. Not one little bit."

The Pasdaran with the sap knee-walked to a position directly in front of Davis and rattled off a long string of Farsi, which Patrick couldn't understand. Then he brought the tanned leather bludgeon down on top of Davis's head.

Over and over the sap struck, breaking the skin and cracking bone and causing Buford Davis to cry out in pain. Then the *Newsweek* photographer suddenly went silent. But the sap kept falling as the man wielding it broke out in a sadistic grin.

Before he could stop the words from leaving his mouth, Patrick yelled out. "You dirty son of a bitch! Quit hitting him!"

The man with the sap couldn't understand his words. But he followed the order and quit bringing the sap down on Davis. The problem was, he began beating Patrick.

Wilson Patrick gritted his teeth as he took multiple blows to the skull, wondering with each strike if he would die, and wondering if, even if he didn't, he'd suffer a concussion and permanent brain damage. But finally the bearded man stopped.

Patrick opened his eyes and saw that the Pasdaran had shifted his attention to Wilkens, whose sobbing in the corner of the truck he found irritating. "You are woman," the bearded Pasdaran cried in anger as he slammed the sap against the crying man's nose. "Act like man!" A second blow struck Wilkens squarely on the bridge of the nose. As the Pasdaran withdrew his weapon, blood spurted from both nostrils, spraying toward the man's left.

Because a good half inch left of center was where Wilkens's broken and swollen nose was now situated on his face.

"Leave him alone!" Patrick yelled again without thinking. "He hasn't done anything!"

And for those words, he received two more strikes with the bloody leather cosh—one to the forehead, the other to the jaw.

The bearded man didn't even have to turn around from his kneeling position in front of Wilkens. He just twisted his neck so he could see, then backhanded both blows to the other side of the pickup.

Wilson Patrick felt the lead-filled leather strike him both times. And his last thought before passing out was that if he was going to sleep, he hoped he wouldn't wake up until this real-life nightmare was over.

CHAPTER TEN

The men in the Hummers and jeeps felt the wind blowing against them as they saw the outskirts of Isfahan in the distance. McCarter and the rest of Phoenix Force had commandeered the lead Hummer, and now the former British SAS officer held up a hand as they came to an oasis on the plateau. It was a slight detour, but it provided the only place to dump the Hummers and jeeps without just leaving them out in the middle of the plateau where they'd be spotted from the air.

Best of all, the oasis appeared to be deserted. McCarter had noted increased air traffic as they drove toward Isfahan. All of the planes had been American-built F-14s. He was sure of only one thing.

Something was up, something way beyond sending out fighter jets on routine flights to spot Kurds or the Iranian Christians.

McCarter could feel it in his bones. He had no idea exactly what was going on. But he had seen several dozen of the F-14s now, coming from the direction of

Tehran. They all had passed over his head, them come back later on their way home.

As the jeeps and Hummers ground to a halt around the oasis pond, McCarter addressed his fellow Phoenix Force warriors. "Drink every drop you can hold and fill your canteens to the brim," he said. "We've got a long, hot, dry hump ahead of us."

McCarter followed the rest of his men, the Kurds and Tex's Christian Iranians with Tex by his side. "Even without the women and children, we've still got way too many people here," he told the American missionary. "A group this big made up entirely of men? Even without the Hummers and jeeps, and our weapons hidden, and dressed like Kurds..." He paused to shake his head. "We're still going to attract a whole lot of unwanted attention."

"Well," Tex said, "let's thin out the ranks a bit, shall we?" He paused, still looking toward the water. "You remember the Old Testament story of how King David picked out the warriors he wanted with him in a similar situation?" he asked the Phoenix Force leader.

McCarter stopped dead in his tracks. "Yes," he said. "I do." He and Tex stood there watching as several of the Kurdish and Iranian men dropped their rifles on the ground and practically dived headfirst into the water. They paid absolutely no attention to the others in the group, or watched out for the possibility of enemies approaching the oasis while they drank.

Other men, some Iranians, others Kurds, walked slightly out into the water, then turned back toward the vehicles. Lifting water to their mouths with cupped hands, they kept their eyes on the horizon as they drank.

By now, Abbas had joined them and picked up on the gist of the conversation.

"Let's weed them out," McCarter said, and he and Tex went around the oasis, telling the men who had remained vigilant while they drank that they would be going into Isfahan while those who had paid no attention to possible danger were ordered to take the Hummers and jeeps back to protect the women and children.

McCarter saw no reason to explain to the men why some were being sent back or how they'd been separated.

When their canteens were full, McCarter assembled the men who'd be accompanying Phoenix Force into the city. Abbas translated his words as he said, "You were chosen because you never let your guard down while you were drinking," he said. "I want you to keep up that kind of alertness. And keep all weapons hidden until I say differently. Everyone understand?"

The men waited until Tex had translated, then they all looked at McCarter and nodded their heads.

McCarter had taken on the chore of watching Hamid for any tricks himself, and now he looked at the young Iranian soldier. Sweat was dripping down the kid's face. He had changed into the colonel's uniform, but the Phoenix Force leader had forced him to wear a Kurdish robe and turban on top of that. Being a member of the military—especially a high-ranking one—might come in handy somewhere along the line. But right now, it would look incredibly odd for an Iranian Army colonel to come walking into town with a bunch of nomads.

As the Hummers and jeeps disappeared back in the direction from which they'd come, McCarter led the re-

maining warriors away from the oasis and onto the
plateau. They had several miles to cover on foot, and the
way things were going they'd get into Isfahan shortly
after sundown. But nighttime was preferable to a daylight entry anyway. There would be more of a variety
of people who came out at night, and new faces would
be the norm rather than an oddity.

More F-14s flew overhead, turned around somewhere south of them, then returned to whatever base
they had come from. McCarter found himself frowning
again. What were they doing? They were leading up to
something. What? Surely it wasn't just to check on his
band of ragtag warriors walking toward the city. Of
course, he reminded himself once again, that didn't
mean that a byproduct of at least one of the flights
would be to bring back intelligence information about
the strange group of men on the plateau.

Patting the M-16 hidden beneath his robe, McCarter
continued to lead the way. Finally, after what seemed
like days rather than hours, the sun dropped and along
with it, the temperature. Now McCarter and the men of
Phoenix Force were grateful for the robes covering their
blacksuits, and pulled them tighter around the neck-
lines. The sweat that had formed beneath the robes was
absorbed into the heavy cloth, and kept them from
freezing.

When the lights of Isfahan appeared on the horizon,
McCarter picked up the pace. He wanted to get into the
city quickly now, and force Hamid to guide them to the
metalworker's shop. The young Iranian with the
colonel's uniform beneath his Kurdish robe was directly

behind him, being watched carefully by the rest of Phoenix Force. All McCarter had to do was drop back a step to keep pace with him as they walked.

"I want you right next to me, every step of the way that's left," he said. "Especially once we're in town. So if you've formed any plans in your head about escaping once we're inside the crowds, forget them. They'll only serve to get you killed."

The young man nodded vigorously. "I will do as you say," he said in a soft voice.

McCarter estimated they were still roughly a mile from the city when they heard the sound of hooves hitting the ground. And a moment later, the sandy plateau actually began to shake with the vibrations.

The Phoenix Force leader turned to Abbas, who had come forward when they'd first heard the noise. "Who do you suppose that is?" McCarter asked him.

"Brigands," Abbas said. "They work these areas around the major cities. They are far enough away to be out of sight from the town. But close enough to find merchants on their way into the city with their wares."

McCarter nodded. It was the same with criminals the world over. The New York mugger used the same strategy when he practiced his trade in places like Central Park, where he'd be hidden from immediate discovery but still not so remote that he couldn't find victims.

McCarter turned to the other four men of Phoenix Force. "You guys hear all that?" he asked.

The four heads nodded as they opened their robes to free their M-16s.

Looking farther back, McCarter saw that both the

Iranian Christians and the Kurds were doing the same thing—bringing out their primary weapons and readying themselves for battle.

McCarter opened his own robe and swung his M-16 out on its sling. He checked to make sure the 30-round magazine was locked firmly in place and that none of the extra ammo mags had fallen out of their carriers built into the blacksuit. Finally he flipped the selector switch to full-auto and braced the synthetic stock against his right shoulder.

As the Phoenix Force leader raised the barrel of his assault rifle, he looked out through the darkness to see what looked like the shadows of at least forty men atop camels and horses. They were racing toward McCarter and his small army at top speed, their robes and the tails of their turbans and kaffiyehs trailing behind them in the wind.

Bullets began to fly both ways.

LYONS, SCHWARZ AND BLANCANALES all dropped their rifles and other gear on the carpeted floor of the remodeled Concorde and took seats in the stuffed reclining chairs. They had been flown back to the larger Kansas City, Missouri, airport by Grimaldi, who had just returned from Bosnia, dropping off Mack Bolan at the Farm.

As the Concorde lifted off into the air, Lyons pressed a button on the arm of his chair and opened the direct line to Stony Man Farm. As soon as Hal Brognola was on the line, he said, "It's me, Hal. We just took off your way."

"Well, you're headed in the right direction," the

Stony Man Farm director said. "But you aren't coming home quite yet."

"Oh?" Lyons said. "A side trip, huh? Need us to bring home a loaf of bread and a gallon of milk, do you?"

Brognola chuckled on the other end of the line. "If only life was that simple," he said.

"It is for most people," Lyons replied.

"In case you hadn't noticed," Brognola said, "we're hardly *most* people."

"I've noticed," Lyons said, his tone turning serious. "Okay. What do you really have next for us?"

"It's a strange situation," Brognola stated. "But you're heading for the Big Apple. A kidnapping case."

"What?" Lyons said, looking from Schwarz to Blancanales and then back at the speaker in the arm of his chair. "I'm not a detective anymore, Hal," he said. "What do you want with us on a routine kidnapping case?"

"It's anything but routine," Brognola said. "The abducted man is a famous Swedish orchestra conductor who just arrived in the U.S. to conduct a concert with the New York Philharmonic. He was snatched from in front of a liquor store near the Bowery. Hans Gustafson. Any of you heard of him?"

Lyons looked up to see if there were any signs of recognition on either Schwarz's or Blancanales's face. He saw none.

"Sorry," Schwarz said, leaning forward in his chair slightly. "But I'm a little bit country."

"And I'm a little bit rock 'n' roll," Blancanales chimed in.

"I'm not real big on that kind of music, either, Hal,"

Lyons said. "But I still don't see what makes it a case for Able Team."

"It was very different than most kidnappings," Brognola said. "It happened in broad daylight, in public. Two carloads of men, all wearing Iranian Pasdaran uniforms, grabbed Gustafson. They all carried AK-47s, and shouted out for all the people frozen in shock on the sidewalks that Allah was going to send them straight to Hell."

"Okay, Hal," Lyons conceded. "You've convinced me. That definitely brings them into our little circle."

"Yes, it does," Brognola said. "What they're doing here is thumbing their noses at the U.S. and at the same time telling the rest of the world that America is still the Wild West and nobody, anywhere, is safe."

"You have any leads yet?" Lyons asked.

"Yeah," Brognola said. "Most of the people on the sidewalks made themselves scarce when the Pasdarans started firing randomly. Miraculously, no one was hit. But there's one man who was there through it all. Exactly how reliable he is, I don't know."

Lyons had known Brognola long enough to sense there was much more to this story. "Well," he said. "Who is he, and why are you worried about his reliability?" he asked.

"Ex-NYPD cop," Brognola said. "Now a Bowery alcoholic."

"Oh, that's great," said Lyons. As a former LAPD detective, he'd seen many a cop take to the bottle as an escape from the horrifying things they'd witnessed. And like most men addicted to alcohol, they often began to lose the distinction between reality and their own tortured imaginations.

That was what Brognola had meant when he'd questioned the man's reliability.

"Have you told Jack yet?" Lyons asked.

"I'm on with you." Grimaldi's voice came from both the front of the Concorde and over the line. "I've already changed course for New York City."

"Then we're on our way," said Lyons.

"NYPD has already been alerted to the fact that some 'top federal agents' will be in charge of the case." Brognola paused for a moment, then went on. "They don't like it, but they'll go along with it. I'd suggest changing out of your blacksuits into some civvies before you meet with them, though."

"Will do," Lyons said. He noted that Schwarz and Blancanales had already risen from their chairs and were opening two of the lockers bolted to the walls of the Concorde. "Of course you realize we'll never pass for FBI," the Able Team leader went on. "None of us can afford those thousand-dollar suits your overpaid FBI agents wear."

Brognola laughed. "They aren't my FBI," he said. "I'm just a poor Department of Justice man like you guys."

Lyons snorted into the line. "That's affirmative," he said. "Anything else?"

"Not at the moment. I'll ring you back and we'll talk more right before you land."

"That's a 10-4," Lyons said. "AT-1 clear."

"SMF clear," Brognola came back, and both men tapped the buttons to end the call.

"This is going to feel a little strange, Ironman," Schwarz said when Lyons had reached the locker next to the one he had opened.

"What is?" the Able Team leader asked.

"Wearing real clothes." The Able Team electronics expert pinched the arm of his blacksuit and stretched it out, letting it snap back into place. "You kind of get used to these things."

Lyons was already twisting the dial on his lock. "Well, Gadgets," he said, "when this is over, you can put your blacksuit back on and wear it all over that dingy little apartment of yours if you want."

Schwarz laughed out loud. "Like that's ever going to happen," he said. "As soon as all this is over we'll be on our way to some other crisis somewhere on the planet."

Carl Lyons started to speak, then realized there was nothing to be said.

Schwarz was right. The life of a Stony Man Farm operative never slowed down.

But he'd have had it no other way.

THE BRIGAND IN THE LEAD wore a black robe and headdress, with a black mask covering his face from the nose down. His horse was a pure black stallion, and the animal seemed to be as evil as its rider as it approached the men on foot.

The only thing not black about the man was the medium brown tone of the skin around his eyes and the shining steel scimitar raised above his head.

He began to strike down with the wickedly curved sword when he was still several feet from David

McCarter, who simply raised his M-16 and fired a 3-round burst into the black face mask.

The man in the black robes turned a backflip as he fell backward off the black horse.

Bullets of all calibers, from all manner of weapons, had already begun zipping back and forth. But the attacking brigands, who thought they'd spotted nothing more than a group of merchants trying to sneak their wares into the city by night, were suddenly the ones who were surprised. Without having to be told, all of the men from Phoenix Force grouped into formation, back to back.

The Christian Iranians and Kurdish warriors followed their lead.

The initial assault took many of the brigands all the way through the groups, knocking several of the men to the ground. Among them, McCarter noticed, was T. J. Hawkins. Hawk was known for fighting "cold." But as he bounded back to his feet, McCarter would have sworn he saw fire in the young Phoenix Force warrior's eyes.

Hawkins, McCarter and the rest of the men from Stony Man Farm opened up with full-auto fire on the brigands.

Two of Abbas's Kurds were hit almost simultaneously, and dropped to the ground. As McCarter pulled back the trigger of his M-16, he saw that one of them was obviously dead—the entire right side of his face gone. The other had been hit in the knee, and now struggled to get back to his feet, using his old British Enfield rifle as a crutch.

The brigand who had shot him in the knee also wore

black—but not exclusively. As he tried to swing the camel he was riding back around for another shot at the wounded Kurd, McCarter saw that he wore faded blue jeans beneath his robes. Swinging his assault rifle toward the man, the Phoenix Force leader cut loose with a short stream of rounds. The 5.56 mm fusillade stitched the man on the camel from the ribs to the armpit and up into his neck.

The fall from the camel's back was farther than from a horse. And the man in the blue jeans lay still on the ground after he'd made it.

His camel looked around, appearing to be lost and stepping all over his master's lifeless body.

McCarter turned his weapon on a brigand riding a spotted horse and cut loose once again, sending a steady stream of rifle rounds into the man's chest. The brigand's eyes seemed to glow in the moonlight as he froze in place and stared back at the Phoenix Force leader. Then they closed and he, too, fell from his ride.

To his side, McCarter could see Calvin James had just used his Crossada to ward off a scimitar attack from a man on a small gray pony. Trapping the long curved blade in the guard and Spanish notch, he twisted the weapon out of the man's grip and sent it dropping harmlessly onto the ground.

A moment later James had buried his knife deep into his attacker's chest. James pumped the weapon up and down as he withdrew it, and blood shot forth from the brigand's chest as if fired from a water cannon.

Gary Manning had stepped slightly away from the group to avoid an oncoming camel. He waited until the animal and its rider had passed, then lifted his M-16 and fired a 3-round burst into the back of the man's neck. The brigand man fell from the side of his camel saddle to join the other dead attackers on the ground.

Rafael Encizo was on McCarter's other side. As the former British SAS officer opened fire again on a mounted brigand, he saw Encizo use his M-16 to block a rifle barrel pointed at him from yet another man on horseback. The man's AK-47 was moved to the side a split second before he could pull the trigger, and several rounds exploded harmlessly into the sandy earth. Then, aiming upward, Encizo sent a 3-round burst into his attacker.

Yet another brigand fell.

By now, the brigands had realized they'd bitten off more than they could chew. The black-clad man who appeared to have taken over command from the first brigand who'd fallen to McCarter's M-16 screamed out orders. A second later the remaining camels and horses had turned to begin an undisciplined retreat. The men of Phoenix Force and the Christian soldiers and Kurds all sent rounds streaming after them.

Several more of the brigands fell to this final assault.

When they had gone, McCarter glanced around. He had lost track of Hamid during the gunfight, but now he saw the cowardly little man rising from atop two dead bodies where he'd been pretending to be dead. In actuality, McCarter's combined forces appeared to have suffered only two casualties—both Kurds. The Phoenix Force leader ordered all of the men to gather around him. As he spoke, Tex translated into Farsi and Abbas turned his words into Kurdish. "Abbas," McCarter said, "send one man back to get a burial party going for your men."

Abbas nodded, spoke a few words to one of his men and the man jumped up and started away from the group. McCarter called him back and Abbas translated again. "Tell him he might as well take one of the horses or camels," he said, and Abbas translated once more.

A moment later the man had gotten the camel to kneel to climb aboard. And a second after that, he was riding away in the night.

Several other camels and horses were standing around, obviously lost without their riders. "Change of plans," McCarter said. "We ride in style from here on in." Taking a few steps to his side, he grabbed the reins of the black horse the original leader had ridden, then motioned for the other men to pick out camels or horses. When they had done so, a good half dozen of the men were still without mounts.

"We'll go on ahead," McCarter said, and waited for the translation process. "You men on foot, follow at your own pace. We'll meet you in the bazaar area down-town. At this metalworker's shop."

The heads of the men still on foot bobbed in under-standing after Abbas and Tex had translated.

David McCarter swung up into the saddle of the stallion. "Let's move out," he ordered.

THE PRECINCT to which the lone witness to the kidnap-ping had been taken was little different from most NYPD stations. The walls were all painted a stomach-bile green, and the wood-and-steel table in the interro-

gation room looked as if it had been there since The-
odore Roosevelt had been New York City's police com-
missioner.

Jim Ritholz and Shelly Cirillo were handling the case
and the two detectives were waiting for the three Able
Team warriors when they walked through the front door.

Lyons had traded his blacksuit for a navy-blue blazer
and khaki slacks, and Schwarz looked almost the same
except for the fact that his sport coat was black.

Rosario Blancanales was dressed in a banker-gray
suit. Lyons flashed the Justice Department credentials
that Hal Brognola provided for all of the operatives
from Stony Man Farm, and the men shook hands all
around.

"I won't lie to you and tell you I like you guys coming in and taking over," Cirillo said. "But this is one case
in which I understand it. The kidnappers weren't your
average criminals. From all reports, they were Iranian
Pasdaran special forces soldiers, and they made sure
everyone knew it."

Lyons nodded in agreement. "I understand your
feelings completely. Before this, I was LAPD. And I
couldn't stand the Feds, period."

All five of the men laughed. A little uncomfortably
at this stage, perhaps. But laughter all the same.

"And now I am one," Lyons said. "Life loves to play
little tricks on you, doesn't it?"

Ritholz smiled in agreement. With the ice now officially broken, he said, "By now you probably know
we've only got one witness. Used to be a cop. I even
worked with him for a while years ago at the old 2-1."

Lyons rested an elbow on the counter between him and the desk sergeant on duty. New York's Twenty-first Precinct was famous among police officers all over the country for being one of the most violent, and dangerous, areas in the world. "What happened to him?" Lyons asked. "I understand he resigned and that he's trying to drink himself to death."

"Well," said Ritholz. "You heard right."

"Then I guess the next appropriate question would be why?"

"You want the short version or the long?" Ritholz asked.

"None of us has time for the long version," Lyons said.

"It happened on a simple drug raid," Cirillo said, taking over from his partner. "He was one of the first through the door, and his job was to run through the living room and secure one of the back bedrooms. It was night, and the bedroom was dark, and he saw a shadow lifting a pistol in the light coming in from the doorway."

Lyons felt his gut tighten. He could pretty much guess what was coming.

"So he fired," Ritholz continued. "Two rounds, right in the X-ring." He pointed to his chest. "Then he turned on the light and saw that he'd just killed a five-year-old kid with a toy gun."

Carl Lyons shook his head. "He couldn't have done anything else," he said.

"No," Cirillo broke in. "I imagine any of us standing here now would have done the same. But we've been lucky. He wasn't."

"So what happened from there?" Blancanales wanted to know.

"It was a good shoot," Ritholz said. "He was cleared of any criminal charges, and there was never any civil action brought against him. But he was off duty with pay for a couple of months while the wheels of bureaucracy slowly ground to that conclusion, and he started drinking his way through each day. He never came back. His wife finally had enough of it and she divorced him and moved back to Indiana or someplace like that. Where she was from."

"What I'd like to know is what this big-time conductor was even doing in the Bowery in the first place," the Able Team leader asked.

Cirillo paused for a moment, then said, "You were an L.A. cop, didn't you say?"

"Right," said Lyons.

"How well do you know New York?"

"Not as well as Los Angeles," Lyons said. "But well enough to know that the two cities are very different. In L.A., you've got good neighborhoods and bad. Here in New York, it goes from block to block. You can cross the street from an exclusive restaurant or store and suddenly find yourself surrounded by nothing but pimps, whores and drug dealers. Walk on another block, and you're back among the wealthy and tame."

"Exactly," Cirillo said. "The liquor store wasn't actually in the Bowery. Just next to it. Randy—that's Randall Hathaway, the ex-cop-witness we've been talking about—had panhandled enough coin for a bottle of rotgut wine. He had stopped for his first swig in the alley next to the store when all hell broke loose."

"Where is he now?" Lyons asked.

"In one of the interrogation rooms," Ritholz said.

"Let's go talk to him."

Without another word, Cirillo and Ritholz turned and led the way past the desk sergeant's counter to a swinging, waist-high door. The men of Able Team, dressed as federal investigators rather than the warriors they actually were, followed the two detectives down the hall.

The smell of alcohol, vomit and urine filled the nostrils of each of the men, growing stronger as they neared the door behind which Randall Hathaway sat waiting. But both units—the two NYPD detectives and the three Able Team men—were used to working in the trenches. They barely noticed the smell.

Cirillo opened the door and ushered them all inside.

What Lyons and the other two men of Able Team saw was a man who was broken. And had been for a long time.

Randall Hathaway wore a decent blue suit. At least it had begun life as decent. Now it looked as if he'd worn it every day and slept in it every night for the past ten years. The body odor emanating from him was mixed with the alcohol escaping through the pores of his skin, and filled the room like some tangible object you could actually grab and hold.

"Hey, Jim," he said in a hoarse voice. "Shelly." He gave off a truly pitiful smile.

"These guys are Feds, Randy," Ritholz said. "But they're good guys. I want you to talk to them, okay?"

"Okay," Hathaway said.

Ritholz whispered a few words to Cirillo and then

turned to Lyons. "We're gonna get out of your way," he said. "Too many cooks spoil the broth and all that."

"Thanks," Lyons said.

The two men closed the door behind them as the Able Team warriors took seats around the table. It was then that Lyons finally noticed how badly Hathaway was shaking, and that he was scratching both arms not unlike a heroin addict needing a fix. "How long since you've had a drink?" Lyons asked in a polite manner.

"Too long," Hathaway said. "The uniforms who responded first at the scene took my bottle from me."

Lyons looked closely at the man. He was dying. But that had been his choice, and nothing Lyons could do now would save him. The problem was, he had reached the stage of alcoholism where he was more rational when he was high than when he wasn't. And in the condition he was in, he'd be no good at all.

"Randy," Lyons said. "We know all about your problems and how you got here, in this state. And none of us is judging you."

For a moment Randy Hathaway brightened. "I was a good cop," he said. "Except for that—"

"We know about it and there's no sense in going over it again," Lyons said. He glanced toward Schwarz and Blancanales. "Any of us would have done the same thing."

For a moment the interrogation room went silent. Then, with tears in his eyes, Randy Hathaway said, "Thanks, guys." He went back to shaking and scratching the skin off his arms.

"Randy," Lyons said, "if you could have anything you wanted to drink right now, what would it be?"

The man going through alcohol withdrawal furrowed his eyebrows. Then he said, "Do I have to pay for it or is it free?"

"It's going to be free," Lyons said. He smiled at the man whose attention had suddenly returned from some other place and time to the here and now. "Just tell me what you want and it'll come to you."

"Any single-malt Scotch," Hathaway said.

"No problem," Lyons said.

"And a six-pack of beer to chase it with." The former cop smiled.

Lyons turned to Schwarz. "Gadgets," he said, "I think I saw a liquor store just down the street."

Schwarz was already out of his chair and heading for the door. "I saw it, too," he said.

"Hurry," Lyons said.

"I will."

Ten minutes later the Able Team explosives expert had returned with the whiskey and beer. He pulled them both out of a paper bag and set them in front of Hathaway.

The former cop smiled like a kid on Christmas morning as he twisted the cap off the Scotch and downed at least four shots before switching to a beer.

Suddenly the shakes were all gone and his arms no longer itched. When Hathaway started to lift the Scotch bottle again Lyons reached out and caught his hand. "Wait just a little bit, Randy," he said. "We need to ask you a few questions before you get totally out of it."

The broken-down police officer looked up with fear in his eyes. "I get the rest of it, though, right?" He rubbed his nose nervously. "After the questions, right?"

The man was so pitiful that Lyons was almost embarrassed. "You get the rest of it," he reassured the man. "Just as soon as we're done. And you can keep drinking the beer while we talk if you want." Lyons watched Hathaway's face relax and once again felt embarrassed for the man. But there was a fine line he had to walk. And if he was going to get any useful information, he'd have to make sure the Bowery drunk walked that same fine line between the shakes of too little alcohol and the abyss of too much.

By now, the single-malt Scotch was working its way through Hathaway's system and he was smiling. "Hey, you guys have been great to me," he said. "Don't you want a drink? I'd say I hate to drink alone. But I don't." He seemed to think this was a particularly clever thing to say and burst out laughing.

"Okay, guys," Hathaway said, taking a gulp of beer. "Remind me why we're here, will you? Did I do something I shouldn't have? You know I used to be a cop myself until—"

Lyons reached out slowly and took the beer bottle out of the drunk's hand. "Let's take the beer away for a few minutes, too," he said.

Hathaway clutched at the bottle as if it were a million-dollar bill in a hurricane. "I will get it back, right?" he asked suspiciously.

"You'll get it back," Lyons assured him. "But first, tell me what you saw earlier today outside the liquor store."

"Man, it was *crazy*." Hathaway's tongue was growing thicker and his words came out slightly slurred.

"I'm just standing there at the mouth of the alley, un-screwing the cap on my wine bottle, and suddenly there are these soldiers all over the place. They were shooting off AK-47s and I don't think they were American. Too dark-skinned and speaking some other language. Span-ish maybe. Hey, they might have been Cubans! Has Castro invaded us?"

Lyons was doing his best to remain patient. But his limits were being taxed. "No, Randy," he said. "They weren't Cubans and it wasn't Spanish they were speak-ing. They were Iranian special forces soldiers, and their language was Farsi."

Hathaway's attention had returned to the Scotch and beer, which now rested on the table in front of Blan-canales. He looked at it, then at Lyons.

Lyons nodded his head and waved his hand in disgust. "Go ahead," he said. "But just a short one. I don't want to see another sword-swallowing act like you did earlier."

"Okay," Hathaway said. Blancanales handed him the Scotch bottle and he took one swallow, then handed it back with the pride of a child who'd just won some sporting event. "I think I'm okay now," he said.

"Then go on with your story," Lyons prodded the man. "About the Iranian soldiers and what they did."

"I don't think they robbed the liquor store, although I can't be sure," Hathaway said. "It looked like their main mission was to just create havoc and kidnap that old man."

"You saw that?" Lyons asked.

"Oh, yeah," Hathaway said. He scooted his chair

back from the table and swept his jacket to the side, his right hand coming to rest on his belt. "I went for my gun...but, of course, I don't carry one anymore." With these final words, his voice took on a sad, lonely tone.

"Is there anything else you can tell us?" Lyons asked. He was beginning to think they were on a wild-goose chase. The kidnappers had not even made contact with the police yet.

"Well, there was the one Cuban...er, Iranian...who came around to the alley to talk to me," he said.

"What?" Lyons asked, frowning. "We hadn't heard that part. Tell us."

"Well, he didn't look much different than the others," Hathaway said. "But he spoke English."

"So what did he say?" Lyons asked, leaning closer to the man now.

"Something about tonight at eight p.m.," Randy Hathaway said. "I can't remember what."

"Was it something *they* were going to do at eight o'clock?" Lyons asked. "Or something they wanted you to do?"

"I don't remember," Hathaway said. "I'd started looking in all my pockets for my gun but I couldn't find it...." He started looking through those same pockets now. His voice trailed off as did his mind, leaving the pain of the present and returning to the days when he'd been a well-respected NYPD officer. When he stuck his hand into the back pocket of his filthy slacks, he came out with a scrap of white cardboard. "Oh yeah. Hey, I forgot all about this," he said. "The guy gave it to me."

Lyons looked at Schwarz and Blancanales. They were both losing patience with the alcoholic, too.

"And you didn't think that was important enough to give to the detectives earlier?" Lyons demanded.

"Well...I just forgot about it. I couldn't find my gun. No matter where I looked...." His attention wandered once again.

Lyons snatched the scrap of cardboard out of the man's hand and looked down at it. He saw the date, the words *eight o'clock p.m.* and then a phone number. "Did the man, the soldier, tell you to call this number tonight at eight o'clock?" the Able Team leader asked, hoping to jog a little more of Hathaway's alcohol-infested memory.

"No," Hathaway said. "I don't think he knew I'm a cop. I couldn't find my gun, you see, and he told me to give this to the police." As if a lightning bolt had suddenly hit him, Randy Hathaway suddenly blurted, "Yeah! That *is* what he said. 'Have the police call at eight o'clock p.m. or the conductor dies.'"

Lyons didn't know whether to shake the man's hand or slap him. "Did he say anything else?" he asked the semidrunken man.

"'If you don't make contact, the godless Swede dies,'" Hathaway quoted as if he was reading it out of a book. "Yeah, he said that, too. I was busy looking for my gun and badge. Have any of you seen my—?"

Lyons looked at his wrist. It was almost seven o'clock.

"PRF dash 58 something," Hathaway suddenly blurted as if the numbers and letters had just fallen from the clear blue sky. "Yeah. PRF-58…I can't remember the last number."

"The last number to what?" Lyons said.

"The license tag of the Mercedes," Hathaway said. "The Mercedes that took away the man from the liquor store."

It took every ounce of control for Lyons to keep from slapping the man. He had once been a cop. He should have given them that information first rather than last.

The Able Team leader reached across the table and lifted the Scotch bottle. Setting it down in front of Hathaway, he said, "Have yourself a ball, Randy."

A moment later he had Kurtzman on the satellite connection at Stony Man Farm. "Got a partial tag number for you to run down for me, Bear," he said. "And we don't have much time."

"Give it to me," Kurtzman said.

Lyons complied.

"What state was it from?" asked the man in the wheelchair at the other end of the call.

Carl Lyons turned to the drunk. "Randy, what state tag did the tag come from?"

Hathaway looked surprised for a moment. "What tag?" he asked innocently.

CHAPTER ELEVEN

Isfahan had always been something of an enchanted city with its dramatic mixture of ancient and new architecture. The general atmosphere of this ancient Persian city, at least to the casual observer, was one of peace. And occasionally, a lucky tourist caught a glimpse of the gardens, flower beds and well-kept pools of water hidden behind the walls surrounding the many small palaces.

But behind similar walls, invisible from the streets and sidewalks, were the *madrasahs,* or religious schools. And it was from these sites that the Iranian Islamic radicals indoctrinated their students into becoming self-destructive conduits for explosives and other suicide missions. But, as always when such brainwashing occurred, there were some who resisted the twisted propaganda. And out of these same *madrasahs* had come a still secret and subtle movement for democracy.

In other words, the students growing up in modern Isfahan had come to realize that with the overthrow of

the Shah and the appointment of the Ayatollah Khomeini, they had achieved nothing more than replacing
one authoritative dictatorship with one that was even
more repressive.

Many wanted the government restructured into a
secular system.

And a few members of the resistance movement were
also ready to die to achieve their goal.

David McCarter's ragtag army entered the brightly
lit city of Isfahan, spreading out and mixing in with
other Iranians either heading home for the night or
entering the city for a night on the town. McCarter has
always been gifted when it came to sensing the moods
of those around him, and he noticed no change in
demeanor among the strangers with whom they mixed.
They continued walking as the natives around them
kept speaking and arguing in Farsi, or remaining silent
as they went.

Abbas sidled up next to the Phoenix Force leader as
they passed a huge, rectangular park. "That's called the
maidan," Abbas said. "And it belongs to *me.*"

McCarter glanced down at the shorter man and saw
him grinning. The Kurd went on. "Okay," he drawled.
"Maybe it doesn't exactly belong to me. But it belonged
to another Abbas. In the past. The Abbas I was named
after."

"Do tell," McCarter said as he shook his head to the
many men and women who were now approaching
them, trying to sell anything they could lay their hands
on, as they neared the bazaar area.

Waving a hand to indicate the park, the Kurd said,

"It was Shah Abbas. Ruled from 1587 to 1629. It's 550 yards long, and used to be a polo field." He smiled proudly. "Right over there," he said, pointing in the direction of a pair of marble posts. "Those are the original goal posts."

"Very nice," McCarter said. "Your country—"

"It is not *my* country," Abbas cut in. "We Kurds don't pay attention to fences or signs." The sentiment belonged to the Kurd. But that means of expression had to have come directly from Tex.

"Of course, mate," McCarter said. "Allow me to rephrase my wording. Somewhere during the past, undoubtedly while a band of very wise Kurds were passing this way, one of them had the good sense and landscaping talents to remodel the old polo field into a garden."

Abbas, who was walking on his right side while Hamid was to his left, threw back his head and laughed. "You know what my good friend Tex would say to that?" he asked.

"No. What would he say?"

"He'd say it's getting so deep around here I should have worn taller boots." Abbas laughed.

"And he'd be absolutely, one hundred percent correct," McCarter added. "But if his tall boots have as many holes in them as the ones he has on now, at least some of it would seep through anyway."

By the time Abbas had quit laughing they had entered the bazaar. McCarter stepped into a doorway, out of the way of the pedestrian traffic, and Abbas followed. There was just enough room left for Tex to shove Hamid in with them, then step up on the single step that led to the doorway.

The rest of the Stony Man Farm warriors crowded in as closely as they could, with the remaining Kurds and Tex's Iranian Christians mixed in with them.

When they were all finally in place, McCarter said, "It's time for a little up-close-and-personal recon work." He waited as Tex and Abbas translated his words into Kurdish and Farsi.

Then the Phoenix Force leader went on. "Cal," he said to Calvin James. "This is your forte. If any 'waste management' needs to be done during this scout-out-only, it'll need to be done quietly." He paused to take a breath and when he did the combination of odors that made up the bazaar all entered his nostrils and shot up through his sinuses into his brain for identification.

McCarter's brain registered the faint odors of the dye as block printers up and down the street stamped out designs on links of material laid out on the ground. The rich scent of olive oil also entered his nose, and he looked beyond the men crowded around the doorway to a huge millstone being turned by roped camels. By far the faintest odor his olfactory senses picked up on was that of hot metal being pounded with hammers.

These were the hardest to smell. But the easiest to hear. And, no doubt about it, McCarter thought, the most important of all.

McCarter looked past the metal pounders and saw that they were now on the far edge of the bazaar area. So far, the narrow streets had been for pedestrians only. But beyond the clang of the hammers, the street widened and cars and trucks—most of them looking as if they'd been overhauled several times—zipped back and forth.

Turning his head toward Hamid, McCarter said, "You go with Cal. But I don't want either of you seen. You understand?"

Hamid nodded. "But please," he said, "I must at least have a weapon of some sort." He looked to the black Phoenix Force commando.

"You know he's right," James said to McCarter. He reached inside his robe and withdrew a small, plastic-handled Spyderco Delica folding knife with the trademark opening hole and pocket clip. He handed it to Hamid.

"But this," the young Iranian said, "is not *half* the knife that he carries."

"No," McCarter said. "It isn't. But that's because we don't trust you half as much as we do him." He nodded toward James. "If you two come back here and you've proven yourself, we might renegotiate the nature of our relationship."

Hamid placed the Delica inside the left sleeve of his robe and fastened the black clip to the outside. It blended in well with the pattern on the robe, and McCarter knew it would not be seen unless someone took special notice.

"Okay, Cal," he said. "Take note of the exact location, all entrances and exits and any other peculiarities you come across. And write down any equipment we're likely to need which we don't already have." He reached inside his robe and pulled out a small notepad and ballpoint pen. "Not sure why I just told you all that.

You already know what to do. You've been through this type of recon mission at least a thousand times in the past."

James laughed. "At least once or twice," he said. "But you know the only thing I've ever really learned from them?"

"What's that?" McCarter asked.

"Every single one is a brand-new ball game with brand-new rules."

Before McCarter could answer, James had reached up and grabbed the collar of Hamid's robe. Jerking the young man along, he said, "I'm going to let go of you now. But remember one thing. If you end up over a foot away from me in this mob out here, you're going to feel all twelve inches of that knife of mine you like so much." When Hamid didn't answer, James said, "Now, take me to the metalworker's shop."

Hamid began leading the way through the throngs of people crowding the street. They passed by the Sheikh Lutfallah Mosque, and then the Shah Mosque, both of which featured blue tiles with scriptures from the Koran handwritten on them. Then, just past the far end of the *maidan,* they came to another metalworking shop. Again, they saw camels tethered to a huge wheel. But this time instead of providing the energy for squeezing the oil out of olives, the camels were generating power for the fire that would heat the metals that eventually became pot and pans, pitchers and trays.

Men wearing fire-seared, heavy canvas aprons over their robes were noisily pounding out the metals as Hamid reached out and grabbed James by the sleeve of his robe. "This is the place," he said. "The Americans will be downstairs in the basement."

James frowned. "You sure about that?"

"Yes," Hamid answered. "This was the place to which they were to be taken."

"So how do you get down there?" James asked.

Hamid raised his arm to point but James grabbed it and pulled it back down. "Don't be stupid," the Phoenix Force warrior growled. "I don't know whether you were trying to draw attention to us or if that little gesture was innocent. But either way, it's stupid. Because if you try it again, it'll get you killed." He tapped the Crossada beneath his robe. "You do understand?"

"I do understand," Hamid said. This time, pointing only with his nose, he said, "Inside the small office building there are stairs. Stairs that lead down to what was once a large wine cellar. Since alcohol was banned with the fall of the Shah, it has been used for other purposes."

"Any other way down there?" James asked as he pretended to watch the metalworkers hammering out their wares.

"None of which I am aware," Hamid said.

James looked just past the office and saw an overhead door. It was closed. But through the glass windows in the top half of the door, he could make out the lines of what looked like an old red pickup. Crumpled into a ball in the pickup's bed was what looked like a light blue tarp with ropes attached to the metal reinforcements around the holes along the edges.

Turning his attention back to Hamid, he studied the

man's eyes, looking for any sign of deception. He saw none. What he did see was a kid who wished he'd never gotten involved in this crazy, mixed-up world of hostages, distorted religion and gunfire.

James turned back toward the metal workers. Although he was a knife-fighting expert rather than a bladesmith, he had watched many a knifesmith forge blades over the years. The process was quite similar to what the coppersmiths were doing, and he could sense that the men doing the hammering of these pots and pans were not well-practiced in the smelting arts. They were simply going through the paces, making it look like the shop was up and running.

James looked closer, to the men's waists, under their arms and to other areas of the body where weapons were most likely to be hidden. Occasionally, as the men twisted slightly or leaned over, he saw unnatural bulges in their robes.

They were armed with hidden weapons just like Phoenix Force and the rest of the men helping them. These men were fighters, not forgers as they pretended to be.

So where were the real metalworkers? James didn't know. They were very likely dead. After all, he thought both angrily and sarcastically, what were a few dead metalworkers when it was all done in the name of Allah?

"Follow me," James whispered as he tugged on Hamid's sleeve again. "And be prepared to do the talking if we have to." He patted the Crossada across his back. "And don't forget that one wrong move will be your last."

Hamid nodded.

James prodded the young man toward the closed office door, walking with the determined pace of men who knew exactly where they were going and what they were going to do once they got there. A few seconds later James reached out and twisted the doorknob, then pushed it open while Hamid stepped through.

"I don't know what to say." Hamid whispered over his shoulder.

"Tell them you placed an order a few weeks ago. See where it stands."

Hamid turned back around as James entered the tiny office area. The first thing he noted was a man sitting behind a desk. Dressed in the same Islamic robes as the men with the hammers outside, he was sitting behind a scuffed and dented metal desk. To his left was an open door to the garage where the red pickup was parked.

To his right was a stairwell that led out of sight beneath the ground.

Hamid spoke to the man behind the desk in Farsi.

James watched Hamid's face as he spoke.

The man answered in the same language. His voice was gruff, as if he didn't like being interrupted. But he leaned down and began opening drawers.

James got the distinct impression that the man was simply putting on an act for his and Hamid's benefit. He had no idea what he was looking for or where to find it.

A moment later he looked at his watch, then spoke again.

Hamid nodded his head and smiled, then placed his hands together and bowed slightly. Then he led the way out of the office.

"I saw what I needed to see," James said when they were back among the throngs of people outside between the two mosques. "Tell me how your conversation went."

"I told him I had placed an order for a copper pitcher, tray and cups several weeks ago. He tried to find the order form but couldn't, of course, since I'd done no such thing."

James remembered the man looking at his watch. "What was the watch thing all about?" he said.

Hamid frowned. Then suddenly it was as if he had been filled with enlightenment. "Oh, yeah," he said. "When he made such a big show of looking at the time?"

"Right."

"He was telling me that he was just the manager. The owner was gone but would be back in the morning. He would find it then if I'd come back."

"He looked through *all* of the drawers," James said. "Wouldn't you think that a manager, who probably has to look up orders several times a day, would know where the waiting order forms were kept?"

"I would think so." Hamid nodded.

"Well, we know where they are," James said. "But there are bound to be more armed men down in that basement." He quickened his pace as they neared the spot where the other members of Phoenix Force, the Kurds and the Christian Iranians had all come together near a grove of trees in the park. James took a seat on the grass next to where McCarter lay on his side. Several baskets of dates—purchased from a vendor a half block away, were making the rounds.

The black Phoenix Force warrior grabbed a handful

as one of the baskets went by, but held them in his hand while he spoke. In only a few brief and concise sentences, he had run down the situation to McCarter. The Phoenix Force leader nodded, then stood. "I think we'd better hit them sooner rather than later," he said. "That brief conversation may have gotten their suspicions up." He let Abbas and Tex translate.

All of the heads around him nodded.

Keeping their weapons hidden beneath their robes, they walked in pairs, trios or alone as they retraced the steps James and Hamid had just taken. But by the time they reached the metalworkers, the camels had been taken away, the men had stopped pounding and left and the office was dark.

The shop had closed for the night.

James looked in all directions to make sure none of the men who had been there earlier were still around. A smile was forming just beneath his neatly trimmed mustache. If all they had to face were the guards down below, this snatch-and-run was going to be a lot easier than he'd expected.

Cupping his hand above his eyebrows to look through the glass in the overhead door, James noted that the red pickup was gone. A sinking feeling began in his stomach and the smile he had worn a second earlier began to fade.

Going to the door to the office, James twisted the knob as far as he could, then leaned against it with his shoulder. The wood around the frame had rotted years before and easily splintered open now.

By the time he had entered the small office area,

Calvin James had his Beretta 92 in his left hand and the Crossada in his right.

The other odd conglomeration of warriors from Phoenix Force, the Kurds and the Christian Iranians followed him inside, weapons drawn.

James sheathed the Crossada and pulled out a small flashlight. The man who had sat behind the desk, going through the motions of being in charge and trying to find the order forms, was gone.

James led the way down the steps with his flashlight illuminating the way. The strong, moldy odor of infested limestone filled the warrior's sinuses as they descended to a lone, ancient door with a large window in the upper half. The window was covered with iron bars.

James pushed on the door and it swung open. Not only was it unlocked, but it also wasn't even closed all the way.

A sinking feeling filled his chest. And when he directed his flashlight into the cold, underground room he felt yet another wave of discouragement sweep over him.

The cellar was as empty as the office and yard above. But the odor of frightened and unwashed bodies still hung in the air like a man at the end of a noose.

They had been so close. The pickup had been there when he and Hamid first came upon the scene. Which meant that the hostages were still down inside this cellar. Perhaps he should have quietly cut the throat of the man behind the desk, gone downstairs with Hamid and freed the men then.

But logic and common sense told him that would have done nothing but gotten them both killed. And it could have meant the lives of the hostages, too. He and Hamid—who had not impressed him as possessing too many warrior skills regardless of whether he was in the Iranian military or not—would have been between the downstairs guards and the armed men upstairs pretending to hammer out pots and pans.

James stepped into the room, sweeping his flashlight back and forth across the walls and floor of the dingy area. His beam went past a white rectangular object on the floor next to the wall. But before he could pull the light back again to further investigate, McCarter stepped into the room. "Don't blame yourself, Cal," the Phoenix Force leader said. "You did all any man could do. Just a stroke of bad timing, this."

James nodded his head. While he'd never say it out loud, Calvin James knew in his heart that he was one of the world's best fighting men. But he had simply been far too outnumbered. And dying here, under these conditions, would not have gotten the important intelligence information he'd gained back to McCarter and the others.

James nodded, then focused the flashlight on the white rectangle on the floor. He could recognize it as looking like a business card now, and the Phoenix Force man holstered his pistol and walked forward, bending to pick it up.

Shining the bright lithium flashlight down onto the card, he read the words *Newsweek magazine* next to the weekly news magazine's logo. Below that was the name *Wilson "Pat" Patrick,* and then *Senior Journalist.* He handed the card to McCarter, leaving the flashlight beam up so the Phoenix Force leader could read it.

"Well," McCarter said, "at least we know they were here a few minutes ago." Pulling his satellite phone from the blacksuit under his robe, he tapped in the number to Stony Man Farm.

Barbara Price quickly transferred him to Kurtzman.

"Bear?" McCarter said when he heard the man answer.

"We've got a bad connection," said the wheelchair-bound computer expert. "You sound like you're in the bottom of a cellar."

"You don't know how right you are," McCarter replied. "Hang up and I'll call you back." He heard a click as Kurtzman disconnected the line.

The Phoenix Force leader called again, and this time both Price and Kurtzman could understand him. "How busy are you at the moment?" McCarter asked.

"Oh, just the usual needed-it-yesterday stuff," said the computer wizard. "Able Team has me running down a license tag at the moment." He paused, then said, "What is it I can do for you?"

"We need you to take a look at the satellite photos in and around Isfahan for the last fifteen minutes, Bear," McCarter said. "We need current status as well as a projected path for a red..." His voice trailed off as he realized he didn't know the make or model of the pickup. "What kind was it, Cal?" he asked.

James remembered his quick glance through the overhead door. "Chevy," he said. "A few years old, I'd say."

"A red Chevrolet pickup," McCarter told Kurtzman. "Not new—several years old."

"There are going to be hundreds if not thousands of

red pickup trucks fitting that description moving through the streets of Isfahan," Kurtzman said.

"I know," said McCarter. "But this one will have started at…" Again, he realized he had more information. But in a form that he couldn't understand. "Hamid," he said, handing the Iranian the phone. "Give him this address."

Hamid spoke a few seconds, and when he handed the phone back to McCarter the Phoenix Force leader could hear Kurtzman tapping the keys on his keyboard. A moment later the wheelchair-bound man said, "That's right by the Shah and the Sheikh Lutfallah mosques."

"It is," McCarter said. "We can see them both from the ground level."

"So you really are in a cellar?" Kurtzman said.

"That's what I told you," said McCarter. He paused, cleared his throat and then said, "The truck we're interested in will have a bed full of bound and blindfolded men in the back. It will have started at this address within the last fifteen minutes, and will be heading out of town about now, if it hasn't already."

"Bound and hooded men out in the open like that won't draw attention?" Kurtzman asked uneasily.

"Of course they will," said McCarter. "But this is Iran, Bear. People are used to seeing mujahideen and their weapons and prisoners. They mind their own business and thank Allah it's not them. But there's more. James spotted a blue tarp in the pickup when it was empty."

"Now it's making a little more sense," said Kurtzman. "You have a GPS reading you can give me?"

McCarter mentally kicked himself for not thinking of that earlier. Pulling a small hand-held unit from one of the blacksuit pockets beneath his robe, he passed on their latitude and longitude to the man in the wheelchair.

"Okay," Kurtzman said a second later. "I've got you zeroed in and I'm moving outward.

"Affirmative, Bear. I'm going to appropriate some transportation, but then we'll wait on your call. No sense in going the wrong direction."

"I'm on it," said the computer expert. "I can run Able Team's tag search on a different computer." He hung up.

McCarter glanced around him. The cellar was crowded now with his men, the Iranian Christians and the Kurds who had gradually drifted on down once they'd seen there was to be no gunfight.

Turning to Calvin James once more, the Phoenix Force leader said, "We need wheels."

"Ask, and ye shall receive," James quoted. "Knife-fighting wasn't the only thing I learned growing up on Chicago's South Side."

McCarter laughed. "That's why I picked you, Cal. Keep in mind how many people we need to carry," he said. "We'll either need some kind of really big transport rig or a lot of little ones."

"I'll try to beat Kurtzman's call coming back," James said. Then the black Phoenix Force warrior turned and made his way through the throng of men toward the steps leading up from the cellar.

David McCarter watched him go, and couldn't help but smile. He glanced at the other three men who made up Phoenix Force. Every last man was a leader of men, and the former British SAS officer felt his chest swell with pride.

It was a privilege to command such men.

"I'VE RUN YOUR TAG with every possible last number," Kurtzman said as soon as Lyons answered the call. "There are about a dozen states that came back with hits, but my guess is that it was a local vehicle."

Lyons drew in a long breath. It wasn't the definitive answer he'd hoped for. But they had to start somewhere. "How many are right here in NYC, Bear?"

"Three," said Kurtzman. "Want their names?"

Lyons let out his breath. "Yeah, I do," he said. "But my guess is that it's a stolen vehicle."

"I've already run a 10-29 on it, Ironman. If it's stolen, it hasn't been reported as such yet. Here are the names— Phillip K. Yancy, Michelle Jordan and Ollie Martinez."

Lyons felt his eyebrows narrow. "Spell that last one for me, will you, Bear?"

"I'm assuming you mean the first name," Kurtzman said. "My guess is you know how to spell 'Martinez.'"

"Right," said Lyons.

"O-L-L-I-E," Kurtzman said. "Not the A-L-I you were hoping for."

Lyons felt a thousand ideas racing through his mind at the same time. Then, all at once, the pieces settled and fell into place. "Back in my LAPD days," he said, "when I was assigned to the Narcotics Division, there were two schools of thought on what names you used undercover. Some guys thought it best to change both the first and last. Others just changed the last so in case their partner or snitch screwed up and used the wrong name, it was actually still the right one. Did that make sense?"

Lyons heard Kurtzman chuckle over the line. "Barely," the man in the wheelchair said.

"Well, put yourself in the place of a Pasdaran who, for the most part, is trying to blend in and go unnoticed. I'm talking about a sleeper here, Bear. A guy who may have been here in the States for years, just waiting for something like this."

"Okay," Kurtzman said. "I've got you covered, I think. He might be likely to just change the spelling from Ali to. Ollie—as in Oliver and Hardy—so he wouldn't accidentally answer to the wrong name."

"Exactly," said Lyons. "And it's also likely he'd be masquerading as a member of a different race. Iranians come in all shades, but my guess is he's got some Turk or Arab mixed into his bloodline, and he's fairly dark. Mexican, Cuban, any Spanish-speaking country would fit him. And you don't get more Spanish sounding than 'Martinez.'"

"Everything you say makes sense," Kurtzman said. "But it's a heck of a stretch to put all of those variables together when each one has a half dozen other possible answers."

"I know," said Lyons. "But we don't have anything better to go by."

"No, we don't. So here's Ollie's address." Kurtzman ran off the number and street, then gave the Able Team leader directions on how to get there. "While you're en route, I'll see what else I can turn up on Martinez."

"Thanks, Bear," Lyons said. "We'll be heading toward that address with two NYPD detectives. If you come up with anything else, I'm only a phone call away."

"Affirmative, Ironman," Kurtzman said.

Then both men hung up.

Lyons, followed by the other two men from Able Team, hurried out of the interrogation room and into the hall, where they were met by Ritholz and Cirillo. Lyons gave the two men the address he'd gotten from Randy Hathaway, then showed them the scrap of cardboard with the phone number and "eight o'clock" written on it.

Ritholz looked at his watch and shook his head. "That address," he said. "I know that part of the city. We'll never be able to drive there before the eight-o'clock deadline."

"How about a chopper?" Lyons asked. "We could—"

He was interrupted by the ring of his satellite phone again. "Lyons," he said into the instrument. "Hey, Ironman," Jack Grimaldi said. "I'm in the parking lot outside. Are you guys ever coming out? A little bird told me you'd need a lift. A high lift."

"My guess is that the little bird was named Aaron Kurtzman," Lyons said.

"That's him," Grimaldi confirmed. "He's also found a phone number to go with the address he gave you. Want me to read it to you?"

Lyons was holding the phone against his ear as he used the other hand to push open the front door of the precinct building. "Yeah, let me have it," he said.

Grimaldi read off the number as Lyons reached into his pocket. A second later he had produced the scrap of cardboard once more. But seeing the numbers did little more than confirm what he'd already figured out in his mind. The number Grimaldi had just given him—tracked down somehow by one of Kurtzman's near magic computers—and the one that the police were supposed to call at eight o'clock were one and the same.

Lyons led his squad of warriors around the corner of the building into a parking lot. In the center of the black asphalt sat an NYPD helicopter, blades revolving, and warmed up.

"We've got to stop meeting like this," Grimaldi said from behind the controls as the other men climbed aboard. "These police departments are really getting surly about me stealing their helicopters."

A second after that, they were airborne, weaving their way through the tall skyscrapers that made up the New York City skyline.

CHAPTER TWELVE

"I've got them in my sights," Aaron Kurtzman told McCarter over the satellite phone.

"You sure it's them?" McCarter asked as he moved to a corner of the cellar where the hostages had been only a few minutes earlier. "Remember—even you said there'd be dozens of red Chevy pickups."

"Let's say I'm ninety-five percent sure then, if it makes you feel better. By using the zoom I was able to get close enough to see it was a Chevy."

"And the hostages were in the back?" the Phoenix Force leader asked.

"That's the five percent I corrected myself on," Kurtzman said. "There's a blue tarp tied down over the bed of the truck. But there are 'bumps' in the tarp that move occasionally."

"Kind of like you'd expect if there were men tied up back there, changing positions now and then?"

"Precisely like that. Not to mention the fact that there

are Iranian military jeeps escorting the pickup, both front and back."

"What's their location?" McCarter said into the phone.

"They're still in Isfahan, but it looks like they're headed toward the highway that runs along the Zagros north to Arak. From there, they could be heading into Qom or Dasht-e Kavir or on to Tehran." He paused, coughed quietly, then went on. "Or someplace in the country. But yes, they're definitely heading for that highway."

"Where are Grimaldi and Mott right now?" McCarter asked.

"Both here in the States. Jack just left to assist Able Team in New York City, and Mott's here. But even in one of the new Concordes he'll never make it all the way to your location before that red pickup disappears from satellite view. I'll send him your way but—"

McCarter remembered that Mott had been awakened at the start of the mission after only a couple of hours of sleep, and had been flying one place or another ever since. "Let him sleep, Bear. You're right. He'd never get here in time to help."

"I'll have that ugly new steel bird serviced and ready to go while he sleeps. Then, when he does wake up, I'll get him started toward your general part of the world again," Kurtzman said.

"I've got James out procuring land transport at this very minute," McCarter stated.

"That's not going to be an easy thing to find," Kurtzman mused. "You've got your guys, these Christian Iranians, the Kurds, and by now you've probably picked up a few Beduins and nomads to round out your very own rainbow coalition. It wouldn't surprise me if you'd picked up a few of the old Knight's Templar along the way, either." He paused for a breath. "You're going to need a big vehicle, like maybe a semi, to haul them all in."

McCarter was about to answer when one of Tex's Iranian Christians came running down the steps, whisper-shouting in Farsi.

Tex was in the center of the mass of men in the cellar and he looked across the room toward McCarter. "Your man's back," he said. "And he's got wheels."

"Never mind explaining," Kurtzman said. "I could hear him. But let's keep this line open so I can direct you out of town."

"You've got it," McCarter said as he fell into the odd assortment of warriors sprinting up the concrete steps. By the time he reached the ground level he could see a large yellow bus parked just outside the building.

And Calvin James was sitting behind the wheel.

Abbas was right next to him as the men pushed out of the office door and up the steps of the bus. McCarter couldn't read the letters painted in black on the side of the bus. So Abbas translated. "It's one of the *madrasah* buses," the Kurd leader said. "There must be one of their religious brain-washing schools close by."

McCarter nodded as he waited for the other men to board the bus. And while he did, he looked around. The streets they had been on ever since entering Isfahan had been walking streets, and James had barely managed to squeeze the bus between the buildings. McCarter's guess was that, as soon as they were loaded, he'd back up, then turn around and head back out on the vehicular passages.

And Phoenix Force's blade warrior would have done just that, the former SAS man thought to himself as he finally entered the bus. Except for the fact that three jeeps of Pasdarans, all armed to the teeth, just pulled in behind them.

With the option to back up onto the wider vehicular street now blocked off, James ground the bus's stick shift into low gear and tore off through the bazaar. McCarter stayed at the front of the bus with him, holding on to the shiny steel pole next to the driver's seat and leaning over to press down on the horn. As the warning wailed away, James shifted into second gear.

Both men watched as the shocked Iranians darted into doorways or behind the many open stalls selling their wares.

At one point the street narrowed even further and the outer right-side mirror was torn off. A second or two later, the entire left side of the bus scraped against the centuries-old brick building and the other mirror went the same way as the first.

Behind them, McCarter could hear shots ring out as the Pasdarans began firing into the back of the bus. Glass splintered, and one man screamed out in pain. There had been more men than the bus could seat. But now there were no arguments as to who would ride on the floor.

Now everyone wanted the floor.

"Man down!" came Gary Manning's voice from somewhere in the back of the bus.

McCarter had continued to grip the steel pole next to the driver's seat with one hand. But now he pushed himself away from it. As James guided the bus down the narrow passageway, occasionally scraping the sides of the buildings and sending sparks flying through the darkness, the Phoenix Force leader staggered over Tex's and Abbas's men on the floor, toward where the other members of Phoenix Force had gathered beneath the broken glass.

All four of his men looked up at him.

McCarter knew that the only thing that had prevented them from returning fire was the possibility of collateral damage. None of them wanted to kill or injure any of the innocent civilians on the walking street. But the men and women who were still ducking into doorways or behind other protective cover were already in danger of being hit by the Pasdarans' rifle-fire, which was indiscriminate. By not firing back and ending that threat, Phoenix Force was putting the citizens of Isfahan in more peril than if they started shooting themselves.

"Take 'em out, mates," McCarter said, and the men of Phoenix Force scrambled for positions at the broken windows in the back doors. Encizo and Hawkins immediately rose to their knees and directed steady streams of fire through the shattered glass toward the lead jeep.

"Who's down?" the Phoenix Force leader asked to no one in particular.

Hawkins looked over his shoulder as he held the trigger back on his M-16.

McCarter followed the man's eyes and saw Adel

"The Rat" Spengha stretched out on a bus seat next to him. Their reluctant informant looked as if he'd taken several 7.62 mm rounds directly to the chest. His eyes were wide open.

But they were staring upward and seeing nothing.

And they never would again.

The bus gained a little ground as the lead jeep automatically slowed and began weaving back and forth to avoid Phoenix Force's 5.56 mm rounds. Far more narrow than the school bus, the vehicles could maneuver easier, and faster, than James could drive the bus.

The Pasdarans could see this as easily as McCarter. And that knowledge seemed to spur them to even more furious pursuit.

Many of the rounds from the men of Stony Man Farm were striking the lead jeep. But its body was armored with Kevlar and the windshield appeared to be made of bullet-resistant glass. Most of Phoenix Force's counterattack struck the windshield, then glanced up and over the two jeeps following.

McCarter had the answer to that problem. But he couldn't use it. Not yet. Not with so many civilians around.

By now, however, they had reached the park and McCarter turned and yelled to the front of the bus. "Cal! Cut over onto the flower beds!"

A split second later Calvin James had twisted the wheel and jumped the curb into the old-polo-field-turned-garden. The bus cut a swath through the carefully tended flowers and plants, and for a second McCarter felt a twang of guilt for destroying an area of such beauty.

But the flowers would grow back.

Adel Spengha, and the rest of the men on the bus, wouldn't.

All three of the jeeps jumped the curb behind them and McCarter held on to the back of a seat as he made his way to where Hawkins and Encizo were still firing. "Give me some room, chaps," he said, and both men scooted to the sides.

McCarter pulled the last fragmentation grenade he had from under his robe, jerked the pin then leaned out the window.

A flurry of lead buzzed past his face as he raised his arm and threw.

The grenade lobbed over the windshield and fell somewhere in the jeep. There was a moment of silence while the Pasdarans stopped firing and scrambled to find the bomb and throw it out.

Then the grenade went off and bodies—and pieces of bodies—came flying out of the vehicle.

What was left of the jeep turned to the left and, without slowing, ran straight into a date tree. There was another explosion, and then the entire vehicle erupted in flames.

One down, McCarter thought.

But there were still two to go.

MIDWAY DOWN THE BLOCK of old brownstone apartment buildings, Carl Lyons spotted the empty lot. Piled high in places with old scrap wood and other debris, he would never have even considered asking Grimaldi to land there under other conditions.

But the time was 1955. In five minutes, they—or rather the police—had been ordered to call the phone number on the scrap of cardboard. If they didn't, Hans Gustafson—who was undoubtedly confused and wishing he'd stayed at home in Stockholm—was going to get a Pasdaran bullet in the head or a blade across his throat.

And Carl Lyons didn't intend to let that happen. He'd be making contact within the next five minutes, all right. But it wouldn't be over the phone.

The Able Team leader intended for his team and Detectives Ritholz and Cirillo to make a personal visit to the apartment where Gustafson was being held. And their initial greeting would come in the form of bullets rather than handshakes.

Grimaldi had been described as a pilot who could set the space shuttle down on a dime, and he proved that that was no exaggeration as he lowered the NYPD chopper onto the only fairly flat ground that was free of rubble. The site was barely large enough to permit the whirlybird to settle without the overhead blades striking the adjacent buildings and being sheared off. And even then, the chopper had to land atop a pile of scattered plywood scraps.

"Nice job, Jack," Lyons said as he unlatched the door. The weight of the hatchway, combined with the angle at which they'd landed, pulled the door open on its own.

"Don't mention it," Grimaldi said. "Need me to wait for you here?"

Lyons turned toward the pilot, nodded, then dropped out of the open hatchway to the ground. He was followed by the other two men of Able Team and the two NYPD detectives.

With a glance at his wristwatch that told him that Hans Gustafson had roughly two and a half more minutes to live, the Able Team leader sprinted toward the sidewalk in front of the lot and made a sharp right-hand turn. Passing the first two brownstones, he turned right again and bounded up a set of dirty and cracked concrete steps.

With the noise of the city all around him, Lyons could not hear the footsteps of the five men running behind him.

But he knew they were there.

A tall, burly man dressed in an elaborate doorman's uniform, complete with braided epaulets and cap, watched Lyons running up to him, then moved in front of the door. "I'm sorry, sir—" he started to say.

Lyons knew he had no time to hassle with this man, or even show him the phony Justice Department credentials. So without breaking stride, he cocked a fist and sent it squarely up and through the broad doorman's chin.

The man in the fancy uniform dropped immediately.

Schwarz and Blancanales each grabbed an arm and jerked the unconscious form to the side of the doorway. Lyons opened the door and let the other men through.

The staircase stood right next to the elevators, and Lyons chose the faster route. Bounding up the stairs three at a time, he felt the burn in his quadriceps muscles as the lactic acid built up.

It was a pain he had learned to ignore years ago.

Now, in the quieter interior of the brownstone, the

Able Team leader could hear the other men behind him. He could even make out the difference between Schwarz's and Blancanales's rubber-soled Converse combat boots and the leather soles of the shoes Cirillo and Ritholz wore.

Lyons turned the corner at the top of the first flight of stairs and bounded up a second flight. Another quick glance at his forearm told him it was now 1959 hours.

If no one called the number on the scrap of cardboard in the Able Team leader's pocket in one minute, Gustafson would die.

The apartment registered to Ollie Martinez was on the third floor, and the numerals 307 had been tacked on the door. Again without breaking stride, Carl Lyons lifted his right foot as he reached the door and kicked.

The kick not only swung the door open, but it also broke the hinges and sent the aged wood flying back into the apartment. Lyons followed it in as it struck the head of a dark-skinned man wearing a New York Mets T-shirt and blue jeans, knocking him as cold as the doorman outside the building. A second later, the Able Team leader was leaping over the man's sleeping body and running through the living room.

There were Pasdarans of every size, shape and mode of dress from battle fatigues to Brooks Brothers suits sitting on the couches and chairs. And to say they were surprised would have been an understatement.

But all had weapons either on them or close by. And they all went for those weapons as Lyons lifted his M-16 and fired into them.

With the explosions of more rifle fire behind him,

Lyons glanced to his left and saw a small kitchen area. Empty. Turning his attention toward the only other door in the living room, he saw that it was closed. So while the rest of Able Team went to work with their M-16s, and Cirillo and Ritholz opened up with their NYPD-issue 12-gauge shotguns, Lyons sprinted on and kicked yet another door open.

Only two men were in the bedroom. One was an elderly gentleman wearing a white tie and tails who sat upon the bed, handcuffed to the steel frame. The other wore the complete Pasdaran BDU uniform, including the red scarf around his neck.

The guard was holding a Glock semiautomatic pistol to the head of the man on the bed.

It didn't take the brain of an Albert Einstein or Stephen Hawking to figure out who was who.

Lyons reacted automatically, lifting the M-16 and switching the selector to semiauto mode at the same time. One pull of the trigger was all it took to send a 5.56 mm hollowpoint into the brainstem of the Pasdaran.

It was as if someone had pulled a main electrical switch that shut down everything within its power range. The man's entire body, including his trigger finger, went limp and he fell to the floor.

In the living room, the shooting had died down. Lyons walked to the bed, at the same time pulling out a handcuff key from the blacksuit beneath his blazer and slacks. "Are you all right, sir?" he asked the man in the tails.

"A little bit shaken up," Hans Gustafson said in a strong Swedish accent. "But as you Americans say, I think, I am no worse for the wearing." He lifted his wrist so Lyons could free him. "Did I say that correctly?"

The Able Team leader smiled. "Close enough," he said.

"My English is not so good," the Swede said as he stood up.

"It's better than my Swedish," Lyons came back. "Which is nonexistent."

The orchestra conductor laughed. "I must remember that one," he said.

Lyons took the man by the arm and led him into the living room. Gustafson's eyes grew wide as he looked around the room, his eyes falling on the dead faces, the blood and the lifeless limbs. "I do not understand this world that men like you live in," he said.

"It's not my world," Lyons said. He pointed to the remains of three Pasdarans who were dead on a couch. "They're the ones who create it."

Gustafson nodded. "Yes," he said. "I am sorry. I did not mean to say you were to blame. In fact, I am grateful for violent men such as you who protect us."

"I'm not a violent man," Lyons corrected. "I just happen to be good at it."

Schwarz and Blancanales had lifted the front door off of the man it had struck, and Schwarz was trying to slap him back into consciousness. Ritholz and Cirillo were making the rounds, checking for any sign of life left in the Pasdarans who had kidnapped the Swedish conductor.

Lyons dropped the older man's arm but turned to him. "Are you hurt at all?" he asked. "Do you need medical attention?"

Gustafson shook his head.

"Great," Lyons told him. "I'm going to turn you over to these two detectives, then."

"My concert was to begin at eight o'clock," the conductor said.

"I'm afraid you're going to be a little late." Lyons turned away and looked back to where Schwarz and Blancanales had gotten the man on the floor conscious once more. "Bring him with us," he said. "We've got to get out of here before more cops arrive and try to bog us down with reports and statements."

When they heard that, Cirillo and Ritholz turned toward Lyons at the same time. "You're leaving?" Ritholz said.

Lyons nodded.

"But how are we supposed to explain all this?" Ritholz asked.

"Hey," Lyons said. "It's your collar. Take credit for it. It's got promotion written all over it."

Ritholz frowned. "The buckshot we can explain," he said. "But what are we supposed to say about the rifle rounds?"

Lyons slid out of the M-16 sling and handed it to the detective. "This was on the premises when you got here," he said. "One of you picked it up when your shotgun ran dry."

"They're going to run ballistic tests," Cirillo said. "The only person that particular rifle shot was in the bedroom."

Schwarz and Blancanales had the man who'd been hit by the door on his feet again. They took turns slipping out of their own M-16s and handing them to

Ritholz and Cirillo. "That should cover the markings on the rest of the rifle rounds," Schwarz said.

"This is going to smell worse than the box we keep for my daughter's cat," Ritholz said.

"Don't worry," Lyons said, picturing Hal Brognola in his mind. "Whoever ends up investigating this shoot from internal affairs will be getting a phone call from the Justice Department. It'll not only skid the case to a halt, but you two will also probably end up getting the medals you deserve."

The Able Team leader turned away, looked at Schwarz and Blancanales and said, "Let's go. Bring our new friend with us."

The Pasdaran held between the two men was awake now. But he had a huge, egg-shaped knot on the side of his head.

"What's your name?" Lyons asked while he was still in a state of semiconsciousness.

"Iraj," the awakening man answered.

As the men of Able Team hustled him out the door, he came fully awake. "Where are we going?" he demanded.

"We're all going for a helicopter ride," Lyons said pleasantly. "And you're going to answer a few questions for us."

"I refuse to speak," the Pasdaran said. "And I demand an attorney."

"He's been watching too much of that decadent, satanic American TV, Ironman," Schwarz said.

Lyons nodded as they walked the man down the hall. "You're going to find that we don't play by those rules, Iraj," he said.

"And if I refuse to speak?" the Iranian said.

"Then we're going to find out if you've got a magic carpet that can fly," Lyons said and shoved the man out of the brownstone and down the steps to the sidewalk.

MCCARTER FELT LIKE a drunken sailor aboard a ship on the high seas as he made his way back to the front of the bus. When he was halfway there, James suddenly twisted the bus's steering wheel and took off in another direction to confuse the pursuing Pasdaran jeeps.

The sudden turn sent McCarter flying between two of the bus seats, and then smashing up against the window on that side of the bus.

As James straightened out again, the Phoenix Force leader resumed his staggering march toward the front of the bus. When he'd reached the shining silver pole again, he grabbed hold of it and said, "Cal. You have any grenades left?"

"Just one," said the man behind the wheel. The Phoenix Force warrior reached under his robe, pulled out the pineapple-looking bomb and flipped it up into the air.

McCarter caught the grenade and started back down the aisle between the seats once more. When he had reached the shattered windows again, he knelt and leaned out through the hole. But this time, the Iranian Revolutionary Guards were ready for him, 7.62 mm volleys peppered the bus on both his sides, as well as above and below his head.

The Phoenix Force leader was no fool. He ducked back into the bus again and dropped below the window line.

"It appears that the Iranians have heard the old expression," he said to Gary Manning, who was crouched beside him.

"What saying is that?" Manning asked.

"'Fool me once, shame on you. Fool me twice, shame on me.'"

The bus skidded slightly as it came out of another flower bed and the tires hit a long stretch of open grass. McCarter risked a quick glance over the window, then ducked back down. There was only one way to get the last grenade to take out the second jeep, and it would require almost superhuman timing.

But the Phoenix Force leader knew he had to try it.

Raising his eyes up for another quick view, McCarter yelled, "James! Hit the brakes! Hard!" He knew the warrior driving the bus would wonder why he'd been given such a seemingly self-destructive order. But he also knew James was disciplined enough to carry it out without having to know why it had been given.

Dirt, flowers and grass flew from the rear tires of the bus as James stood on the brakes. With his eyes still just above the bottom of the window, McCarter could see that the grass, which had looked almost as perfect as a golf green, was quickly looking more like a freshly plowed wheat field during planting season. He pulled the pin on the grenade and dropped it next to him. Taking in a deep breath, the Phoenix Force man relaxed his grip on the handle, activating the three-second timer.

"One thousand one," the man from Stony Man Farm counted out. "One thousand two—"

The second jeep that had given chase had closed the

gap when James hit the brakes, and its front bumper was only a few feet from the rear of the bus. With roughly one second standing between him and doom, McCarter reached up and dropped the grenade out of the window.

A break in the gunfire allowed him, Manning and Encizo to hear the grenade hit the concrete behind them.

The jeep drove over the explosive just as it detonated.

As the nearest jeep burst into flames, skidded then turned onto its side, Manning looked at McCarter. "Why don't you cut it a little closer next time, chief?" the Canadian commando said.

But he was grinning when he said it.

Only the last of the three jeeps that had pursued them still remained. And McCarter saw now why it had chosen the rear position. Even among special forces troops you sometimes found cowards, and the driver of the last jeep wanted nothing more to do with the bus after seeing what had happened to the other two Iranian vehicles. It pulled to a halt behind the flaming mass of steel and flesh in the overturned jeep.

McCarter knew that the official report to their superiors would say something to the effect that they had ceased pursuit in order to render aid to their fellow soldiers. But the truth was, the men in the last jeep just didn't want to have the same thing happen to them.

Reaching the other side of the park, McCarter called out to James. "Cal! Head this thing back north! Toward the highway Kurtzman told us about!"

From the front of the bus, James called back, "I don't know how far we're going to get. We're losing oil fast."

McCarter looked over his shoulder and saw James

pointing at the dashboard in front of him. Then he turned back and saw the steady stripe of black that the bus was leaving in its wake. Only then did the acrid smell of burning oil declare itself to his brain.

At least one of the Pasdaran rounds had ruptured the bus's oil case.

By now, the mixture of Stony Man Farm, Christian Iranians, and Kurds had risen from the floor of the bus and were back in their seats. With the threat from the rear eliminated, McCarter hurried to the front.

A red light burned brightly on the oil gauge.

"We might as well drive this thing until it quits on us," he told James. "But we've got to get out of this area. That third jeep back there has to have radioed for more troops by now."

James nodded as he continued to accelerate. Occasionally, the bus jerked. But it kept going.

"Anybody got a map of this area?" McCarter called back to the men, then waited for Tex and Abbas to translate.

One man reached into his pocket and pulled out a whole series of crumpled papers. McCarter hurried back to where he was holding them up in the air, and Abbas met him there. The Kurdish leader spoke briskly, and the man shuffled through the worn papers until he found a map of the Isfahan area.

McCarter took it from him and looked down as smoke began to rise from the hood of the bus. The writing on the map, of course, was in Farsi. But along with the highway they were heading toward, he saw a parallel line with crosshatches extending from both sides. It ran from Isfahan to Tehran, following almost the identical route taken by the highway.

"Is that a railway?" the Phoenix Force leader asked Abbas.

The Kurdish leader nodded.

McCarter turned his attention back to the bus as they finally reached the highway headed north to Tehran. In the distance, he could see the railroad tracks running alongside. Looking down at James, he said, "How much longer before this thing throws a rod?"

James shrugged. "No way to know. I'd have thought it would have quit on us already."

McCarter knew that finding another vehicle, or vehicles, to continue their pursuit of the red pickup and the hostages would be nearly impossible. But then, just as he was about to order James to pull over and begin hot-wiring all the automobiles they could find, McCarter heard the whistle of a train in the distance.

He hurried back to the rear of the bus again. A locomotive was coming from the south, almost directly toward them. McCarter ran to the front again. "You hear that whistle?" he asked James.

Calvin James smiled, showing a bright white line of perfect teeth. "I did," he said. "But you're not really thinking what I think you're thinking, are you?"

"I'm afraid so," said McCarter. "Relax. I've seen it done in almost every American Western movie I've ever seen."

"Yeah, but that was in the movies," James said. "And on horses. I'm not going to be able to get this bus as close to the train as horses could get. *If* this bus even lasts that long in the first place."

"Well, we've got to try, mate," the former SAS man said. Then, turning to face the rest of the men on the bus, he called out loudly, "Quiet! Let me have your attention!"

Tex and Abbas translated as usual, and the murmuring conversations that had been carrying on in different languages suddenly stopped.

McCarter cleared his throat, then said, "We have only one chance, and that's to jump from the bus onto the train. It'll take us in the direction we want to go, toward Tehran. When we pass the pickup with the hostages, we'll stay on the train for another mile or so, then jump off again. This means we'll be attacking the Pasdarans escorting the hostages from the ground. And that, in turn, means some of you are very likely to get killed. That is, if you survive jumping on, or off, of the train." He paused for a deep breath while Tex and Abbas translated again. Then he added, "I've already given you all a chance to go back to the rest of your people. And I'm giving you that chance again. So if any of you want out, now's the time to say so. No one's going to hold it against you."

Only one hand shot up from the bus seats. And it belonged to Hamid.

"Understandable," said McCarter to the young man. "Now, get your arse up here. You've just become our chauffeur."

When Hamid reached the front of the bus, James stood and jumped to the side, still holding the steering wheel. But now the bus was choking and coughing, and

McCarter knew it was only a matter of seconds, rather than minutes, before the engine seized.

Hamid slid behind the wheel and took over the steering duties.

"I want you to get us as close to the train as possible," McCarter said. Then he pulled his .40-caliber Browning Hi-Power from its holster beneath his robe, and pressed the muzzle against Hamid's cheek.

"What is that for?" the Iranian asked.

"That's in case you don't do exactly what I tell you," McCarter answered. "The train's going to be going considerably faster than we are, so there's only going to be a very short window of opportunity for these men to catch it. If you do anything to impede their chances, you're going to find out that you're a suicide bomber without a bomb." He paused a second, feeling the ground rumbling beneath the bus's tires as the train continued to near. Behind him, the mixed army of warriors who had coalesced into one unit had already opened the windows. Some had even climbed out onto the roof of the bus where they were clinging to the large luggage rack. McCarter moved to the seat directly behind Hamid and stuck out his head. The train was only a few seconds away. But it was long, with a tail of boxcars extending rearward so far he couldn't see the caboose.

At least that would be in their favor.

Returning to grasp the steel pole, he jammed the Browning into Hamid's neck. "All right," he said. "Get off the road and up to the tracks."

The bus was only moving in a series of jerks, chugging along erratically and promising to die altogether soon. "Faster," the Phoenix Force leader told Hamid. The closer they could get to matching the speed of the train, the easier it would be for the men to make the transfer.

Not that anything was going to make it easy. Just easier.

"It will not go faster!" Hamid shrieked. "I am trying!"

Then, almost before he knew it, David McCarter saw the engine flash by the bus. Several men jumped from the roof of the bus, landing on top of the boxcars or grasping hold of the handrails along the steps between the cars. Most of them made it.

But one man, a Kurd McCarter had seen but not met, slipped off the steps, bounced into the side of the bus, then screamed as it knocked him directly beneath the train on top of the rails. By the time McCarter looked down, the man—or rather the pieces of the man—had disappeared as if he'd never even existed.

As the train continued to pass, more and more men jumped from the roof of the bus to their new transportation. McCarter noted that the men of his own team were still inside the vehicle, staying at the back, helping the Kurds and Iranian Christians out the windows and onto the roof. They continued making the leap, most of them being successful while others suffered the same fate as the man who McCarter had watched fall.

Finally the bus quit altogether. McCarter pressed the Browning into Hamid's neck and said, "Get it started again or I'll kill you."

Hamid tried the key. Again, then again. Finally, he

threw up his hands and with tears in his eyes, screamed, "Go ahead and kill me! I cannot stand this anymore. It will not start!"

McCarter had seen the flames coming up from under the hood even before he'd told Hamid to start the bus again. "I never thought it would," the Phoenix Force leader said. Then, without another word, he holstered his pistol, climbed out of the window directly behind Hamid and pulled himself up onto the top of the bus.

Looking down the line, he saw that the other four men from Stony Man Farm were the only other warriors still atop the bus. "How come you haven't jumped yet?" he called out.

"We were waiting for our fearless leader," Hawkins called back.

McCarter smiled. "Well, here I am," he said, then lifted his arm and pointed past the rest of the Phoenix Force men. "And there's the caboose." The end of the long train had finally become visible.

"What am I supposed to do?" Hamid screamed from inside the bus.

McCarter looked at the flames leaping up from under the hood and said, "Well, if it was me in your situation, I believe I'd get out of that bus before the gas tank explodes." He paused a second. "But you're on your own now, Hamid. Do whatever you want."

McCarter turned and leaped from the roof of the bus onto the steps between two boxcars. As he flew through the air, he again felt the pride of a man privileged enough to lead other leaders. Even if he missed the rail, and became sliced to pieces on the tracks like the man he had watched earlier, he would go to his grave knowing he had done his best to rid the world of all the evil he possibly could.

The Phoenix Force leader felt his fingers curl around the cool steel of the railing, and a second later he was firmly seated on the steps and waiting.

Fifteen minutes later the train passed the red pickup with the blue tarp being escorted, front and back, by the Iranian military jeeps.

Still dressed in his traditional robes, McCarter smiled at the soldiers in the jeeps as they passed. The soldiers smiled back, then saluted. McCarter saluted them back.

A mile or so later, the Phoenix Force leader jumped from the train and rolled down an embankment between the tracks and the highway. As he came to a halt, he saw the rest of his odd assemblage of men jumping, too.

CHAPTER THIRTEEN

The NYPD helicopter, with Grimaldi at the controls, was just lifting off when Carl Lyons's satellite phone rang again.

"Lyons," the Able Team leader said into the phone.

"Phoenix Force has located the hostages on the road from Isfahan to Tehran," Aaron Kurtzman's voice said as the chopper continued to rise in the sky. "David and his boys are on a train paralleling the highway right now."

"A *train?*" Lyons nearly shouted into the phone. "How the—"

"Don't ask," Kurtzman said on the other end. "It'll take too long to explain." He paused, cleared his throat and then went on. "What I called about is that while I was running down the leads that both you and McCarter gave me, I kept my eye on the CIA. It seems a whole convoy of semi-tractor-trailer trucks came from Russia into Iran last night. Using their infrared satellite cameras, the spooks watched them unload what looked like F-14 fighter jet parts. Then they refueled and started back toward Russia."

"Sounds to me like the Russian black market is helping Iran rebuild its air force."

"Yes, it does," Kurtzman agreed. "Never thought I'd miss the old Soviet Union."

"Me, either," Lyons said. "But at least they helped keep a lid on this sort of thing."

By now, the helicopter was high in the sky over New York City. "Where to?" Grimaldi asked, turning toward Lyons.

The Able Team leader glanced over his shoulder to where Iraj—the Pasdaran who'd been knocked out by Lyons's door kick and had an ever-growing egg-shaped knot on his head—was squeezed in between Schwarz and Blancanales. "Just hover for a minute," he said.

"What?" Kurtzman asked over the phone.

"Nothing, Bear," said Lyons. "I was talking to Grimaldi." He stopped for a moment while his mind raced. Finally he said, "All of this is nice to know, Bear. But it doesn't have much to do with us here in the States."

"*Au contraire,*" the man in the wheelchair retorted. "There's more. I've also just gotten some on-the-ground intel about a ship that pulled into port in Venezuela earlier today. It was flying French colors but the CIA's South American desk says that several of the men were overheard speaking Farsi instead of Spanish or French."

"So what do they say about the ship's cargo?" Lyons asked.

"Not sure where this came from, but they suspect there were nuclear warheads aboard."

Lyons paused for a moment, taking it all in. Then he said, "Venezuela has its own air force that could get the nukes at least as far as the southern States, Bear. But the Venezuelans aren't Muslims. And I doubt any of them have been converted into crazy-assed kamikaze jocks."

"Which is where the Farsi speakers come in," Kurtzman said. "My guess is that it'll be more Pasdaran pilots flying the Venezuelan F-14s with the nukes on board."

"Not that that's not enough," Lyons almost growled into the phone. "But is there anything else?"

"Oh, yeah," Kurtzman said. "There was an aircraft carrier flying the Portuguese flag which left Iran a few days ago. The satellite pictures showed the deck covered with tarps. But they're certain it was planes of some type beneath the coverings."

"Then they're trying to get their planes close enough by water to attack the northern States," Lyons said. He paused, then went on. "It sounds like a great job for McCarter and his boys. But once again, I can't see where—"

"Where you come in?" Kurtzman finished for him. "I'm about to tell you. There's more intel that at least one nuke has already been smuggled into the U.S. It's to be detonated by hand at the same time we're getting bombed by both Iran in the north and Venezuela in the south. And an unnamed source warned his CIA handler that at the same time we're getting nuked, they're going to hit Israel, too."

"That little rat-looking Iranian potentate really is trying to start World War III," Lyons said. "He can't be so stupid that he doesn't know we'll bomb the hell out of Tehran in retaliation. And Israel? I don't even want to guess at what extremes they'll go to in retaliation."

He paused, took a deep breath, then let half of it out as if he was about to trigger a precise rifle shot. "Iran can practically send their nukes into Israel on camel back."

"The Iranian president knows all that," Kurtzman said. "But he's willing to take a huge loss of innocent civilian Iranian lives just for propaganda use. His real objective is to get America and Israel bogged down on the ground inside the country after the bombings. Pretty much like we are in Iraq right now."

"That's true," Lyons agreed.

"Anyway," said Kurtzman. "There's one more thing you need to know."

"Well, then give it to me."

"Kidnapping the Swedish conductor was only step one for the Pasdarans you wiped out back at the brownstone," the computer genius said. "They're also in charge of detonating the smuggled nuke, as well."

"Any idea where it might be hidden?" the Able Team leader asked.

"No," Kurtzman said. "Nothing concrete, anyway. But the rate at which all of these things are all coming together, and the fact that they kidnapped the conductor in New York City makes me think it's close by."

Lyons felt a twitch in his chest. He looked over his shoulder at Iraj. They had come across nothing even remotely resembling a nuclear bomb back at the brownstone, which meant it had to be hidden and waiting somewhere else. And they had killed all of the Pasdarans who were there.

But were there others in that cell? Lyons wondered. Men who had been out at the time of attack? Someone who had gone out to pick up burgers or coffee or for some other reason while Able Team eliminated their enemies?

He had no way of knowing. So he would be forced to work on the assumption that there *were* others willing to sacrifice themselves to wipe out thousands, or perhaps even millions, of New Yorkers.

"Hold on a minute, Bear," he said into the phone, then rested it on his shoulder. Turning toward Iraj, he said, "Where's the nuke you guys smuggled into the country? The one you were supposed to set off at the same time the F-14s attacked with other nuclear warheads?"

The fact that Lyons knew that much about their plan seemed to startle the man in the backseat. "I know nothing about that," he said.

Lyons turned toward Grimaldi. "Fly us up over the Empire State Building," he said. Then, into the phone he said, "Bear, I'll call you right back."

The Able Team leader folded his satellite phone closed again.

Grimaldi chuckled, knowing what Lyons must have in mind as he turned the NYPD chopper that way.

A moment later they were hovering over the building that had once been the tallest in New York City, and had returned to that position when the World Trade Center towers had come tumbling down due to the work of men just like Iraj.

"Look down, Iraj," the Able Team leader said as Grimaldi returned the helicopter to its hovering state.

Schwarz grabbed the man's neck and forced his face against the window.

"What do you see?" Lyons asked.

"A very tall building with a needle-looking thing on top," Iraj choked out.

"That needle-looking thing is an antenna," Lyons said. "Now, keep that in mind while we change the subject for a few seconds."

Iraj's dark brown skin had taken on a gray color.

"Do you know who Vlad the Impaler was?" the Able Team leader asked.

"No," Iraj muttered in a shaky voice.

"Well, I don't have time to give you his whole history," Lyons said. "But he was an ancient Prince of Wallachia, sometimes referred to as Vlad Dracula. Does that name ring a bell?"

Iraj nodded. "Dracula," he said. "The vampire." The expression on his face had grown curious now.

"Yes," said Lyons. "That's who Bram Stoker's original Dracula was based on. But the real Dracula didn't bite people on the neck and suck their blood out. He just liked to impale hundreds of people at a time on sharpened wooden posts sticking out of the ground while he ate dinner and used them as a floor show."

Now, Iraj's eyes had grown wide and he trembled with fear as he said, "You are going to bite me and suck out my blood?"

"No," Lyons said. "I'm going to toss you out of this bird and see if I can impale you on that 'needle-thing' as you called it." Without waiting for a reply, he said, "Even if I miss, it's no big deal. You'll get to experience what the people in the World Trade Center felt when they were forced to leap to their deaths rather than be burned to a crisp."

Now, Schwarz didn't have to force Iraj to look out of the window. The Pasdaran did so on his own.

And his pale face looked as if its lips might spew forth vomit at any minute.

Lyons opened the door next to him and the wind suddenly rushing in made the NYPD chopper's tail fish-tail back and forth with the force.

"Don't worry," Blancanales said to Iraj. "The fall won't hurt at all. It's the landing part that's a bitch."

Blancanales reached over and unsnapped Iraj's seat belt. Then he and Schwarz shoved the flailing and kicking man into the front of the chopper onto Lyons's lap. With the door already open, the Able Team leader said, "You want one more chance to tell me where the nuke's hidden?"

Iraj's eyes were closed and he was muttering some kind of prayer.

"Guess not," Lyons said, and with a quick twist at the hip he pulled Iraj across him and shoved him out the door, holding on to the collar of the man's leather jacket with both hands. "Take it a little to the right, Jack," he told Grimaldi. "I really do want to see if I can't stick him on the top."

"Say hello to King Kong for us," Schwarz said from the back seat.

"No! Stop! Pull me back in!" Iraj screamed in a high-pitched voice of terror. "I will take you to the nuclear device!"

The satellite phone that Lyons had set down next to him suddenly rang.

"Get that for me, will you, Pol?" Lyons said. "I've got my hands full. No pun intended."

"I will take you to the bomb!" Iraj screamed again as Blancanales took the call.

"You sure you even know where it is?" Lyons asked. "Answer quick. My arms are getting tired."

"Yes! Yes! Yes!" Iraj cried with the tears of a woman streaming down his face. "I will take you there!" he screamed again.

Lyons pulled the man back up into the chopper and closed the door. "Just remember that if you change your mind, we can always come back up here," he said.

THE MEN OF PHOENIX FORCE, the Iranian Christians and the Kurds all lay flat in the bar ditch as the red Chevy pickup and the two Iranian army jeeps neared.

"Wait until I fire!" McCarter shouted at the top of his lungs. Then he said, "Go for the tires first!" He saw the last man at the other end of the prostrate warriors raise his hand to indicate that they'd all heard.

The seconds ticked away, feeling like hours.

Finally, when the lead jeep appeared, McCarter watched it drive past the other hidden warriors as he waited for it to get to him. He wanted all three vehicles in a tight little bunch before he set loose the fires of hell so none of them could turn back.

The lead jeep was almost even with him when the Phoenix Force leader finally rose to his feet and opened up with his M-16. Three rounds exploded into the front tire, rupturing it into strips of hot rubber that flapped through the air. By then the back tire had driven into his sights, and McCarter did the same with it.

The lead jeep swerved to the right, leaving the highway and skidding down the embankment on its rims.

The red pickup was next, and McCarter watched as Gray Manning took careful aim to avoid hitting the hostages beneath the blue tarp. It followed a similar route, skidding to the shoulder of the highway and stopping.

Two Pasdarans rode in the pickup's cab. Encizo and Hawkins made short work of them with carefully placed shots from their own M-16s.

Farther down the line, McCarter watched as Tex Karns, Abbas and their respective followers took out the trailing jeep with a massive attack of lead. Both the Iranian Revolutionary Guardsmen and the jeep they were riding in seemed to fly apart in pieces.

McCarter stepped to the side as the lead jeep rolled down the embankment, then turned over onto its side. Only two men came tumbling out alive, and they began screaming and firing indiscriminately.

Teaming up with Calvin James, McCarter put the two Pasdarans out of their confused misery.

Suddenly all went quiet. As if to emphasize the silence, the train from which they'd jumped sounded its horn, far in the distance. As the rest of Phoenix Force began checking the downed Pasdarans for vital signs, McCarter ran forward, drew his Fairbairn-Sykes dagger and sliced the tarp off of the pickup.

As the plastic blew away in the wind, the Phoenix

Force leader saw the frightened and confused faces of the five newsmen.

"My name's Jason Kapka," one of the men said. "*Newsweek* magazine. And I'm sure hoping you're an American."

McCarter couldn't keep from laughing out loud. "No, I'm not from the colonies. But I *am* on your side." He looked up at the Zagros Mountains in the distance. They had no operable vehicle at all now, and the Phoenix Force leader resigned himself to another hard crossing through the rocks.

Calvin James leaped up over the side of the red pickup with the agility of an NBA star slam-dunking a basketball. Pulling a six-inch knife from somewhere beneath his robe, he began cutting the tape to free the men who had been held hostage.

McCarter was about to call the men together and get them started toward the mountains when the satellite phone in his blacksuit began to vibrate. Reaching under his robe, he flipped the instrument open and said, "McCarter here."

Barbara Price, the Stony Man Farm mission controller, said, "Hello, David. You found the hostages, we see."

McCarter looked up at the sky. Apparently the staff back at the Farm had watched the entire battle via satellite.

"That's affirmative," the Phoenix Force leader said. "And now we're about to start the long yet scenic romp back through the Zagros and into Iraq."

"I may have a better idea for you," Price said, and even

as she spoke McCarter heard the distinctive sound of one of Stony Man Farm's recently purchased Concordes in the distance. As he looked up into the sky to see the strange-looking aircraft fly into view like some stone-age predatory bird, another click sounded on the line.

"Mind if I join you, David?" Charlie Mott's voice said on what had now become a conference call. "I couldn't sleep anyway."

And even as the words came out of his mouth, the Concorde appeared above the Zagros Mountains, flew past the men on the ground, then banked to the left and began descending onto the flat plateau behind them.

"And I thank God for your insomnia," David McCarter said.

Now there was another click and Hal Brognola said, "Okay, guys. I think it's about time we all got on the horn here and figured out what we're going to do." McCarter could almost see the ragged end of a cigar clamped between the Stony Man Farm director's teeth. "Hold on a minute."

McCarter heard a series of clicks as Brognola tapped in what he suspected was Carl Lyons's satellite number. As he waited, the Concorde came to a halt not thirty feet away from them and the men of Phoenix Force shook hands with the Kurds and Iranian Christian warriors and said their goodbyes. McCarter had offered any and all of the men of the two groups safe passage to the U.S. and an easy green card.

But this was their home. And both Kurds and Christians had chosen to stay and fight for it.

Not so the newsmen who had been held hostage.

They practically flew up the steps to the Concorde as the folding staircase descended.

McCarter was the last man to hoof it up the staircase to the remodeled interior of the plane. As he took a seat in the reclining chair he'd claimed as his own, the Brit was surprised to hear Blancanales, instead of Lyons, answer the call.

"Where's Ironman?" were Brognola's first words and, although it rarely showed through the director's rough exterior, the care and worry he constantly lived with concerning his troops became transparent in his voice.

"Oh, he's here and he's fine," Blancanales said. "But at the moment, he's teaching a new Iranian friend of ours how to fly. Hang on a minute."

Over the airwaves, on the other side of the world, McCarter could hear the shrieking voice of a terrified man above the rush of wind. There was also an almost throbbing sound that told him that Able Team was probably in the air in a helicopter.

A few seconds later Lyons was on the phone. "You rang?" McCarter heard him say as he tapped a button to switch to speakerphone.

"That's affirmative," Brognola said. "It's just about time for the final act. Have we got everyone on stage here?"

The chorus of responses told the Phoenix Force leader that in addition to him and Brognola, Barbara Price, Aaron Kurtzman and Carl Lyons were now on the line.

"Okay," Brognola said. "Here's where we stand at the moment. Javid Azria has teamed up with Venezuelan President Gomez and shipped nuclear warheads to

South America. From Venezuela, those warheads can reach most of the southern United States on Gomez's own F-14s. Since the Venezuelans aren't suicidal, Azria has sent his own Iranian pilots to fly the Venezuelan planes."

McCarter waited while Brognola let it sink in. Then the Stony Man director went on. "Gomez had also shipped spare F-14 parts to Iran. David, you've spotted the planes flying overhead, right?"

"Right," McCarter said. "And they're definitely gearing up for something."

"Well," Brognola continued, "that something is one of two things—Azria is sending some of his nuked up F-14s toward America by ship. They can stay in international waters without invading our waterways and still be within F-14 range. They'll be so close they can fly on in before we can shoot them down. At least some of them."

"What's the other possibility?" McCarter asked.

"Israel," Brognola said. "They'll figure they might as well hit them, too. They can't make us any more mad at them than we already are by bombing our very homeland."

McCarter nodded his head silently.

"There's one more item of attention," Kurtzman said, breaking the silence that had fallen over the conference call. "The Russian trucks that delivered more F-14 parts to Iran. I've gone back and looked through their history. This isn't the only trip they've made down there. Which means that Azria is even better prepared than we thought."

"So we've got three problems to solve," Brognola declared. "And calling them 'problems' is the understatement of the new century. Lyons, you and your team need to locate the nuke that's already in the U.S. and keep it from taking out the whole city.

"David, Phoenix Force has got to sink that ship flying the Portuguese colors, and do it without setting off any of the nukes on board. I'm sure I don't have to tell you what the tsunami from that would do to our Eastern Seaboard. Not to mention Canada and Mexico."

"Right," McCarter agreed.

"That leaves us with the nuclear-equipped F-14s coming out of Venezuela," Brognola went on. "Kurtzman's just shown me satellite photos of their northernmost air base. It looks like a used-jet-fighter dealership, and there must be a hundred aircraft mechanics running around like chickens with their heads cut off."

"So, who's getting that assignment, Hal?" McCarter asked. "Striker?"

"Man, I wish," said Brognola. "But Bolan grabbed a couple hours of sleep and then took off for Thailand before all of this intel came together. I could never get him back here in time to help or I'd have already called him in."

"That Venezuelan base and the Portuguese ship," McCarter said. "We've either got to send the whole USAF at them in an air strike or use our own bombs." He stopped to clear his throat, then added, "That's the only way we can be sure all of the planes are neutralized. And we've got to use conventional bombs and not activate the nukes in the process."

"I'm no expert," Carl Lyons cut in. "But Schwarz has

told me that a simple concussion shouldn't detonate the nukes—they aren't set up that way." He paused a moment, then said, "Manning, are you where you can hear me?"

Phoenix Force's explosives expert, Gary Manning, had dropped into a chair next to McCarter's, and now he said, "I've gotta agree with Gadgets, Ironman. Nukes are a whole different ball game. Either Schwarz or I could explain the difference to you but there's no sense in wasting the time."

"Okay, then," said Brognola. "David, you're still close to Russia. So take your men north and take out the trucks that brought the F-14 parts. If we don't, they'll just send more parts when this is all over. As soon as that's done, head toward the ship with the Portuguese flag." He paused again, then said, "Ironman, Able Team has got to find that nuke that's already inside our borders, and have Schwarz defuse it."

"That still leaves the Venezuelan AFB," McCarter said.

"And that assignment's a first-come-first-serve job," said Brognola. "I've just been on the phone to the President. Whichever team gets to South America first will have the entire 101st Airborne as backup."

"How much you want to bet that we beat you there, Mac?" Carl Lyons said over the airwaves. "Say, a hundred?"

"Dollars or sterling?" asked the British SAS man.

"You pick," Lyons said.

"Then dollars it is," McCarter stated. "I'll collect the bet when this is all over."

"We'll see," Lyons said.

McCarter ended the call.

Charlie Mott had listened to the whole conversation on speakerphone and already banked the plane to the right and headed north. "Take a nap," the ace pilot yelled back over his shoulder. "I'll be flying below the radar, and I mean that literally."

But David McCarter, his fellow Phoenix Force warriors and the former hostages had already closed their eyes.

CARL LYONS had been forced to kill many men in his long career of protecting the helpless and innocent. And to men with his experience, the line between righteous killing and murder was distinctive. Rarely had he ever even wanted to murder anyone, let alone carried out such a nefarious act.

But if the little wimp in the back of the helicopter again didn't quit sniveling like a four-year-old, he was really thinking about hanging him out of the chopper's door again.

And this time he'd let go.

Lyons looked over the seat to where Iraj was huddled between the other two Able Team men. He insisted that the smuggled nuke was right here in New York City. And that he could get them there in a matter of minutes.

As the NYPD chopper continued to hover, Lyons twisted in his seat, reached into the back and dug his fingers into Iraj's throat. Pulling the man forward, he stopped when Iraj's head reached the space between the seats. "Give us our directions," the Able Team leader growled. "And do it quickly." He dropped his fingers from around the man's windpipe.

"Do you know Duane Park?" Iraj said hoarsely as he rubbed his throat.

"No," Lyons said. He looked into the back of the chopper and watched both Schwarz and Blancanales shake their heads. "Who is he?"

"It is not a person," Iraj said, still rubbing his neck. "It is a place."

"Okay," Lyons said. "It's a park?"

"Yes. A small one at the intersection of Duane and Hudson streets in the Tribeca area. Lower Manhattan."

Lyons glanced to Grimaldi, but the pilot had already headed that way.

"So this smuggled nuke is in Duane Park?"

"No," Iraj sniveled. "But it is close by. The park would be a good place to land."

A minute or two later, the chopper was hovering over a tiny triangle of grass where Hudson Street met Duane. As Grimaldi set the helicopter down, Lyons looked around and saw that the entire area was made up of nine-teenth-century buildings that conjoined to give the essence of stepping back a hundred years into the past.

"One six nine Duane Street," Iraj said, his voice still hoarse from Lyons's hand. "That is the address."

Lyons found that number on the curb and looked past it to see a redbrick building with rounded arches, Romanesque detailing and a mansard roof. "The nuke's in there?" he asked.

"Yes," Iraj confirmed. "Please do not kill me. I have brought you here."

Lyons got out of the chopper and waited for the rest of his team to exit, pushing Iraj ahead of them. Leaning back into the open door, he said, "Just wait on us here, Jack. I don't see any signs of sentries or other guards. They may be relying solely on secrecy to keep this nuke safe and sound."

"I'll be here when you need me," said Stony Man Farm's number-one pilot.

With the men of Able Team still dressed in sport coats, shirts and ties, Iraj led the way to an iron gate in front of number 169. It was not locked, and that fact made Lyons frown.

If it had been him hiding a nuclear weapon at some obscure location, he would have taken full advantage of all locks and other obstacles that would keep curious people out and away from it. The Able Team leader shrugged silently. On the other hand, everybody made mistakes. Timothy McVeigh had masterminded the Oklahoma City bombing of the Murrah building with careful attention to even the smallest of details.

Then he'd been caught because he'd driven away in a car with no license tag.

Inside the gateway the men of Able Team found a rock garden with evergreen shrubberies seeming to grow up out of the stones. Iraj knocked twice, and then a third time on the ancient wooden door. Then he dropped his arm to his side. Ten seconds later, he knocked again with the same staggered cadence.

Carl Lyons would never know whether the thought that suddenly popped into his head was from some tiny detail his subconscious had picked up on or was purely a gut instinct. But before he even knew what he was doing, the Able Team leader had shouldered Iraj out of the way and kicked in the door.

The two knocks, followed by one, then repeated a few seconds later, formed a code.

And it didn't mean "Let us in." It meant "Detonate the nuclear bomb immediately."

Lyons saw the suitcase in the middle of the otherwise empty front office. At the same time, he saw a dark-skinned man with a bushy mustache appear from somewhere in the back of the complex.

The man held an Uzi in his hands. But he never got a chance to fire it.

Lyons put two rounds from his Beretta 92 into the man's chest, then a third into the bushy mustache. The terrorist fell backward, but was caught before he could hit the floor by another man wielding a 1911 Government Model .45. Before the man could raise the pistol, Schwarz had put two more 9 mm rounds into his neck and ear.

Behind him, Lyons could sense Blancanales and Iraj. A split second later he turned their way and saw Blancanales throw the Iranian down onto the carpet. Schwarz had disappeared down the hall to secure the other offices, and the Able Team leader heard gunfire erupt from that direction.

As always, the warrior ran toward the fire, not away from it. Lyons was almost to the hall when another spontaneous thought caused him to turn around. Blancanales was right behind him and stopped cold in his path. Together, they looked back into the empty office and saw that Iraj had knelt next to the suitcase, opened it and was reaching inside.

The Iranian looked up at them, and his dark brown eyes drilled holes of hatred through both men from Able Team. Lyons realized that all of his cowardly behavior had been an act, leading up to this moment.

Iraj was just as crazy in his suicidal fanaticism as the other Pasdarans. And now he was about to detonate a bomb that would likely wipe Manhattan and the other islands that made up New York and Brooklyn off the map.

Both Lyons and Blancanales raised their pistols at the same time. The 9 mm rounds from both Blancanales and Lyons struck his face at almost the same instant, and wiped the hatred from his expression. They also obliterated both eyes and the majority of his nose.

Iraj fell backward onto the carpet as Blancanales and Lyons rushed toward him.

"Go get Gadgets," Lyons commanded, and Blancanales did an about-face and took off to the back of the offices.

Lyons looked down at the contraption he didn't understand. But he could tell it was far more sophisticated than any of the bombs they'd come across at the Kansas City mall or at other sites. A keyboard with both numbers and letters looked back up at him, and flashing on a screen were the numerals 703.

A second later Able Team's electronics expert was kneeling next to him with a small pair of wire cutters in his hand.

"I take it there were others in the back?" Lyons asked him.

As Schwarz's eyebrows lowered almost to his nose, he said, "Yeah. But they aren't in any shape to cause us further trouble."

"How about this thing?" Lyons asked.

"It's causing us further trouble," Schwarz said. He continued to study the nuclear bomb inside the suitcase, his eyes following the different-colored wires that wound their way through the contraption. "It takes a four-number code," he finally said. "And you got this maggot just before he hit the fourth key."

"Which would have meant…" Lyons let his voice trail off.

"One word," Schwarz said. "Blewie!"

"So what are your plans?" Lyons asked.

"Well, Ironman, after a little prayer, I'm going to have to take a chance." He closed his eyes for a moment, then said, "I think the blue wire will shut this thing down. Unless there's some trip or trick I've missed."

"What happens if you do nothing?" Blancanales asked, moving up toward the suitcase now, too.

"My guess is it'll detonate anyway after a certain length of time. How long, I can't say—it'll depend on how the thing was set up, and I can't find that part without tripping it."

"Then go ahead and cut the blue line," Lyons said. "We aren't likely to be able to get this thing out of here to a safe zone before it goes off. What do you say, Pol?"

Blancanales nodded. "We might as well try," he said.

Schwarz reached out with the wire cutters open. The top blade of the instrument went over the blue wire while the bottom cutter slid under it. The Able Team electronics expert looked up for a minute and said, "You guys ready?"

"I don't know exactly how you get ready for something like this," said Blancanales.

"Me, either," Lyons said. "Just cut the thing.

Schwarz took a deep breath and then clamped down on the wire cutter. The blue wire snapped in two. For a full five seconds the empty office went as silent as a graveyard. Then Lyons said, "Close that thing up and bring it with us. I've got a bet to win in Venezuela."

MCCARTER HAD MOVED from the rear of the Concorde to the seat next to Charlie Mott as soon as the Stony Man Farm conference call had ended. And if it had been any other pilot but Mott or Grimaldi behind the controls, he suspected he'd have ordered him to take them higher. Because when Mott had promised to fly under the Russian radar, he had meant *way* under. There had been several occasions in which McCarter had been sure they were about to clip off the top of one of the Zagros foothills or other structures along the road.

But they hadn't, and Mott had proved once again that he could fly anything, anywhere, anytime and any way.

Now, perhaps fifty feet in the air, they were following a convoy of trucks. "That has to be them," McCarter said.

Mott yawned. "Yep," he said as he pulled his California Angels baseball cap down tighter over his head. "What do you want me to do?"

"These Concordes are new to all of us," said McCarter. "May I assume they've been outfitted with machine guns of some type?"

"Oh, yeah," Mott said. "Twin M-61 Gatlings. But seriously updated." He glanced toward the control board in front of McCarter. "Grab that mouse-looking thing right in front of you. I've got one over here, too."

McCarter frowned as he reached out and removed what did indeed look like the mouse to a computer. And when he lifted it off its clip, a flat panel automatically slid out. In the screen atop the panels, he saw the exact same view he could see by looking out of the front windshield of the Concorde.

"Just set the mouse down on the screen, move the cursor to the spot you want blown away and press the red button."

McCarter set down the mouse, moving it up and down on the photolike screen and getting the feel of it. His thumb rested on the red button in the center of the instrument, which was connected to the screen with a plastic-coated wire.

"Tell you what, mate," the former SAS man said. "Why don't you do a fly-over, turn around and we'll take them all out as we pass back over them."

"Just what I was thinking," Mott said. "I'm certain this is the right convoy. But it doesn't hurt to make sure."

He manipulated the controls and the Concorde jerked suddenly forward.

"They saw us," McCarter stated. "And it's definitely the right trucks."

"I'd say so," Mott said. "Those AK-47s hanging out the windows and shooting at us aren't exactly standard issue for the Russian trucking industry."

"No," McCarter said. "And it's time they were ticketed."

Mott banked the plane sharply a mile or so in front

of the convoy, then guided it straight back toward the trucks. When they were a hundred yards from the lead truck, McCarter centered his cursor-sight on the engine and thumbed the red button.

Both McCarter's and Mott's rounds struck the first truck almost simultaneously, and the big rig suddenly exploded in smoke and flames. The convoy behind them was forced to slow, and together the two Stony Man warriors took out the second, third and fourth trucks with more M-61 rounds.

By then they had flown over the remaining five trucks, which had been forced to stop on the highway. Banking to the left and back again, they got three more on their return swoop.

"Two left," Mott said. "Right in the middle. Why don't you take the first and I'll take the second?"

"Sounds fine to me," McCarter agreed. He watched the first of the remaining two trucks explode in more fire and smoke as Mott flew them back over the convoy, then pressed the trigger on his own machine gun to take out the final vehicle. A lone man had jumped out of the cab of the last truck and now, with an AK-47 slung over his shoulder, tried to sprint away from the carnage along the highway.

McCarter shifted his cursor slightly. A half second later, the Gatling practically cut the man in two.

"What do you want to do now?" Mott asked as McCarter let up on the trigger one final time.

"Head toward the ship with the Portuguese flag, which should be somewhere in the Atlantic by now," McCarter said. "Before the Russian air force spots us and shoots us out of the sky." He unfastened his seat belt, stood and started toward the back. But before he went he said, "We'll check in with Kurtzman in a little while and get its exact location from him." He stopped talking for a second and reached up to scratch the three-day growth of beard he hadn't had time to shave off. "We've got to sink them and then beat Lyons and his team to Venezuela. We do that, and I'll split the bet with you."

"Wow," Charlie Mott said as he banked the plane a final time. "Fifty whole dollars? My sister can finally have that operation and walk again, and I can buy that little farm in Nebraska I've always wanted."

DAVID MCCARTER caught a little over an hour's nap before awakening and heading toward Charlie Mott. Stony Man Farm's number-two pilot had plugged his earphones into a CD player and was singing "The Silver-Tongued Devil" along with Kris Kristofferson.

McCarter tapped him on the shoulder as he sat again. "You're supposed to fly us around, Charlie," he said. "Not kill us."

Mott laughed. "You getting ready to call Kurtzman?" he asked as he pulled the plug out of the CD player and inserted it in the control board again.

"Yeah. He's tracking the phony Portuguese ship for us. A couple more hours, and we should be over it."

"Has anybody thought about what we're going to do then?" McCarter asked.

Mott shrugged his shoulders. "We're equipped with four Hunting JP .233 dispensers under our fuselage. They can deliver 120 SG-357 pavement-cratering weapons and 860 small HB-876 area-denial munitions.

Together, that's more than enough to completely incapacitate an airfield."

"That's nice to know," McCarter said. "But we aren't going after an airfield—at least until we hit Venezuela. I still want to know how we sink this ship without setting off the nukes it's carrying."

"I don't understand it all myself," Mott said. "But Kurtzman assures me—and Schwarz and Manning both agreed—that nukes are a different breed of cat. There's all kinds of somethings that have to make contact with other somethings to set them off. And those somethings are kept separate until the very last moment, when the bomb is actually used. It's a safety precaution."

"But these Iranians," McCarter said, "are all planning to die anyway. How do we know they haven't already set everything in motion except the last step?"

Mott shrugged his shoulders again. "We can't know—at least not for certain. But keep in mind what motivates them. They want to bring the U.S. to its knees. And they don't mind dying to get it done. But if even one of their nukes goes off before they can get close enough for the F-14s to take off, they fail in their mission." He paused and drew in a breath. "So they don't want any early surprise explosions any more than you or I would. They're likely to be just as careful as we'd be. But for a different reason."

McCarter's satellite phone rang suddenly, interrupting the conversation. "McCarter," the Phoenix Force leader said.

"You're getting close," Kurtzman's voice said over the airwaves. "Tell Mott to slow her down and start looking. We're counting on the individual bombs still being in pieces. But just in case they're already set..." His voice trailed off. Then he went on, "In case they've already set them, you couldn't be in a better position to strike. There'll still be some unbelievable tsunamis. But they'll be dying down by the time they reach land."

"What about us?" McCarter asked.

There was a long pause over the line. Then Kurtzman finally said in a quiet voice, "You guys won't make it."

McCarter nodded silently. Being caught up in a nuclear explosion might not be the ideal way to die. But he had known such things were possible when he'd joined Phoenix Force. "Just curious," he said into the phone.

"If it's any consolation," Kurtzman said, "there are probably no more than one or two of the Pasdarans who've been trained in nuclear warfare and would even know how to put the bombs together."

"Quite comforting," McCarter said. "Anything else we need to know?"

"Only that the whole Atlantic fleet is less than a hundred miles away and ready to move in after you've disabled the ship. The SEALs are itching to join the fight."

"Then we'll do our job and meet Able Team in Venezuela," McCarter said. "Over and out."

"Over and out," Kurtzman said in a low voice, and McCarter could tell that the Stony Man Farm computer genius was hoping those weren't the last words he'd ever say to the men of Phoenix Force.

EPILOGUE

After everything that had led up to it, the attack on the aircraft carrier flying the phony Portuguese flag was almost anticlimactic.

All of the men aboard Stony Man Farm's new Concorde had crowded up into the cabin to watch through the windshield as Mott zoomed them down toward the ship. It was standing room only, and none of the men worried about seat belts.

If things didn't go right, they'd be instantly pulverized and the thought of worrying about a seat belt was almost comical.

On the first pass, Mott dropped 60 SG-357s, which proved they could crater a ship's deck just as easily as the concrete runways they'd originally been designed for. Two huge holes—one in the aft, the other in the bow of the ship—cracked the craft into thirds and sent the pieces spinning in circles as water poured in like tidal waves.

Smoke rose from the debris on the water below, rising high enough to encompass the Concorde and

block out the view. Mott flew them on, out of the bil-
lowy black cloud, into the clear blue sky once more,
then banked the plane and turned back.

There was plenty of smoke, all right, McCarter smiled
to himself. But, at least so far, no mushroom cloud.

"We need to make at least one more pass just to make
sure," the Phoenix Force leader said, and Mott dropped
their altitude slightly. Perhaps fifty feet above the fast-
sinking ship, they looked down to see that several small
fires had broken out. What was left no longer even
looked like a ship, and here and there bodies, lay on the
floating rubble.

"Want me to hit them again?" Mott asked.

McCarter shook his head. "No reason to waste
ammo," he said. "Let the SEALs and the nuclear experts
have their fun. Let's go to Venezuela."

THE RACE was on.

Carl Lyons could hear the chatter over the Concorde's radio as Grimaldi flew them closer to the Venezuelan air force base near Puerto la Cruz. He didn't
speak Spanish. But he recognized one of the voices answering what sounded like an angry dispatcher on the
ground.

Rafael Encizo.

A moment later his satellite phone rang. "Hello,
David," he said without bothering to look at the Caller ID.

"Greetings and salutations, Ironman," David
McCarter said. "Your 10-20?"

"We're still a few miles out. But I can hear your
Cuban talking to someone on the ground."

"Yes, indeed," McCarter replied. "It seems they want to know who's invaded their airspace. Rafe is doing his best to convince them that all personnel should vacate the base. We've given them ten minutes."

"They know who we are?" he asked.

"CIA, Marines, SEALs, take your pick. They've accused us of being all of those things and more. Encizo had told them pretty much the truth—that we're an international unit and that we intend to destroy all of the F-14s down below. By the way," he went on, "nice job on the ship. Barbara tells me you did well and weren't blown up yourselves, which of course I know now, since you're speaking to me."

The Concorde continued through the air, slowly losing altitude as Grimaldi guided it toward the base. "You have any ideas on how to handle this yet?" Lyons asked McCarter.

"Yes, but I'd like your input, too."

Lyons nodded unconsciously. "My suggestion would be that we destroy the runways, then let the 101st float down from the sky and disable the planes. We're not dealing with a bunch of crazy Muslims anymore. Except for the Iranian pilots, my guess is that they'll get out of there as quickly as they can. And if not, too bad for them."

"My thoughts exactly," McCarter said. "Five of their escape minutes are up. Let's both do a fly-over to encourage them to leave, then we'll strike."

Lyons closed his phone as the Venezuelan shoreline appeared in the distance. "Keep her about this height, Jack," he told Grimaldi. "Let's see what's going on."

Grimaldi nodded.

As they flew over the base, Lyons saw line after line of the F-14s lined up in formation on the ground. There had to be at least one hundred fighter jets ready to take off, and possibly already nuclear-equipped. Farther back from the shore, around a number of office buildings and hangars, people were running toward cars and other vehicles, then speeding away from the base as fast as they could.

But the man on the radio continued to speak in a threatening voice.

The Able Team leader snapped his phone open again when he saw the other Stony Man Concorde come flying over the base a few hundred feet away. A second later, he had McCarter on the line again. "Looks like we tie as far as the bet goes," he said.

"Yes, it does," McCarter agreed. "So, shall we begin the fun?"

"Whenever you're ready," Lyons said. Then, turning to Jack, he pointed at the men and women escaping the air force base as quickly as they could. "Kind of nice to deal with folks who have some common sense again, isn't it?"

Before he could answer, Grimaldi had dipped the plane slightly and targeted one of the runways. On the other side of the base, Charlie Mott did the same.

Both planes made multiple passes, dropping SG-357 bombs that cratered the runways.

"We got 'em, Ironman," Grimaldi said. The Stony Man pilot turned the Concorde around again and did one final fly-over as at least two hundred USAF planes suddenly appeared on the horizon. Soon the paratroopers from the 101st Airborne squadron were free-falling through the sky. Among them, Lyons knew, would be a good many trained in nuclear defusion. And there were more than enough troops to hold back other Venezuelan military and police until the cleanup was over and they could all fly back home.

It was going to be a diplomatic nightmare. But that wasn't the concern of either Phoenix Force or Able Team. Their mission had been to keep the United States from becoming a wasteland.

And they'd accomplished it.

As both Mott and Grimaldi drew their aircraft parallel to each to other and gave a thumbs-up, McCarter spoke into Carl Lyons's ear.

"Where to now?" the former British SAS man asked.

"Back to the Farm," said Lyons. "I'm hungry and I want some sleep."

The sound of a feminine voice clearing her throat sounded over the phone, indicating that Barbara Price had just tapped into the call. "Sorry, Ironman," the mission controller said. "I hate to tell you, but you aren't coming home yet. You're needed in Detroit. Hal will brief you while you're in the air."

McCarter's laugh could almost be heard from the other plane as well as over the phone. "Tell you what, Ironman," he said. "We'll eat and sleep for you."

"Not unless you plan on sleeping in the reclining chairs," Price said. "You aren't headed into the Farm yet, either."

"What do you mean?" McCarter asked.

"I just hope you like Thai food," Barbara Price said.

TAKE 'EM FREE
2 action-packed novels plus a mystery bonus
NO RISK
NO OBLIGATION TO BUY

AleX Archer
PARADOX

What once may have saved the world could now destroy it...

Archaeologist Annja Creed reluctantly accepts an assignment on behalf of the U.S. government to investigate what is thought to be the remains of Noah's Ark. Annja must escort a group of militants through civil unrest in eastern Turkey, but the impending war is nothing compared to the danger that lies hidden within the team. With lives at stake, Annja has no choice but to protect the innocent. Legend says the Ark once saved mankind...but this time it could kill them all.

Available November wherever books are sold.

GOLD EAGLE®

GRA21